SWAMPY
GOES TO PROM

JEREMY DORFMAN

ISBN: 978-0692575000

Published in the United States, 2015.

Book design by Jenelle Kleiman.

Cover design and artwork by Perry Shall.

"Whoever fights monsters should see to it that in the process he does not become a monster. And if you gaze long enough into an abyss, the abyss will gaze back into you."

Friedrich Nietzsche

"Tell me how am I supposed to live without you
Now that I've been lovin' you so long
How am I supposed to live without you
How am I supposed to carry on
When all that I've been livin' for is gone."

Michael Bolton

"I'm a dreamer. I have to dream and reach for the stars, and if I miss a star then I grab a handful of clouds."

Mike Tyson

PROLOGUE

Rumors spread. It is their most fundamental characteristic. Spreading is as essential to the nature of rumors as growing is to hair or itching is to testicles.

One can't just start a rumor and expect it to sit still, stifled, and stagnant in a corner somewhere, content to expire as fodder off the lips of a single mouth, caught by a single pair of half interested ears. No. A rumor needs to be passed around to stay alive as crucially as humans need oxygen to keep breathing.

One moment Bobby Crumpler seems to take an extended glance towards Angela Waymentooth in the lunchroom because a crumb of Pop Tart launched into his eye and soon enough the entire school just KNOWS he's got a giant crush on her.

Mr. Wilkinson is a few bucks short at the grocery store and has to put back a can of peaches. By the end of the week EVERYONE is whispering about the Wilkinson family's financial troubles and the inevitable bank repossession of their house.

Ginny Detwiler, drunker than she intended to be at the beginning of the evening, blows a kiss to a gentleman in the shadows of the alley outside of Monahan's pub at 12:32 on a Saturday night and the very next morning the entire town is ABSOLUTELY CERTAIN, without a shadow of a doubt, that she has a second career as the town whore.

The problem with rumors' overzealous need to appear in the passing conversation of every Tom, Dick, and Charlene they come across is that their ultimate plausibility takes a hit each time it turns out that Ginny Detwiler is not actually a whore. (Four times so far, for the record). And when people stop believing what they hear, they sometimes ignore the evidence of something quite fantastic that is staring them right in the face.

This is precisely what happened with...

THE BLUFORD SPRINGS SWAMP MONSTER

(Cue scary move music in your mind. Or on your smart phone if imagination isn't your strong point. This is the 21st century after all. The theme from "Halloween" is always a good starting point.)

For four decades in this small, valley-tucked town, folks told tale of a horrifying creature lurking in the murk. A revolting humanoid confabulation of sludge and slime, with an eyeball that hung inches below it socket, connected only by a repulsive string of nerves, and a pimply pus filled mouth that would haunt your dreams for the rest of your life were one of the lucky few who survived seeing it.

The first rumored incident took place on July 20, 1969. The day of the great moon landing. While a nation of Americans were glued to their seats watching newly born heroes traipse around the earth's closest celestial buddy, shouting a subtextual "fuck you" to the Russians by planting our flag in it, some Bluford Springs teenagers of the free love generation hit the swamps for a day long session of marijuana induced revelry and mosquito hindered sexual passion.

The problem was – THEY NEVER RETURNED.

A week later, in the swamps, a local fisherman (with very poor instincts for where fish might want to spend their time) nearly fell out of his rowboat when it bumped into the corpses of six sludge covered youths. This dense man initially mistook the blood, guts, & slime splattered all over the teenager's skin for the normal outward appearance of dirty unshowering hippies and their deadness for a drug induced slumber. He finally realized something was amiss when he spotted that their eyeballs had fled their faces and taken up residence in their anuses.

Scandal, of course, ensued, for scandal likes to ensue as much as rumors like to spread. The media invaded the small town with ruthless tenacity. They planted themselves on the lawns of the poor grieving families of those dirty hippies, who just wanted some peace and quiet and told the reporters so in increasingly snippy tones. The viewing public thought the families quite rude even though the tragic loss they suffered probably should have given them a free pass on social manners.

The police investigation was long and frustrating. The detectives on the job presumed the deed was the work of a "sadistic whack job who probably got porked by his daddy one too many times," and they did their best to scour the town for someone who met these key description points.

While the police ran their futile investigation, another less publicized inspection was launched.

Todd Sooter, the younger brother of one of the victims, was not content to sit around and wait for the police force (whose previous biggest case involved an incomplete pair of shoes) to figure out who murdered his big bro. He enlisted a couple of his sixth grade buddies. They packed up their backpacks with flashlights, chewing gum, and duct tape, and ventured to the swamp to gather evidence first hand. Paddling through the muck on an old tire, they got to the corpse cleared scene of the crime, which was still identifiable from the flapping remains of poorly applied police tape.

"What exactly are we looking for?" asked Leo Sunday, a new member of Todd's friendship circle. Leo was secretly terrified by the idea of being in a place where folks where recently murdered, but he joined along on the quest to gain some street cred.

"Evidence," said Todd, with a distant determination.

Todd's buddies kept their eyes peeled for a certain period of time until the repetition of swamp bubbles blurred into each other and they became unsure if they were moving or still. They were bored and scared and the sun was setting but they didn't dare overrule Todd's determination. Their poor friend had suffered an inconceivable loss and he was entitled to several hours of irrational swamp inspection. (*Even if the killer might still be lurking around somewhere, oh god, oh god, mommy*, thought Leo).

The sun set and the crickety reverb of unknown swamp animals sounded in their ears. Todd waited, feeling an uneasy confident assurance that something would reveal itself.

And then they saw him. A pair of burnt yellow eyes shining horrifically through the dark. Green veins dripping around tadpole eyelids. A creature of terror such as they had never set their eyes upon.

Urine escaped Leo's pants like a retreating army. Todd's other friends gripped the tire for dear life and averted their eyes from the terrible sight.

But Todd did not look away. He looked straight into the pupils of the beast. He wanted to see the monster that had killed his brother.

For unknown reasons the Swamp Monster spared them that day. They lived to tell the tale of what they had seen. Todd went straight to the police station with the evidence he had gathered first hand; the dirty hippy murderer was not a "sadistic whack job who probably got porked by his daddy one too many times," but actually a horror creature of the deep. Instead of the gratitude he expected, he was met with a nauseating display of laughter. Glazed donut crumbs were splattered all around in projectile saliva. He was met with condescension and ridicule. To put it mildly, they didn't believe his story.

However, the policemen did tell people about what the Sooter boy had said as a humorous anecdote. And the people they told, told others about it. And those others told yet more others who told some people who had already heard it but also other others who had not. And soon enough the tale of the swamp monster of Bluford Springs got into the hands of the neurotic and suspicious who suggested – "Hey, what if there really is a swamp monster? Those murders were pretty disturbing." And from there the rumor got into the hands of certifiable urban legend addicts who just KNEW it was the truth and claimed they had seen the creature themselves, WITH THEIR OWN EYES (although they in fact had not), and who claimed to have HARD physical evidence like fossilized foot marks and slimy deposits that proved Swampy's existence. (Swampy was the uncreative namesake with which the monster was unceremoniously graced). Eventually they even started to believe their own lies, as is the custom with conspiracy theorists.

As the years passed, Swampy enthusiasts took the lead of Che Gevara worshippers. They smuggled a serious situation over the border into the country of kitsch by plastering a cartoonish version of the creature onto mildly popular t-shirts. Later, 1980s schlock horror icon director Vincent Wells made a horrendous slasher pic about the crimes, further trivializing the brutal reality of the loss of life through an absurd hour and a half of ketchup blood splashing onto exposed breasts.

By the end of the Reagan years it wasn't uncommon for Bluford Spings residents to blame even the smallest of misdemeanors on their mascot of terror. The local 7-Eleven got robbed? Must have been the Swamp Monster. Billy Rudolph couldn't remember where he left his bicycle? Swamp Monster. Old Man Riggins got pranked into stomping out a flaming bag of shit on his front porch? Curse you Swamp Monster!

The legend grew and grew until finally a funny thing happened. Rumors of Swampy became so ubiquitous in that little nook of a town that it was, almost simultaneously, overly obvious to every one of Bluford Springs' residents, from the most ardent skeptic to the most devoted whack job, that Swampy was merely a silly story. There could not possibly be an ounce of truth in the whole thing.

All fear faded away. Youths learned of the legend from their parents and laughed in their folks' faces when they were informed that this yarn of a slimy supernatural murderer was ever taken seriously.

The whole thing became a colossal joke, just as it was destined to. For rumors cannot ultimately restrain their massive ambitions. Their unquenchable desire to become omnipresent dooms them to their own death. Once a rumor has lost any power to convince others of its validity it is no longer a rumor at all – it is a gag; an anecdote of ridicule; a stain on the tablecloth of information which the dinner party actively ignores, covering it with a pot of string beans and then forgetting it was ever there in the first place.

In the year 2010, the McCarter Group put forth a plan to build a state of the art shopping mall where the swamp grounds had stood since the cracking of Pangea. No objections were raised. The swamp had been a zit on the face of Bluford Springs' picturesque landscape for long enough. It was high time to stick an Abercrombie and Fitch over the mother fucker and be done with it.

Not one person raised the objection that it might be dangerous to build a shopping mall where a vicious swamp monster resided because not one person any longer thought there was any possibility that there really was a swamp monster. (Actually, there was the notable exception of grown up, reclusive, and increasingly unstable Todd Sooter, but we'll come back to him later).

So ground was broken. Construction was rapid. And in late September of 2012 the Bluford Springs Mall had its grand opening, heroically saving the locals from having to travel more than fifteen minutes down the road to buy pants. The place was a smash success. Nearly a thousand flocked to its store sized cubbies of goods on opening day.

Everyone in town was happy because, as we all know, nothing makes people happier than the acquisition of material goods.

But little did they know... they had awoken a monster...

1

On Friday the fifth of October, less than one total month into the new school year, Lindsay Morpletopple was asked to the junior prom for the first time. The culprit was Teddy Bigshartz, a five foot five male of mediocre social standing and mediocre looks who put all his money on red and bet that lovely Lindsay would be too kind to say no. He was confident that the wheel would land in his favor and he would lock her up simply by being the first one out of the gate. He overestimated her benevolence. She let him down with a chilly rendition of: "I'm just not ready to think about that yet. I'll let you know when it actually gets closer."

The poor sap wandered away with hunched shoulders and dragged feet, knowing full well that Lindsay would never get back to him. She'd end up going with Bobby Fusilage or Tommy Questinghouse or any one of the jacked, ham-brained, popular studs who roamed the halls, barely able to keep their balance without slamming into an open locker.

Lindsay watched Teddy slump away with the greatest sympathy. She got no satisfaction from shattering the hopes of a sweet, plain faced peer, who deserved a girlfriend but had probably yet to even receive a first kiss. It was going to be a long year. She was bound to be asked to the prom by at least a dozen boys. She wasn't being egotistical. She knew the way guys looked at her. She tried to play it down. She often wore lumpy sweatshirts and applied minimal make-up but she was a naturally beautiful, big breasted blonde and nothing could be done to hide it.

Teddy was sadly correct in his assumption that Lindsay would never get back to him. But he was incorrect in thinking that her rejection was born in her desires for Bluford Springs High School's handsome goons. In actuality, Lindsay's soft refusal was not punctuated by thoughts of Bobby or Tommy but of William Denworth, the suave teenage vampire who was the love interest of the tweenage girl protagonist in the wildly popular "Midnight" series.

The series was made up of seven books: *Midnight*, *After Midnight*, *Midday*, *Where Wolf?*, *Boogey Man - Tissue Wrapped*, *Mummy Dearest*, and *The Lust Kiss Goodnight*.

Each of the seven books had been given a viscous drubbing from literary critics worse than the last and each book had sold more than twice the amount of its predecessor.

Lindsay was well aware that literally every girl and her mother had read the canonical seven, and yet, the series felt like her own personal escape to a land that no one else knew, not even its author. She had read each book at least three times and felt closer to the fictional characters who populated their pages than she did to her own friends.

More than anything though, she was in love with William Denworth.

Yes, William was a viscous bloodsucker who gruesomely bit off the throats of his enemies and chewed on their nerves. But he was also a handsome, sensitive, charmer who teared up at the sight of a dying chipmunk and kissed in a way that made Lucy, the protagonist of "Midnight," see a white light and fill with a blissful rush, as if chocolate flowed through her veins.

William read poetry and communicated through romantic clichés that melted female hearts when spoken through his butterscotch voice. He understood women. He was the complete opposite of all the sweaty, horny, self-serving, animalistic *children* who roamed the halls of B.S.H.S. He was mature. He was technically a teenager (although an immortal one), but really, he was a man.

SWAMPY GOES TO PROM

Just thinking about the fictional frame of William Denworth got Lindsay all excited in parts of her body that were entirely inappropriate to talk about in public.

Lindsay liked to think that she was in love with this storybook chap in spite of his dark side, but the truth (which she was not fully ready to admit to herself) was that her infatuation was actually, in great part, because of it. William's red rose words made her heart swoon, but it was his sadistic clawing and biting and murdering with a gluttonous abandon to feed his orgasmic blood cravings that really got Lindsay's loins burning as she read.

She imagined herself making love to him, both of them covered in blood, his teeth locked into her neck, stretching out her skin like a rubber band.

Suffice it to say, Lindsay had a real problem on her hands. She was madly in love with a man who didn't exist. Even more disconcertingly, a great part of her passion came from the fact that he was a vampire who butchered the bodies of his victims into unrecognizable slabs of meat. The cherry that topped this hot fudge sundae of existential agony was the looming prom, which she, like any teenage girl, had dreamed of going to since she first walked through the orange rusty doors of her educational institution as a freshman. However, she couldn't imagine actually attending the prom because she couldn't imagine saying yes to any real life boys. The only image in her head that ran in sync with her desires was her, in a slink pink dress, held by gorgeous William Denworth, dressed in all black, swaying back and forth to some cheesy ballad on the dance floor of her junior ball. William Denworth, kissing her as the clock stroked midnight. William Denworth, taking her back to his stone castle and plucking her virginity from her like an unwanted hair.

"You alright Lindsay?"

Our heroine was stirred from her stupor by the chewing gum in liquid gears voice of her friend Jane.

"Yeah, fine," she said, excited in her nether-regions by all this thinking about William Denworth and hoping that Jane couldn't tell.

"You look feverish or something."

"I'm fine. Really," she said, turning to a random locker and rotating the numbers wheel on the lock as if she knew the combination.

"That's not your locker."

"Uh, I know that. I just... like to see sometimes if I can guess the combinations on other people's lockers."

"That's kind of creepy. And maybe illegal."

"Just because you like to play by all the rules Jane, doesn't mean I have to."

"I don't play by all the rules."

"Oh, yeah?"

"Of course not. You know me better than that. Speaking of which, want to take some X later?"

"What?" said Lindsay abruptly – certainly not having forseen that turn of the conversation coming.

"I took some a couple nights ago with Ivan Mussivitch. You'd never believe the things he can do with his pecks."

"Uh..."

"I stole one from him and I'm sure he'd hook you up with one if you gave him a hand job. He's got a bunch more."

"I think I'll probably pass."

"Your loss. It was amazing. It was like having butter slathered all of my body and licked off."

"We are talking about the ecstasy right? Not whatever you did with Ivan?"

"It's hard to say. It all sort of blended together."

"Well, I don't think I want to hear anything else about this, thank you very much."

"Anyway, I came over to ask if you want to go with us to the new mall tonight."

"Oh. Who's going?"

"Me, Kelly, Chris, Dustin, and Sean."

"Huh. I don't know."

"C'mon! It's Friday night! And besides, I think Sean's got the hots for you."

"Oh. Well hooray then."

"You should give him a chance. He's really cute."

"He thought that Abraham Lincoln was 'that guy on the cereal box'."

"They look alike."

"No. They don't!"

"You haven't really talked to him one on one. He's new here, he just needs some time to get adjusted."

"I don't know."

"Come on! Come with! The new mall's supposed to be awesome!"

"Well... okay."

"Yay!" Jane hugged her. Then licked her cheek.

"Uch!" Lindsay blurted out pushing her away.

"Sorry," said Jane. "I think I might still be high on the X. I took like five of them."

...

They picked Lindsay up at 7:34. Chris drove. He was the first of the group to acquire his license. For his birthday his parents had bought him a used 1996 Ford Taurus station wagon. He thought they were being uncharacteristically generous but in reality the purchase had only occurred after his mother and father had each insisted that they would never let their moron of a son sit behind the wheel of their BMW (Chris's father) or Mercedes (Chris's mother). A previously owned clunker seemed the best option for everyone involved. Chris had already damaged the front bumper and the back fender but the other parties in the accidents were a light pole and a tree stump, so his insurance premiums had yet to be affected.

Chris loudly blasted the horn to alert Lindsay of their arrival, letting out an unintentional warning call to the rest of the neighborhood to stay off the road.

Lindsay, who had been waiting at the window for the past ten minutes, hesitated for a moment, so as to not appear overeager, kissed her mother goodbye and proceeded to Chris's lime green wagon.

Six foot Dustin stepped out of the back to allow petite Lindsay into the middle seat, ensuring that her thighs would spend the ride in direct connection to both his and Sean's. Jane sat in the front middle and Kelly in the front passenger seat. Lindsay was greeted with a chorus of sunny "Heys," a too seductive grin from Sean, and the statement: "Well look who decided to leave her fucking box for the night," from the always classy Chris.

"Delightful to see you too Chris," she said.

The ride only took five minutes but the search for parking took another ten. It seemed the entire county had left their dens of pie eating and crime of the week TV show watching to witness the rare sight of something new in their cookie cutter suburbs.

The mall was quite something to behold. It was a three floor palace of brightly colored signs over a backsplash of the purest white. Individuals streamed in and out of the doors like maggots in and out of a corpse. Commerce and materialism gave off a capitalistic scent even fifty yards from the automatic doors.

As the posse proceeded towards the gleaming entranceway, Kelly and Jane got to quick work trashing a group of girls from their grade who were marching down the parallel lane of cars (as the other group of girls, out of earshot, got to work trashing them). Meanwhile, Sean attempted to isolate Lindsay and work his magic.

"So... you had a lot of homework so far?" he said smoothly.

"I guess. Not too bad," she replied.

"Yeah, I know right."

"You know what?"

"I know!"

"I'm sorry. What are we talking about?"

"Just... homework. It sucks right?"

"I guess," she said, already regretting her decision to have come this evening.

Sean went silent as he searched his cavernous mind for a new strategy. They all entered the mall.

Even the hundreds of cars outside did not prepare them for the sea of excited faces deliriously parading up and down the marble floors. People of all ages had come to witness the infancy of the giant hall of overpriced stores. Infants wailed, running off into the crowd, away from their stressed out mothers who made the mistake of looking at a purse in a window for more than five seconds and then had to pay the price of running an Olympic sprint to catch up to their child before they tumbled down an escalator. Senior citizens puttered along, tripping over essentially flat marble tiles from the inability to lift their feet more than a centimeter off the ground, constantly bumped by eleven year old skateboarders who were chased by sad sack potbellied security guards working in too few numbers for the outrageous crowd sizes. Teenagers popped their heads around every corner, blocked every storefront with obnoxious loitering, laughed and giggled and shouted at each other creating a ceaseless earsplitting hum that drowned out the Muzak playing over the loudspeakers.

"I'm in heaven," declared Kelly, who closed her eyes and breathed in the air of the shopping oasis.

"I guess that means you died. Can I have your stuff?" said Dustin, designated "guy who thinks he's funny but is not that funny" of the group.

"This really is kind of incredible," said Jane. "It sure doesn't look like the old swamp anymore."

"I bet old Swampy's still lurking around somewhere though," said Chris.

"Swampy?" asked Sean.

"The swamp monster," said Dustin.

"He was supposed to have lived in the Swamp," said Lindsay.

"Half off tops at Hollister!" said Kelly.

"Supposedly he killed a bunch of hippies," said Dustin.

"That's pretty freaky," said Sean.

"Only if you believe in horseshit tall tales made up by a bunch of losers," said Chris.

"I believe he existed," interjected Jane.

"You would. You also believe in magic crystals and psychic fortune tellers," said Chris.

"Denying ESP is like denying your own skin. There's lots of proof."

"I don't know. I always thought skin was just a holographic illusion covering our bones," said Dustin.

"What do you think?" Sean asked Lindsay.

"About whether skin exists?" she replied.

"No," he said, "About this swamp monster."

"I think he probably spends most of his weekend nights with Santa Claus, double teaming the tooth fairy," said Lindsay.

"Really? Like anal and stuff?" said Sean.

"I like it when you show your spunk Linds," said Chris.

"Hey, where's Kelly?" asked Jane suddenly.

The group stopped their aimless forward march into the mall. They looked around themselves on all sides. Kelly had in fact disappeared.

"Well that's weird. No one saw her go off?" asked Dustin.

They all agreed they had not.

"She must have just gone into one of the stores," said Chris. "She was practically foaming at the mouth at all of the clothes around here."

"It would have been nice if she had said something," said Lindsay.

"The woman can't control herself," said Dustin. "She's a shopaholic. I've been trying to get her to attend meetings but she's still in the denial stage."

"I'll call her," said Jane.

There was no answer.

"We should look for her," said Jane.

"She's the one who decided to run off," said Chris. "She'll find us."

"What if her phone's not working?" said Jane.

"I don't know, she'll figure something out," said Chris.

"Let's at least look in the stores we passed," said Jane.

They all agreed – Chris, somewhat reluctantly – but it made no difference. There was no sign of her – not even in the Hollister she had so excitedly referenced.

"This is really weird," said Jane.

"It's like she vanished – *straight through the walls*," said Dustin in a strange British accent. They all looked at him with confusion and condescension.

"Shutter Island! Didn't anybody see it?" he said.

Apparently, they had not.

"I don't really like Leonardo DiCaprio," said Lindsay.

"Are you kidding me? Do you want to fight?" said Dustin, in what must have been a joke, but which certainly didn't seem like one from his tone.

"Maybe she lost her phone and is waiting back at the car so she doesn't lose us completely!" suggested Sean animatedly, believing he had experienced a stroke of insight.

But she wasn't there either. They tried calling her again but there was still no answer.

"What should we do?" asked Dustin.

"Let's just walk around the mall. At some point she'll either call us or we'll run into her. This doesn't have to be such a crisis," said Chris.

None of the others had a better solution so they all agreed.

For a while they halfheartedly explored the three floored structure, weaving in and around long purchase lines that went well beyond the borders of store entrances. Their enthusiasm was notably diminished as time ticked on and the mystery of Kelly's sudden separation became more and more pronounced. The particular nervous ticks of the group's members began to outwardly emerge. Jane's skin transformed into a landscape of goosebumps. Dustin's left eye commenced a rhythmic twitch. Even supposedly impervious Chris's armpits unleashed a flash flood of sweat as uncertainty lowered its bitter cage around them.

As for Lindsay, all of the color had drained from her face. But the reasoning for her concern was less pure than she might have liked. Sure, she was worried about her friend/acquaintance's whereabouts, but she was also oddly, uncomfortably, excited. Something dramatic was happening for once. It would probably turn out to be some mundane misunderstanding and they would soon come across Kelly making out with some goon on the benches beside the fountain, but for the moment she found herself in the middle of a full-fledged *plot*. Needless to say, she kept these dangerous thoughts to herself and her pale look probably came more from worry that the others might suspect her mental betrayal than from anything else.

For his part, Sean, whose mind was the mammal equivalent of a candleless jack-o-lantern, saw all this quiet as a good opportunity to resume his flirting with Lindsay.

"I like your shirt," he said. A real Don Juan.

"Oh. Thanks," she replied with minimal enthusiasm.

"You know, I listen to you in class sometimes. When you answer questions and stuff. You're really smart."

"That's nice of you to say."

"I mean, I know I'm not that smart, but I can tell who is smart, so I think of that as a kind of smart, you know?"

"It's practically the same thing," she said sarcastically.

"I like to think so."

Silence.

"So," Sean continued, "It's nice hanging out, outside school."

"Yep."

"Maybe you'd hang out with me again sometime."

"I'm sure we'll all hang out again."

"Yeah, but I mean, like, just with me. You know, like, just me and you. You know, like, just you and me."

"Me and you? Or you and me? I'm confused," said Lindsay, deciding somewhat uncharacteristically to mess with her suitor, because she just couldn't take his unsavory brainless genuineness at the particular moment.

"Well, like, either one!" he said wholeheartedly.

"Hmmm. I don't know. I mean, maybe you and me. But me and you? I'm just not sure I see it."

"Oh, I see," he said with concern. Then a small smile was sketched on his blank canvas. "Wait, are you messing with me?"

His question never got answered. It was interrupted by a scream from Jane.

"Look!" she said following her vocal outburst. "Those are Kelly's shoes!"

Sure enough, a few feet down the hallway that led to the still acceptably clean, but doomed to be revolting first floor public bathrooms, sat Kelly's pair of Steve Maddens, covered in a strange puddle of yellow-green liquid.

"Ewww, what is that?" said Dustin. "Is it pee?"

They cautiously preceded over to the muck covered shoes.

"That's not like any pee I've ever seen," said Chris as they got a closer look. "It looks more like slime."

"Oh god. What the fuck is happening?" said Jane through fear induced stuttering.

"Guys, look," said Lindsay. She pointed further down the hallway. Drops of the unidentifiable slime formed a path to a door marked "Employees only."

"Maybe we should get the mall cops," said Dustin.

"Yeah right. Those assholes will just think we're a bunch of prankster teenagers trying to mess with them," said Chris, as behind them a mustached mall cop tripped over his own feet while chasing a ten year old punk who had stolen a decorative potted plant.

"So what do we do?" asked Sean.

"We follow the trail," declared Lindsay with confidence. "We see what's behind that door."

All five took a moment to stare at the door and imagine the dark depths which might lie behind it.

"Well," said Chris, deciding that a male should lead this mission even if Lindsay had suggested it, "Let's get to it. Follow me."

Chris went first. Then Lindsay. Then Sean, who awkwardly inserted himself in front of Lindsay in line, in order to protect her. Then Dustin (both eyes now twitching). Then finally the unreservedly panicking Jane, who sung a chorus of "Oh gods," that all of the others did their best to ignore.

Chris slowly pushed the door open. On the other side was a rather unassuming, completely unornamented hallway. The track of green slime continued down the floor.

"C'mon," their self-appointed leader said and they all followed.

They tiptoed down the tiles. An oppressive silence smothered them as the blank walkway continued on and the globs of green on the ground grew in size. Heavy breathing rotated like a choral baseline.

Lindsay's heart beat faster and faster but not from fear. She had never been so excited in her entire life. Though she hadn't ever consumed any hard drugs, she imagined that this anticipatory thrill had to measure up to the highs gained from certain uppers.

At the end of the hallway was another door. Underneath its frame rested a full pond of the green scum.

"1. 2. 3!" Chris said quickly before kicking the door open in a completely unnecessary feet feat that made everyone nearly jump out of their shoes (or so the expression goes – in reality one would have to be wearing unreasonably large shoes for this event to occur).

"What the fuck Chris?!" shouted Jane, who briefly thought she was having a heart attack.

"Yeah, dude, was that really necessary?" said Dustin.

"I just felt like, fuck it, let's show them that we mean business," said Chris.

"Who are we showing that we mean business?" asked Dustin.

"I don't know. Them. You know. Whoever's doing this."

"Doing what?"

"Okay, now you're just being contrary."

"Am I?"

"There you go again."

"Guys...," said Sean, interrupting the squabble, "Look."

The other four heads turned in sync and saw what waited for them on the other side of the kicked open door.

A dark dank flight of stairs descended into a dreary basement of pipes and heaters. The sight of the dirty underground room of behind the scenes practicality would have creeped them out anyway from the contrast it held to the bright, smooth, product laced spaces open to the public eye. But there was a much more frightening, clearly unintended, feature of the subterranean chamber: Where the stone floor should have been, there was a two foot deep *swamp*, complete with floating pieces of rotted wood and vines extending out of the muck, up onto the walls.

"I guess this is what happens when you build a mall on swamp land," said Chris, wishing to diffuse the tension, though no one really bought his explanation.

"Maybe we should turn back," said Jane.

"I like that idea," said Dustin.

"No," said Lindsay. "We can't turn back now." Then she added, as a personal afterthought but as a crucial piece of motivation to the others, "Kelly, might be down there,"

"Lindsay is right," said Sean forcefully, who was clearly prepared to agree with any suggestion Lindsay made, even if it was – "hey, let's all kick Sean in the balls!" Not that there's any reason she would have ever suggested that, but the point remains that Sean really wanted to have sex with Lindsay.

Before the others had a chance to agree or disagree Lindsay continued down the stairway. The others, still too entrenched in their teenage years to really think for themselves, followed.

"Kelly!" shouted Chris, "Are you down here?!"

A low toned gurgle responded to his question.

"What the fuck was that!?" said Dustin

The door at the top of the steps slammed shut. The shock of the noise made Jane's feet slip. She let out a high pitched scream as her momentum sent the entire crew tumbling into the slime.

"Gross," said Sean, as he peeled himself out of the gunk. It felt like decayed jello.

"Guys – I'm scared," said Jane through chattering teeth.

"That's enough of this. I'm getting the hell out of here," said Dustin. He trudged his way back towards the steps. Survival instincts kicked in and his friends were no longer his top priority.

"Uh, dude? What's that on the stairs?" said Chris, his sheen of supposed confidence finally breaking as fear wrapped its ugly hands around his neck.

"Huh?" said Dustin.

They all saw it at once. A seven foot high, four foot wide, monster in the shadows. It was dripping. And twitching. Its eyes were corpulent and gray, but only one eye was in its socket. The other dangled on a thinly connected string of nerves. They couldn't make out the rest of its features in the darkness but there could be no doubting that it was...

THE BLUFORD SPRINGS SWAMP MONSTER.

"Swampy," Lindsay whispered to herself, in awe of what stood before her. The room was dark, but for Lindsay, a bright heavenly light was shining.

Dustin, however, didn't have the same positive perspective.

"SHITTTTTTTTTTTTTTTTT!" he screamed as the monster descended upon him. He tried to run but it was too late. Swampy wrapped his goopy arms around the class clown and shoved him into the depths of his unhinged mouth. He chewed Dustin up. The murderous grinding sounded like an unregulated jackhammer. It was so loud that it drowned out Jane's somewhat repetitive shrieks. Moments later, Swampy spit his pray across the room. Dustin's body looked like a husk of corn on the cob whose kernels had been thoroughly shucked.

The remaining teens were frozen solid for a good ten seconds, as is perfectly understandable in such a moment of shock.

Finally, Chris shouted, "RUN!" and led the way with an all-out sprint – (he'd been out in front thus far, so why stop now?)

Jane followed with a graceless run, looking like a bird whose wings had been broken and who was learning to escape predators on foot for the first time.

Poor, terrified, meat-headed Sean was about to race after them when he noticed that Lindsay had not moved an inch.

"Lindsay! Come on!" he urged her.

But she could not even hear him. Because right then, she only had eyes for the swamp monster.

"Hi," she said gently, looking back and forth between his mis-leveled pupils.

Swampy took a step closer to her and she was able to see him fully. He truly was revolting. His entire body looked like a runny nose. His snot skin was covered with bulbous bubble pimples that popped and regrew in an almost musical pattern. He had teeth, but they were not inside of his outhouse hole of a mouth. Rather, they jutted out from various random spots along his frame. Oh and the *smell* – it was unbearable – like a collection of first place farts at the gas pageant had been left out for too long in the sun.

For Lindsay, it was love at first sight.

She took a step closer to the beast. Some of the dripping boogers on him rose up and stretched towards her.

She leaned in to kiss him.

"Lindsay! No!"

Then Sean did the bravest and stupidest thing he ever did in his short life.

He ran over and punched the swamp monster in the face. His hand went right through the creature's slimy head and when he pulled his arm back out it burned like it had been dipped in lava. He squealed as he watched his arm melt into sickening radioactive decay.

"I love you," said Lindsay.

Sean started to cry. "I love you too," he said.

"No not you," she specified gently, "*You*," she said to the swamp monster.

And wouldn't you know it – for a brief instant – she saw something human in Swampy's cold dead eyes. She knew then and there that he loved her too.

"Blargggggg," said Swampy.

"What the fuck!?" said Sean.

Swampy reached into Sean's stomach, pulled out his guts, and tossed them on his own head like a hat. Sean's removed lower intestine fell in front of the monster's face and he ate it with a second mouth that resided in his nostrils.

"I don't understand," said Sean with his last breath.

"No one understands love," said Lindsay, never taking her eyes off Swampy.

Sean collapsed to the ground and died.

In the background Chris screamed. "Fuck!" Lindsay heard him say, "There's no other exit!"

"Oh god, oh god, oh god," said Jane, in an endless loop that would take up too much ink to write down in full.

"Okay," Chris said to her quietly. "We just have to run past the thing as fast as we can. I can't see it being that speedy. We run right past it, right for the door."

"I'm so scared."

"I know. But I'm not good at comforting people. It's been a problem in both of the relationships I've been in. I guess it's something I'll have to get over one day if I ever want something long term, but I don't know, part of me thinks it's just how I am."

"What?"

"Nevermind. On the count of 3. Ready. 1. 2. 3!"

At the sound of his count Chris and Jane galloped across the room as fast as their hooves would take them. Chris screamed a guttural yelp, best transcribed as "AHHHH." It was intended to be a war cry.

As they approached, Swampy stood in place. Lindsay did the same. They were mutually unfazed.

Inches away from his horrific foe, Chris had the bright idea to run right at the beast and plow over him like a linebacker to prevent being snatched. He lowered his shoulders, collided into the monster's icky "chest"... and went right through the less than solid creature, emerging on the other side, plastered in flecks of acidic play-doh. His exposed skin immediately boiled to goo and his covered skin got ready to join in the immense pain as his clothes rapidly dissolved. Chris's repetitive scream of "AHHH, AHHH, AHHHH," continued, but now from all consuming pain, rather than from aggression.

While the monster was distracted by the slithering reformation of his body, which briefly contained a Chris-shaped hole, Jane was able to run around him, up the stairs, and out the door. Chris, although aflame both inside and out, mustered up the strength to follow.

Lindsay's heart beat fast at finally being alone with the swamp monster. She wanted to look deep into his eyes and peer into his soul. She wanted him to wrap his arms around her and drip his green globular material into every part of herself.

But at the moment he was distracted. He paid her a quick, dead eyed glance, then turned and raced after Jane and Chris, unleashing a hurricane of nasal passage destroying farts that Lindsay drank in like a desert wanderer at an oasis pool, saved miraculously from the brink of thirst death.

She ran after him. "Wait!" she cried, desperately needing his love.

At first Jane and Chris's reemergence into the bustling mall did not create the chaos it probably should have, considering she was letting out a series of high pitched screams and his face was melting off. Actually it barely even attracted attention beyond a few perturbed glances from those over the age of forty who disapproved of kids running around the mall "high as a kite."

But when Jane's shirt and bra ripped off on the extended branch of a decorative tree (since bare breasts just tend to find their way into these horror situations), the males in the area took notice. And when the males took notice, the females with them took notice, quickly pulling dirty looks out of their expression holsters with the speed of the greatest gunslingers. And when the more observant females looked closely at the object of their derision, they noticed genuine fear on her face. Then they noticed her screaming companion whose body looked like it had been through a garbage disposal. And then they noticed the swamp monster chasing them. And then they kind of flipped out.

Screams ping ponged back and forth across the mall like they were shot out of a canon. A mass exodus began. Frantic shoppers fastened iron grips on their bags of all important items and ran for the doors.

Some on the second and third floor landings stayed put – unable to look away. They saw a teenage girl chasing down the monster screaming "Wait! Wait!" They were amazed at what they imagined to be her bravery in trying to stop the monster from killing her friends. Little did they suspect her trance of desire.

Eventually Chris's legs collapsed into mashed potato stumps and his torso splatted on top of them like gravy. The monster shuffled close to him. He scooped up what remained of Chris with a serpentine tongue, chewed him up, and with an ear splitting belch spit out his head like the pit of a cherry. It shattered the window of the first floor GAP.

Jane neared the door when the monster spit out a wad of vile phlegm that projected into the air and landed on her like a net. She was helplessly fastened to the ground. The monster approached. She screamed. The terrified folks remaining in the mall could only watch as the swamp monster lowered himself, anus first, onto her and swallowed her up through the body end typically designated for disposal.

A bone chilling quiet followed. The beast looked around in different directions with his unsymmetrical eyes. His hunger was not yet satiated. He searched for more victims.

His hunt was interrupted by the approach of Lindsay.

She stepped slowly and confidently towards him. She saw him through a romantic gauze, like he was a figure from her dreams or a guest on a Barbara Walters interview.

He let out a disgusting gurgle. He whipped his head back and forth. He almost looked scared. Like a scared teenage boy about to have his first kiss.

Swampy looked at Lindsay for a long moment. Then, hearing the approaching police sirens, he let himself drip through a crack in the floor and disappeared from sight.

Later that night, after the police had questioned her, and she had been hounded by reporters, and her mother had hugged her so hard she nearly suffocated, as she lied in bed with no chance of actually falling asleep, the spell would crack just enough to let in a beam of guilt and self-loathing. Lindsay would brutally question herself on how she could be so emotionless over the horrific deaths of her friends; how she could be so inhuman; and most of all – how the hell she could be attracted to a nauseating swamp monster to the point of a near comatose daze. She would question it all, knowing how deeply fucked up she must be. But she wouldn't feel any different. She would still want nothing in the world but to be held in those slimy "arms."

2

Minutes after being unceremoniously rejected as a prom date by his dream girl Lindsay Morpletopple, Teddy Bigshartz walked directly to the B.S.H.S. annex vending machine and bought out the entire row of Honey Buns. He skipped geometry, marking the first time he had cut a class during his entire academic career, and gorged himself on those notoriously sticky pastry rolls. He cried a little in the bathroom, got kicked in the knees by a mean spirited stoner who heard him crying in the bathroom, then pulled himself together for his remaining two classes, his eyelids quivering threateningly throughout though ultimately holding strong. As soon as the day-ending bell rang he marched on a torrid walk home, burning excess energy with such vigor that he probably released fossil fuels into the air.

Teddy had been in love with Lindsay for over two years. They had shared a short conversation during freshman orientation that had been enough to cast her as the permanent leading lady in his fantasies of romance most high. The conversation had been about reading. So few girls his age loved to read like he did and even fewer were gorgeous blondes.

He had talked to Lindsay here and there over the years in short snippets, though they certainly couldn't be called friends or really even associates. But she knew who he was – he was certain of that! (Pretty certain anyway).

Every night he dreamed of her. Every day his thoughts were stuffed with her beautiful image. When he went to school he spent the entire day just praying for a fleeting moment of conversation or contact with her. One time at the end of the day, as Lindsay chatted with her friends on the way out of school, he noticed that she dropped a pencil. He picked it up and handed it to her. She said "thanks." It was just about the happiest he had ever felt in his life.

Teddy had been so confident about his prom plan. He would ask her right at the beginning of October – early enough so that no one else would have, but not so absurdly early that he would seem overanxious. She would say yes because she was a kind person who would feel too bad to say no, then he would have almost a full school year as her prom date to be to get to know her. After all, she couldn't turn down hanging out with the guy she was going to go to the prom with.

But she didn't say yes. Turns out she was not too kind to pass. His plan was foiled.

Teddy's emotional devastation had a main course of sadness, but also contained a significant side-dish of anger. The anger was not really directed at Lindsay, but more at himself. He hated the fact that his love for Lindsay turned him into someone he usually was not.

Teddy was a nerd for certain. He was a fan of foreign films and literary fiction, who thought grammar was interesting and sports a bore. But he was a self-aware nerd in complete control of when, and where, and in front of whom, his purest nerdy outbursts took place. He certainly couldn't pass as cool, but he was fully capable of fitting in with the hefty stock of bland normals parading the halls of small town USA high. More importantly, he was a subtly sarcastic intellectual who kept irrational emotions chained up, sentenced to suppression for the crime of doing nobody any good. He didn't let the silly squabbles of typical teenagers affect him for he was above these average Joes and Janes and could outwit them even if they didn't realize it.

He had a high self-esteem, for Pete's sake! How many teenagers could boast of that particular claim?

Yet Lindsay detonated all his rationality and self-esteem into a million unrecognizable shards. She was the closest thing he had ever experienced to a drug. Some substance, or in this case, person, who yielded a sensation of such high that the user's coherent thoughts withered away, replaced only by the repeated notion: I WANT, I WANT, I WANT...

His grades through the first month of junior year were not what they should have been and it was because he spent all his time asking Lindsay to the prom in his head on an endless loop, imagining each and every likely and wildly unlikely scenario of reaction hundreds of times over. This tended to distract him from any other important work he should have actually been focused on.

Now, on his devastating walk home, following his epic failure, he thought of how cruel the mind was to shackle him into a slavery of thoughts about a particular individual, when the object of his yearning had likely not thought of him once the entire time. How often throughout history had a pathetic person been seized by love's oppression, their mind burdened with an endless hunger for another, unable to think about anyone or anything else, left starving without the only meal they are willing to let nourish them, while their object of affection lived their life burdenless, ultimately unaware of maintaining the smallest stronghold in another's mind lands?

Oh this life is painful, thought Teddy. Though the aggressively depressing content in all of the foreign films he watched and the novels he read should have left him less surprised at that conclusion.

So, with nothing else to do following his heartbreak, Teddy returned home to his basement bedroom and masturbated for a little while (a very little while, if we must be honest), pretending that Lindsay had in fact said yes and that she had been uncontrollably in love with him all this time too and had been waiting so desperately for him to reach out that when he finally told her how he felt her passion could not be contained; and in her delirious joy she immediately swept him home and mounted him in a delirious physical culmination of all that had been left unsaid.

After jerking off, he spent an hour or so sifting through love poetry on the internet, hoping to find some lyrically grouped words to match his inner condition. A failed venture. Every poem he came across seemed to be sortable into one of two distinct categories: 1) Poems that sounded like they must be brilliant but contained language so incomprehensible he couldn't make heads or tails of what the hell they might be talking about. 2) Poems so laughably straightforward in their declarations of love that they would probably feel at home in the notebooks of middle school girls who had Justin Beiber posters on their walls.

He then closed the browser to the awful poetry sites the search engine was directing him to and instead searched for porn, figuring he might as well masturbate some more. But watching the porn made him feel guilty – like he was cheating on Lindsay, even though she had just rejected him – and so he closed the screen and thought of her instead. But having masturbated so shortly before made it take an unreasonably long time with no feeling of end in sight, even after ten minutes, at which point his arm was completely exhausted, so he stopped that too and laid down on his bed feeling the most unfulfilled he ever had in his life.

The rest of the evening was an unpleasant trudge. He barely touched his food at dinner, which excessively concerned his overprotective mother, especially when he refused to give any reason for his lack of appetite. He ignored the calls and texts from his best buddy Henry, asking him to check out the new mall with their friend Tom and the rest of the county's youth, sure he couldn't stomach such a place on a night like this. He flipped through the television channels erratically, no program satiating the opposing needs of either hopeful restoration or despairing emotional embrace. He eventually settled on a highly edited for television Rambo marathon, since the incredulity of the violence in parts II through IV was so removed from reality that it provided a brief, but ultimately unlasting, sense of escape. He lay in his bed and stared at the ceiling for hours, wondering if a person could feel stressed enough to induce a stroke and/or heart attack. He pretended that he held Lindsay in his arms and kissed her and caressed her. He wanted her more than ever although her rejection had caused him so much pain and even though she likely had not thought of him once since unknowingly breaking his heart.

Around 8 P.M. he received another call and a subsequent text from Henry but he didn't answer or read the text. He didn' t wish to speak to any human that wasn't Lindsay. He didn't want to be reminded that people who weren't Lindsay existed.

At 8:15 Teddy's dad knocked on his door and entered before receiving a response.

"Hey buddy, you alright?" he said.

"Fine," said Teddy, his face buried in a pillow – not the most convincing context in which to insist on his contentment if he really wanted his dad to believe him.

"You seem a little off to me and your mom," Teddy's dad said, sitting down on the edge of the bed.

"I'm not off. I'm on. I'm fine."

"Teddy…are you getting bullied?"

"What?"

"Look, we know you're not the coolest kid in the world. Hell, you're a bit of a nerd—"

"Uh…"

"Kids are going to pick on you. It's going to happen if you dress like you do and talk a lot about books and computers—"

"How do I dress?" said Teddy, self-consciously, looking down at his outfit, which he had thought was perfectly acceptable.

"—but you don't have to change who you are because of a bunch of assholes. You know what I say? Don't tell your mom I said this. But fuck em. Fuck em!"

"Jesus Christ dad."

"You're better than those assholes and they're just picking on you because they have their own feelings of inadequacy. And who knows, maybe some of them have been molested and they're just taking out their pain on some kids they think are weaker than them."

"I'm not getting picked on dad!"

"I mean I'm not saying I don't feel bad for them, they're victims but… wait, did you say you're not getting picked on?

"No! I'm not!"

"I thought you said you were."

"No, I didn't."

"Are you sure? I mean you talk an awful lot about fantasy."

"I talk about Game of Thrones. Everybody loves Game of Thrones. It's like the highest rated show on premium cable."

"I haven't seen it."

"That's because we don't have HBO."

"Well then how have you seen it?"

"I download it."

"Isn't that illegal?"

"Well yeah, technically, but I mean, everybody does it."

"I don't know how I feel about that. I mean I saw this ad that said piracy is not a victimless crime – but, wait, hold on, we're getting off topic. You're not getting picked on?"

"NO!"

"You don't have to yell."

"Sorry."

"Well then what's bothering you?"

"Nothing. I'm fine."

Teddy's dad looked into his son's eyes for a long moment, trying to assess just why his son was obviously lying to him.

"You're sure?"

"Yeah," said Teddy unconvincingly.

"Well if you ever need to talk to someone, you know I'm always here for you."

"I know Dad."

Teddy's dad departed from the room. Oddly enough, as intensely as Teddy had wanted his father to leave when he had been in the room, he now, suddenly and dramatically, missed the company.

He shoved his head back into his pillow and recommenced wallowing.

At around 8:30, Teddy heard his mother scream. This, in and of itself, was not something so rare or noteworthy. To call Teddy's mom high strung would be a massive understatement. She was strung from the top of Sears tower. She was EVEREST strung. The woman screamed whenever someone unexpectedly entered a room or whenever an object was dropped unexpectedly or when a car door closed outside or when the phone rang or when a light went out or when a crumb dropped or pretty much any fucking time any fucking thing happened, if you get the idea. So if Teddy had no immediate response to her scream, he can be forgiven.

But instead of the usual single ear piercing cry, followed by silence and shame at her own foolishness and then apologies to the surrounding victims of her overreaction who were busy massaging their ear drums, this time Teddy's mom's initial blast of vocal fear was followed by the ellipsis of "NO, GOD NO," then a series of distraught grunts, another half scream (a whispery wail perhaps) and then possible tears, though it was hard for Teddy to tell for sure from inside his room with the door closed and his face wrapped inside of his pillow.

Curiosity overcame heartbroken sloth and Teddy pushed himself out of his bed and towards the living room to find out just what was happening and if he should be calling for an ambulance or something.

His mother and father both appeared to be in once piece but their distressed faces were locked on to some breaking news report on the television.

"What's happening?" he asked.

His father looked over to him. Teddy had never seen him so drained of color or hope. He just pointed to the television, unable to speak.

Helicopter footage showed the Bluford Springs Mall. Police were everywhere. The words on the screen read: "Murder at the Mall."

Teddy's heart started to beat real hard. "What's happening?" he repeated with force.

His mother sobbed and babbled some incoherent nonsense.

"What?"

"Some kids got killed," Teddy's father said softly. "Some fuck job dressed up like the swamp monster."

"The swamp monster?" said Teddy. He did not lack knowledge of the local legend, he was just surprised by what he heard. His parents did not respond to his vocal question mark.

Teddy sat down on the couch next to his folks and closely watched the broadcast.

The anchor communicated the circumstances of the evening's unexpected horror on a frustrating repetitive loop of description that none of the Bigshartz clan (nor any of the parallel families throughout the neighborhood or the state or the country in their own homes, glued to their own television sets) could turn away from. An innocent exciting evening in a brand new complex of commerce had been unexpectedly shattered by a maniac in a monster costume chasing a group of three youths (one of whom was already battered and bloody) through the center walkway of the first floor. He had smothered one male and one female to death with his bare hands but the remaining teenage girl had somehow managed to avoid his intended violence just before chaos broke out and the murderer disappeared from sight. Authorities were investigating to see if there had been any other victims of this sick rampage. Talk eventually turned to the role violent video games played in causing this tragedy. That was when Teddy abruptly remembered Henry's phone call.

"Shit," he said and ran to his bedroom. Normally his mother would have screamed from concern at his sudden exit but she was too deep in her tragedy induced stupor.

Teddy looked at Henry's text message.

It read: "CALL ME BACK. INSANE SHIT AT THE MALL."

He rang Henry up immediately.

"Hey, where were you?" said Henry upon answering.

"At home. I just...missed your call. I heard what happened. Where are you? Are you guys okay?"

"Yeah we're fine, but, Ted, you wouldn't believe the shit we saw."

"Where are you now?"

"I'm back home. We got out of there quick."

"You saw it happen?"

"We saw the whole thing. We were on the third floor eating ice cream."

"A little cold out for that isn't it?"

"Eh, I feel like I can eat ice cream until it dips below forty."

"Interesting."

"Anyway, we're just eating our cones at a bench and all of the sudden we hear this SCREAMING. So we turn around and we see...I mean I kind of feel crazy saying what we saw but—"

"Yeah they said on the news. Some maniac dressed up like the swamp monster."

"That's what they said?"

"Yeah."

"Well, that's not exactly accurate."

"What do you mean?"

"I mean, I can hardly believe that I'm saying this but everyone else around me saw the same thing."

"What?"

"It wasn't some creep dressed up like the swamp monster. It *was* the swamp monster."

There was a long gap of silence.

"It's kind of fucked up to joke about this. People died," said Teddy.

"I'm not joking! It was the fucking swamp monster! It was a gigantic fucking glob of slime and guck with eyes slithering down the mall! It ate Jane Heliotope with its ass! With its ass Teddy! WITH ITS ASS!"

"Henry maybe you're experiencing some sort of post-traumatic stress. Some trauma induced psychosis."

"Ask anyone there. It shouldn't be so hard. It was half the town."

"I don't understand."

"Neither did any of us but I'm telling you, we were all just sitting around, minding our own business, and out of nowhere we hear this screaming and there's the swamp monster chasing Jane Heliotope and Chris Truffleshaw, who looks like he's FUCKING MELTING, and they're being chased by Lindsay Morpletopple and they're all screaming their lungs out."

Teddy's heart ricocheted around his chest like a bullet shot inside a closet that some pretentious modern architect had built entirely out of metal. He hadn't thought to worry whether Lindsay had been there. The thought that Lindsay may have been killed by a murderer or a monster (though he still had his doubts about that part of the story) was enough to make him want to just die right then and there. Just take a pencil from his desk and jam it into his throat and be done with the whole thing.

"Lindsay Morpletopple?" Teddy squeaked out of his unexpectedly vanished voice, which had cowardly retreated inside of him to hide behind an artery or some other shield of an organ. He had never told his closest friend about his life-consuming crush. Henry had no idea that earlier that very day his emotionally secretive pal had asked this very girl to the prom and faced stark rejection.

"Yeah. She was running the monster down! And then it turns and looks at her and she just STARES at it. And then it just shuffles off and disappears. It didn't even touch her after ripping the other two to shreds."

"So Lindsay's alive?"

"Yeah, she's fine. Then the cops came and…"

Henry kept speaking but Teddy didn't hear anything he said. He was too busy undergoing a full body hope reset, like a just flushed toilet releasing tainted water, only to be immediately refilled with a bowl of clean liquid.

Lindsay was okay. It didn't matter what had happened as long as Lindsay was okay.

3

Sleep and Lindsay were not currently on speaking terms. Which is a shame, because Lindsay could have used someone to talk to while she was up all night.

She tossed. She turned. She flipped from back to front to side, but sleep resisted her, holding tightly on to its grudge. It refused to let Lindsay fall into its comforting arms.

Lindsay supposed sleep was mad at her because her thoughts just wouldn't shut up about Swampy and how *dreamy* he was. (Or perhaps *nightmarish*, would have been more accurate). She longed for him. She touched herself as she thought about his slimy exterior. Her heart beat hard as she imagined being held in his booger arms. She wanted to disappear into his goo like a pinhole pricked plastic float slowly descending into a public pool.

The past several days had been a whirlwind. She was the focus of every student's peripheral vision at school, as well as several undisguised direct glances. The school population's intense curiosity was thinly masked by their surface sympathy.

To be fair, many were genuinely saddened by the deaths of their friends and acquaintances, but the whole swamp monster angle definitely diluted the tragedy with all of the questions it raised.

The official national news position was that "a man in a monster costume" had committed the heinous crimes, but the folks of Bluford Springs knew better. They knew that the creature whose attack had garnered over six hundred thousand views on a cell phone camera recorded youtube video was the real thing. The legends were true. Swampy had awoken once again and Lindsay was their only link to him. They were terrified of the monster but in a way they worshipped him. He was their own local mythology. He was a kind of god.

"What did it look like?" Lindsay was asked by a social grace-less freshman boy with fishbowl glasses who must have been on the educational fast track because there was no way he was any older than eleven.

She did not answer the freshman's question. Not because she was too afraid or traumatized to give an inch by an inch description of the monster's "body," but because she was greedy and wanted Swampy all to herself. In a weird way, she felt that talking to others about him would be akin to cheating on him.

Lindsay did take some time out of her busy schedule of longing and being gawked at to question just where along the line her sanity had bought a one way ticket to crazy town. Her attraction to monsters, whether fictional and handsome or real and revolting, was now too strong to be denied in any capacity. And her attempts at convincing herself that her attraction to William Denworth had been due to his handsomeness and attitude, rather than his appetite for destruction were far out the window. It was sick and disturbing, but the truth was that she found gruesome violence to be a huge turn on. She now realized that. Even if the instinct was too powerful to deny, she was determined to figure out where it had come from.

So as she tossed and turned at night and the sweats of emotional fever ran down her forehead, she thought endlessly of a future with Swampy; but she also explored the labyrinth of the past, mining that mucky region of the mind for answers about the birth of her ailment.

She had been born with a severe allergy to wool that she had discovered at age five when her mother had swaddled her in a sweater to shield her from the "devastating" forty degree weather. She had broken out in hives so severe it wouldn't have been surprising if bees had emerged from them. The swelling hadn't receded for over a week. But it probably wasn't her traumatic wool allergy that inspired her sexual proclivities.

She had made out with exactly two boys, neither of whom she particularly liked. She did find the novelty of the first tongue on tongue contact exciting. (Though the second session with more attractive boy number two was kind of tedious.)

She went to four different summer camps in three years from the ages of seven to ten, until her mother dropped the idea, coming to the conclusion that Lindsay just didn't like the outdoors.

When she was twelve she had written a letter to the Vice President for a school assignment and he (or his office) had actually responded. The letter had complimented a tie the Veep had worn. The return letter had thanked Lindsay for the compliment.

Lindsay's thoughts were kind of all over the place, it's true, but the mind doesn't particularly like to stay fastened to its rationality safety wires when it's dangling over the cliff of half sleep.

In reality there were two main sources of probable cause for her craziness. Two people to be precise. Her grandmother and her father.

Lindsay's mother had been born when her own mom was only eighteen. She was born inside of the mental institution in which her young mother lived. Lindsay had never been told who her grandfather was.

Lindsay's grandmother was a loon. Lindsay had visited her periodically over the years when her mother insisted. She never paid too much attention to anything her grandmother said because he words were the incoherent ramblings of a lunatic. All her life she had done her best to try to forget that her crazy grandmother even existed, but now it occurred to her that they might be cut from the same cloth.

What if I'm just as crazy as she is? Lindsay wondered. *What if it's only a matter of time before I go completely insane? What if it's genetic?*

If her grandmother's mental illness was the primary "nature" hypothesis to her disturbing mind, the primary "nurture" cause had to be the adandonment of her father.

Lindsay had *loved* her dad. He was her favorite person in the "hole world," or so she had written in crayon next to a drawing of him on construction paper at age six. Every night she had cuddled up against him as he watched the local news reports of murders in the nearest impoverished neighborhoods. They often ate ice cream together for dinner instead of the meals Lindsay's mother cooked. He told her scary stories when he tucked her into bed; Tales of ghosts and ghouls and haunted houses that gave her nightmares for weeks, but she *loved* them anyway, just as she *loved* her father.

Then, abruptly and without warning, he had run off with a slutty med-school student (or so Lindsay's mother described her) just before Lindsay's seventh birthday.

He left Lindsay a note saying he was sorry and wishing her "an awesome life," which certainly implied that he no longer planned to be a part of it.

The whole ordeal was very traumatic. Lindsay cried for about a month straight. She ripped the heads off all of her Barbies and pooped in the hallway three times out of misguided emotional defiance. Her mother made her talk to a therapist after the third pooping incident, perhaps also worried that Lindsay had inherited her own mother's lunacy. Lindsay saw Dr. Bootstein for three and a half years, until the doc died unexpectedly, choking on a salmon bone from a fish spread at her family's Yom Kippur break the fast dinner. At that point Lindsay's mother decided that her daughter seemed perfectly normal and that all the psychotherapy had been a waste of time and money anyway since her daughter had just been sad about being abandoned by her father, which was completely understandable. (She probably would have felt far different on the matter if she had seen Dr. Bootstein's three years of rather disturbing notes, but she was not afforded such an opportunity.)

There was still a part of Lindsay that held out hope that her father would return someday, or at the very least, would contact her. But thus far this dream in her head had not transformed into any corresponding reality.

Lindsay tossed her covers off violently. She stomped upon them in a release of aggression she had not been prepared for but obviously needed. She masturbated standing up for a little while, imagining Swampy's nerve dangling eye watching her, but the culmination provided no release from her bondage of desire.

And that's when she decided that she could wait no longer. She had to see him again. So she changed her underwear, threw on some clothes and sneaks, and made her way into the night.

She broke her long unused bicycle out of the garage for fear that starting the car might awake her mother. The old pink bike's joints were rusty and its wheels flat, but it managed the job of slowly moving Lindsay forward even if it felt like riding a toaster.

Her destination: the closed down police crime scene known as the Bluford Springs Mall.

...

As she pedaled along through the suburban darkness and her calves ached from not having ridden her handle frilled, two wheeled childhood vehicle for over three years, she thought about the funerals of the five peers her chosen lover had killed.

They had been a gloomy succession of mass crowds shedding oceans of tears over lives lost too soon. Great swaths of black cloth had packed into the three churches chosen for the task. (Two had double duty). Giant media conglomerate news outlets had battled over private property lines for the prime camera spot to catch the ratings gold footage for their twenty-four hour news networks. The President of the United States himself had sent letters of condolences over the "tragedy" brought about by a "deranged costumed killer," and declared that he would do "anything he could" for the grieving families – a claim whose limitations had already become apparent when Dustin's little brother had asked for a tank and promptly been ignored.

It was all quite depressing – at least from an objective standpoint. Lindsay received the lion's share of the non-family comfort provided by the townsfolk who barely knew the victims but felt it socially necessary to attend their funerals anyway. Everyone presumed her to be a broken thing, too shattered by trauma to even be considered fragile, since fragility no longer applies when the object is already in shards. Lindsay found the performance of it all revolting; all of these strangers going through the motions to act like they were sad about her own presumed sadness, which also did not exist.

Lucikly perhaps, the only person who seemed to notice Lindsay's true state of emotions was her own mother.

Her mom's first reaction to the madness at the mall was disbelief so total you might have thought the police had told her that she was out of milk instead of "your daughter was the sole survivor of a public murder spree." Then, a half hour later, when the police left for the evening after questioning Lindsay less intensely than they probably should have (her unconscious determination to protect her love made her answers vague), Lindsay's mom suddenly shed her shell of shock and burst out crying. She clutched Lindsay like her daughter would fall into a bottomless pit if she let go. She both cursed and thanked the heavens for allowing such horror and for sparing her daughter, respectively. For several days Lindsay's mother, like everyone else, assumed Lindsay was devastated and did her best to provide an endless running spout of love and affection and comfort. Eventually however, she seemed to notice the odd fact that Lindsay didn't need any comfort. She noticed that Lindsay didn't seem sad at all, come to think of it. At funeral after funeral, Lindsay had the oddest expression on her face and Lindsay's mother couldn't quite place it.

After three burials she asked Lindsay directly about her odd look.

"Lindsay, what are you thinking? Just what is happening in that head of yours? I'd so like to know," she had said.

Lindsay told her, without the slightest hint of convincing emotion, that she was sad about her friends dying. It should have been a dead giveaway (pardon the expression) that her answer was false just from the fact that it was not said in a series of screams through a downpour of tears and immediately followed by a door slam, (the way most testy teenage girls would have said it).

In actuality, it was the way Lindsay spoke, not the way she didn't, which really disturbed her mother. Lindsay's facial muscles were still but somewhere in her eyes there was a sparkling gleam. A sick joy. A lust even.

After that, Lindsay's mother put on a façade of normalcy, but all the while Lindsay could tell that her mom was looking at her like a piece of meat she expected to spoil at any moment.

...

Breathless from unpracticed pedaling in the brisk autumn night, Lindsay finally arrived at the soon to be reopened mall.

The businesses which had paid handsomely for residence were fed up with the police's seizure of the facilities. They hadn't been able to find the mad-man murderer, known by all of the locals to be Swampy, and this week business would resume. The police's lack of location skills did not deter Lindsay's hunt. Her heart was magnetized to the swamp monster's. It was a romantic compass which would lead her right to him.

She parked her bike by the bushes in front of T.G.I.Fridays and searched for an open entrance. Her hope that the front doors might be incompetently unlocked was dashed but she was not discouraged.

She progressed down the mall's flowery surrounding sidewalks. She kept her eyes peeled for cracks in the fortress's armor. Smashing a panel of glass on a door or a window was not out of the question, but she figured some sort of alarm system was probably rigged for such aggressive break-ins. It was best to avoid destruction. She scanned the right angles where the walls met the ground for mouse holes which might provide some hope that the place was not impenetrable, even if they were far too small for her to fit through. Finally she took a break from looking down and tilted her head towards the sky.

The roof. That was where her entry would take place. She was suddenly sure of it. But how to scale the flat white walls?

Scanning the surrounding area she came across a giant cypress tree that bordered the mall's east end. The tree was far too large and imposing to have been inserted by the mall's landscape crew. It must have been a relic of the swamps. A stubborn, curmudgeonly, grandfather of a plant that refused to budge when all his brethren were removed for the purposes of human shopping. She said a quick prayer to the tree. She apologized on the behalf of humanity for the genocide of his kind and then asked the cypress the favor of providing her with a safe path to her great love.

Lindsay stretched out her legs, threw her arms around in a couple of wide concentric circles like she had learned to do in gym class before climbing the ropes, and approached the massive trunk. She wrapped her hands around the rough bark and shimmied herself up the base. The jagged wood cut her as she slid up the tree but she didn't notice the physical pain because the heartache of being away from Swampy usurped every other feeling. Ten feet up she grasped onto a thick limb and hoisted herself into the bramble of branches. From there the climb was easier. Her foot slipped once, nearly causing her to fall out of the tree to a landing of inevitable broken bones, but her hands instinctually locked on to the branch above her and saved her the pain. Her prayer had worked, she thought. She struggled and scrambled and put forth more physical effort than she ever had in her life, but it was all worth it because she eventually ascended to the roof. She hopped an imposing two-foot gap between the tree and the edge of the building, feeling far more self-assurance than she should have, even when she teetered on the edge for several seconds upon landing.

The roof was painted white for maximum heat reflection. It was ragged and jagged; the only outer part of the building that had not been designed for maximum visual appeal. Lindsay wasted no time scurrying around, letting her instincts guide her to the magical portal that would lead her inside. She thought about launching herself through a skylight window but sensibly halted herself, realizing that halfway to the ground would not be a good time to figure out how to break her fall.

Soon enough, she found just what she was looking for. It was a silver macaroni shaped tube of metal, just wide enough for a skinny girl like Lindsay to crawl in. It likely connected to the heater or the air conditioning or some other temperature related building function (she wasn't very concerned about the technicalities) but she had seen a hundred movies in which a spy crawled through building vents and she imagined it couldn't be too different in real life.

She contorted herself into the oversized pipe headfirst, gave a big push off with her feet and shot down the tube about twenty feet. It was a sensation similar to being on a water slide, if water slides required tetanus shots after each ride. She landed on her hands and sliced open her left palm on a jagged piece of metal. She wiped the blood on her pants and proceeded to crawl into a tight horizontal shaft. Periodically as she slid forward she thought she heard movement behind her, but every time she stopped she heard nothing and her call of "hello" was met with no response. No matter. It was no time to be phased by the creaky sounds or the intense claustrophobic conditions or the darkness. It was a time to continue forward with a marked determination. It was a time to grin and bear the conditions in order to achieve her destiny.

After what might have been ten minutes or might have been an hour Lindsay came across an opening underneath her. It was remarkably small, but she decided to try it. She squeezed herself into the hole and shimmied down a dank vertical pipe. For a moment she got stuck and a hot flash of worry went through her that she was permanently encased and would eventually die where she was from lack of food and water. Just as quick though, her body budged and her resounding hope drowned out any fear.

Suddenly, Lindsay felt something collapse below her. She tumbled downward but unexpectedly landed on a marshmallow soft surface. She opened her eyes, which she had shut instinctively in negative anticipation, and found that she had fortuitously crashed into a mattress store. Her back rested on a fluffy bed. Fate was on her side.

It must have been several hours during which Lindsay searched the mall for her slimy paramour. She ran back and forth throughout the darkened customerless walkways screaming: "Swampy! Swampy! Come out! Don't be afraid. I don't want to hurt you!" She left cheek smudges against the glass and grates of every closed store, peering in to see if her monster was hiding behind a mannequin or a rack of pants. She rotated in an out of the thoroughly disgusting public bathrooms. She went in every stall (both men's and women's) and looked deeply into the toilet bowls (or the ones that were without feces anyway – seriously how hard was it to just push the flush?) to see if a dangly eye extended down the pipes to Swampy's less than solid body. She weaved anxiously around police tape and crime scene debris looking for the door to the overflown chamber where she met Swampy for the first time.

And finally she found it.

Lindsay's heart rate increased as she jogged impatiently down the hall. Her whole body shook with eager anticipation as she pried open the door and walked down the soaked steps. The filthy water now came up to her thighs but it did not slow her progress. She slogged through the indoor swamp like a brigadier general.

"SWAMPY!" she screamed with all her might. "SWAMPY I LOVE YOU! PLEASE! PLEASE COME TALK TO ME!"

For a moment the room was silent but for the steady sound of dripping liquid. This quiet was shattered by an incredibly loud, sickening gurgle reverberating off the walls. Lindsay whipped her eyes around. The gurgle seemed to come from all sides of the room. It was a noise with three hundred and sixty degrees of presence, pushing closer and closer into her ear drums as its loogie hocking, chunk blowing imagery increased with every increase of decibels.

"Is that you?" she said, hope soaring inside of her.

A family of a hundred or more rats raced past her in terror, desperate to escape exactly what she came here to find.

They were followed by a small sphere rocketing through the water, connected to a long oily vein. The sphere's progress stopped when it arrived at Lindsay. It tentatively rose above the surface. It was Swampy's eye. It rotated on its axis until the swamp monster's pupil looked directly into Lindsay's.

"Hi," she said gently.

Frightened, the eye retreated. It shot back to its source like a measuring tape whose lock had been unclicked.

"Please come out," she said.

The eye peeked around a pipe, the shot back again quickly when it was spotted.

"I won't hurt you. I just want to talk."

She smelled him before she saw him. The putrid scent that was like the garbage that garbage would produce if garbage came to life. It was a smell so horrid that even the water seemed to run from it, but Lindsay breathed it in like it was roses smothered in chocolate chip cookies.

Then there he was. Six feet of sewage bubbling over towards her. He breathed heavily (if it could be called breathing – the status of such organs as lungs within his body was undetermined). Snot flecks fell off him as he got closer and closer to Lindsay.

For a moment she thought he was going to consume her whole. She had a brief flash of rationality where she saw the ridiculous situation for what it was. On one side stood she, an innocent teenage girl with serious fetishistic mental health issues – and on the other side stood a horrifying murderous swamp monster. She contemplated screaming the high pitched wail that such a situation would call for under any normal circumstances (well, okay, not normal, but what happens in moments like this in movies anyway).

Her clarity vanished just as quickly as it arrived when he stopped in front of her and looked at her contemplatively with his non hanging eye.

"Hi," she said again.

He was silent for a moment, then gurgled.

"You don't know how happy I am to see you again," she said. "I haven't been able to stop thinking about you."

His eye turned away from her. *He's embarrassed*, she thought. How could she have ever worried that he was going to hurt her? Sure he had murdered her friends in gruesome violence, but he had not touched her from the start. He felt something for her too. She knew he did.

"It's okay," she said. "I haven't been able to stop thinking about you either. I know everyone will think I'm crazy but I can't help what's inside of me. And the truth is...I love you. I love you more than anything in the world. And I'll love you forever."

It occurred to her as soon as she stopped speaking that the protagonist of the "Midnight" series had given this exact speech to her vampire lover at the end of "The Lust Kiss Goodnight" but it now fit so well into her own life that she was not bothered by her plagiarism.

She waited for a response. Swampy belched. Flecks of recently eaten rat guts flew onto her face.

"I want us to spend our lives together," she said. "Please. Tell me you'll take me as your wife."

She reached out for his hand and her own fingers submerged into his goop.

Just then, Swampy whipped himself away and turned his back to her. He roared to the heavens.

"Swampy dear, what's the matter?"

He marched off in the other direction.

"Wait!" she cried.

She ran after him and around him. She looked into his eye once more.

"Please. Don't go. I love you. Can't you see that?"

He slithered around her and continued his retreat. She ran around him once more.

"Wait! I don't understand. Don't you love me too?"

No response. Further exit. Lindsay once more didn't get the hint and ran around him.

"WAIT! I LOVE YOU. I know you're scared but if you just give me some sign that you love me too we'll figure it out – even if the world is against us. We can make this work. I'll tell you what. If you love me just raise your right arm now."

The Swamp Monster stood still and did absolutely nothing.

"Okay, maybe you can't raise your arm. If you love me just turn your eye to the left."

Swampy stared right at her.

"If you love me make a noise."

Swampy was silent.

"If you love me stand still and do nothing!"

Swampy walked around her and continued on forward.

Lindsay felt her ability to breathe leave her faster than Usain Bolt running from a pack of tigers. She held her chest and tried not to suffocate from the unbearable pressure. Never having had a boyfriend, she had never experienced the heartache of a breakup, and never having felt any real passion for anyone before, she had never known the sting of rejection. A lifetime of unfelt pain was dropped upon her all at once and she seriously felt that she was going to die.

She clutched herself hard as the emotional tremors threatened to consume her.

"I don't understand!" she yelled to the swamp monster. "If you don't love me than why not kill me?!"

He didn't even acknowledge her. He moved farther and farther away until he was gone from sight, absorbed by the muck.

She wanted to scream in agony but did not have the vocal strength.

Somehow, after nearly twenty minutes of waiting hopelessly for Swampy to reemerge, Lindsay managed to force herself out of the swamp covered boiler room and back into the mall's main corridor. Focused on her shattered dreams, it did not occur to her to be worried about how she might get back outside. Nor was she aware enough of her external circumstances to properly question the glass of the front door of the mall being completely smashed open so that she could easily exit. She merely saw an opening and naturally passed through it, carried forward like a zombie.

She pedaled her bike steadily home, though she would remember none of the trip later. She reentered her house a half hour before dawn without any consideration for the noise she was making, but, by lucky chance, her mother did not wake up.

She spent the short remainder of her night crying in bed until her tear ducts actively hurt. She wanted to die. Suicidal thoughts raced through her mind but the effort required to take her own life seemed far too great a strain. The notion of getting out of bed again was agonizing.

She thought: *Life is awful. If I can't love Swampy, then I don't want to go on.*

4

It seemed to Teddy that he was the only student on the entire Bluford Spring High roster who had not been at the mall when the killings had happened.

As for all of the people who had been there (which was everyone), they all confirmed Henry's wild claim that it was the actual swamp monster who had wreaked the havoc. (Just for the record, havoc likes to be wreaked as much as rumors like to spread and scandal likes to ensue.)

This fantastic possibility was not even touched on by any of the news programs, local or national, but around B.S.H.S., as well as the larger Bluford Springs area, Swampy's return was commonly accepted truth that Teddy thought, if it were true, folks weren't flipping out about nearly as much as they should be. I mean this was a frickin' real life monster we were talking about.

Nevertheless, all of Teddy's doubts were not expunged. After all, sights can be deceiving. It sure seemed to him, when he used to watch episodes of Mindfreak, that Criss Angel really levitated above the Luxor Pyramid or walked on water but Teddy knew in his rational mind that the guy was just a really good illusionist, not a wizard. (Although one national poll had shown that 10% of Mindfreak viewers thought they were watching "real magic," even though Mr. Angel had made no such claim, due to iron clad reasoning such as: "c'mon, that's some crazy shit.") History was filled with elaborate hoaxes that were all eventually debunked. Teddy was a skeptic. He was a man of science.

A man of reason. A man of… A man of uncontrollable, knee shaking love for Lindsay Morpletopple.

Oh god did he love her. Now more than ever. Now that she was the focus of everyone in the school even more than when she had just been a hottie junior. Now that he saw the grace with which she deflected the attention and the deep inner sanctum she retreated to in the midst of unwanted notice – her eyes glazed over with what was surely existential reflection. God did he love her. God did he want her. He wanted to hold her and comfort her and tell her that the world was a harsh place and that he was sorry about the loss of her friends but that everything would be okay because he was there for her and he would protect her from harm and he would love her to the end of time.

All of which was wonderful to think about and think about and think about (which Teddy did, if you added about a thousand more think abouts) but the fact was that Lindsay had already rejected him and all hope he had of ever winning her over had already been crushed.

At least in theory.

Lindsay had just been through a horrifying scare and experienced life-changing loss. So, maybe, just maybe, things would be different now. Maybe Lindsay would reexamine her life as folks are known to do after such monumental life moments, and realize her priorities were all out of whack and it wasn't Bobby Fusilage or Tommy Questinghouse she needed but a smart, kind guy like Teddy Bigshartz. Teddy, who left her alone in the immediate aftermath of the mall massacre when everyone else hounded her with inappropriate inquisition and oppressive consolation. Teddy, who treated her like a person instead of a celebrity.

So Teddy made the determined decision to lay back and say nothing to Lindsay until all the commotion died down. He knew it was the right strategy even though every time he passed her in the hallway he wanted to fly onto her like a paperclip to a magnet. It was incredibly difficult but he knew if he ever wanted a chance with her it was necessary to stay back now.

In the meantime, he watched a shitload of John Cusack movies.

If anyone knew how to be casually suave, innocently endearing, and unaggressively lovable even when playing characters with severe moral failings, it was John Cusack. If anyone could teach him how to win the girl without being a jock whose biceps couldn't make it through doorways, it was John Cusack. Teddy gave himself over entirely to the religion of JC (John Cusack), ready to worship in his teachings and pour full faith into his messiah. He fired up his Netflix queue and flew through screenings of Better Off Dead, Sixteen Candles, One Crazy Summer, Grosse Pointe Blank, Serendipity, The Sure Thing, and of course, the holy grail of teenage love, Say Anything.

He watched Say Anything twelve times in six days. He took notes. He paused and rewatched individual scenes repetitively, making sure to completely digest Lloyd Dobler's awkward but ultimately successful courtship. He didn't want to miss a single helpful physical tick or throwaway phrase that he might utilize in his own personal mission.

Teddy even branched outside of the Cusack canon to the films of his disciples, Anthony Michael Hall and Andrew McCarthy and Ethan Embry and Michael Cera and basically any leading man in a high school movie who ever managed to win over the girl after an hour and a half to two hours of struggle and manufactured doubt (when really, the audience never expected anything other than that the hero would end up with the heroine). Sure, they were only movies. Sure, Teddy knew that formulaic silver screen tales of seventeen year old love could hardly be taken as solid tracts on reality. But he also knew that girls loved those movies so there must be something to their teachings.

All he had to do was be like John Cusack and there was no way that Lindsay would be able to resist him. He had faith. He believed.

Two weeks after the murders at the mall, he decided to act on his newfound creed. Teddy felt content that he had waited long enough. The camera crews had left town. The mall was to be reopened. Lindsay, resolute in her silence at school, had stopped being hounded by the curious and the sympathetic. Every time he saw her, he swore he saw a look of lovelorn longing in her eyes. He was prepared to fulfill her needs.

Teddy bought a boombox (a harder task than he had expected – apparently the ipod revolution had killed the need for these portable music blasters; he finally managed to find one on craigslist; he picked it up from a man dressed in a tunic who also tried to sell him a lamp, a table, a sega dreamcast, and a bottle of Oxycontin). Teddy preloaded the boombox with Peter Gabriel's "In Your Eyes," just as Lloyd Dobler had. He snuck out of his house in the middle of the night and ventured over to Lindsay's. (He didn't really think about the fact that he would wake up half the neighborhood but it wasn't an issue in the movie so he didn't imagine it would be one in real life).

Teddy set up outside of her window and readied himself to lift the boombox over his head for the song's five minutes and thirty seconds (which, admittedly, his arms weren't in proper shape for). Just as Teddy was about to enact his romantic but horribly misguided plan, he was frozen by the sight of movement.

The garage door to Lindsay's house opened and out of it emerged the love of his life herself, riding a pink bicycle. She closed the door as quietly as she could then pedaled off into the night.

Teddy had a couple of choices. He could do the safe (and not creepy) thing and return home, living to enact his boombox wooing on another night. Or, he could do the risky (and borderline illegal) thing and follow Lindsay on her mysterious late night bike ride, keeping the headlights in his car turned off so that she wouldn't learn she was being followed; while Teddy prayed not to drive into someone's front lawn in the dark suburban streets.

Since love was involved, can there be any doubt as to which choice he made?

Teddy drove as slowly and as noiselessly as possible. He kept at least twenty five feet back. Really, Lindsay still should have heard him. The only reason she didn't was that she was so consumed by her own foolish feelings of love that her physical senses were dialed down to near uselessness. ("You've taken leave of your senses" is an expression for a reason.)

There's no need to thoroughly detail Lindsay's attempt to get into the mall since you just read all about it one chapter ago, so it shall just be said that determined Teddy followed her every step of the way. He followed her around the building. Up the tree. Through the vents. Into the mattress store. And down to the depths of Swampy's lair.

Sweaty, sore, aching, Teddy became more and more angrily curious as to what exactly Lindsay was looking for. At first he thought she might just have some unhealthy emotional need to revisit the scene of the crime; to conquer her lingering distress by placing herself at the place where the shit went down. As he ungracefully followed her around the facility, however, (banging his toe, cutting his forearm, and smashing his head into an overhead pipe in the process) he became certain that her frantic exploration meant she was looking for something specific.

When he saw the basement swamp into which she excitedly frolicked, he had a bad feeling as to what the thing she was looking for might be.

When he heard her scream: "SWAMPY I LOVE YOU! PLEASE! PLEASE COME TALK TO ME!" the confirmation that she was looking for the swamp monster had less of a frightening impact than it should have, because of the bizarre specifics of her words.

Did she just say, "I love you?"

When the rats retreated from the monster, several bit Teddy's legs as they passed. When the monster's putrid smell passed through the room, Teddy vomited inside of his mouth. When the monster emerged, dripping with boogers, his body the consistency of stomach-virus turds, Teddy briefly thought he might gouge out his own eyes with his thumbs just so he wouldn't have to spend one second longer looking on such a terrible sight.

It took everything he had to stop himself from running out of the room. His whole body was convulsing. He was more scared than he had ever been in his life but there is one emotion more powerful than fear – LOVE – and it was love which kept him there.

"You don't know how happy I am to see you again," she said to the monster. "I haven't been able to stop thinking about you."

Just what the fuck was going on here? thought Teddy. *The Swamp Monster EXISTS and Lindsay says she's IN LOVE WITH HIM?* It was a lot to digest.

I know everyone will think I'm crazy but I can't help what's inside of me," she said. "And the truth is…I love you. I love you more than anything in the world. And I'll love you forever."

At this moment, Teddy's mental equilibrium was about as stable as his quickly emptying stomach's. (*Seriously, how could anyone smell that and not blow ALL of their chunks! It's like a shit took a shit!*) He would have thought he was dreaming if not for the brutal throb of the rat bites assuring him of wakefulness.

He listened to Lindsay ask the monster to marry her and watched as he uncaringly retreated from her as she loudly declared her love for him again and again and begged for him to come back. In the midst of Teddy's near fatal overdose of confusion, an unexpected feeling emerged: empathy. He felt for Lindsay. He knew all too well the agony of unrequited love.

As much as Teddy wanted to believe that Lindsay's declarations of love were part of some elaborate act (perhaps a revenge plot against the monster who had killed her friends?), he knew, being a hopeless romantic himself, that everything she had said was completely, and disturbingly, genuine.

He watched her kneel in the muck, holding her hands to her face, cringing in the kind of hope induced pain that can only be caused by love, and he knew it was true. For some ludicrous reason, beautiful, blond, luscious Lindsay Morpletopple had fallen in love with Swampy, Bluford Springs' apparently real urban legend.

And Teddy officially decided that he would never understand life.

Hurting in every way that a person can, Teddy picked himself up and left

Lindsay to her own heartbreak. He had no desire to retrace the labyrinth he had taken into the building so he picked up a decorative rock and threw it through the front door. To his amazement no alarm went off and no security dropped from the sky to seize him. (It was kind of amazing, actually, that the mall had no night security even after murders had taken place there, but maybe no one wanted the job since they were too scared of the monster). He grabbed another rock and smashed what glass remained to open up a human sized hole in the frame, then left the godforsaken place.

...

The next morning Teddy woke from his hour and forty five minutes of sleep with a jolt.

A crazy idea had presented itself to him somewhere in the depths of his dreams. It was more than crazy actually. It was outlandish. It was sick. It was probably suicidal. The men in white coats should have kicked down his front door and thrown him in a padded room right then and there for even considering it.

Yet when he thought of it, he didn't feel so terrible. Last night had been so hard on him. It had been like the prom rejection all over again except worse because it was coupled with bizarre unexplainable circumstances that shattered the very foundations of every idea he had long rested upon.

He had found a medicine to soothe him and he didn't care how crazy it was. If this idea made him feel better, he would do it. He really had no other choice.

It was his only chance of being with his great love in some small way.

The circumstances were as follows:

Teddy was in love with Lindsay.

Lindsay was in love with the swamp monster.

Swampy didn't seem overly interested in Lindsay's declarations of love but he had spared her life now on at least two occasions, which meant that just maybe there was some part of him that felt an affection for her.

Teddy's idea was this: He would somehow convince the Swamp Monster to return Lindsay's affections. He would guide Swampy along the way. He would show the monster how to act, tell him what to say (if he had any power of speech, which remained to be proven). He would live vicariously through this revolting creature of the deep, because if he couldn't love Lindsay himself he would be content to love her through someone (or some*thing*) else.

He would love her any way he could. It was his destiny.

...

At first the local townsfolk felt some trepidation at going to the mall on its Grand Re-opening. No one was anxious to run into the open mouths of the salivating stores that had pushed for the accelerated return to business. They were fearful that they would instead run right into the open mouth of the Swamp Monster.

However, once the store owners agreed to a mall-wide 20% off sale, the public forgot all of their fears and showed up in great heaping numbers.

This time, Teddy was among the swarm. It sickened him a bit that the materialistic public could so easily disregard such a recent tragedy because of a minor discount in pricing. Though really, he was way too nervous to pay much attention to anyone else.

Teddy was preparing to do something quite crazy. He was going to try to make friends with Swampy.

Teddy had spent the last several days doing intense internet research on the legend of Bluford Springs' swamp monster. It was a real rabbit hole of a task. The internet was a medium where a video of a cat wearing a top hat had over 600 million views and where there were entire blogs devoted to obscure pieces of kitchen ware (does anyone really need castironskillets.bloggerplace.

com?) So even a search for an obscure local urban legend like Swampy turned up hundreds of results. Teddy sifted through thousands of words of rambling conspiracy theorist testimony which claimed to be "THE DEFINITIVE EVIDENCE" as to Swampy's existence, then provided nothing which could reasonably be called definitive or evidence. There were blurry photographs that claimed to be images of Swampy, but which looked more liked baked potatoes and dog poop, to give just a couple of examples.

He learned that Swampy's internal organs were made of maggots, he could be transformed into a beautiful prince with true love's kiss, and he HATED jazz music. He learned that Swampy was an alien from outer space, a demon summoned by God to punish humanity for homosexuality, and the illiterate child of Marlon Brando and a female bear. (That last one was a stretch even by internet standards). He learned…nothing of any value whatsoever.

So after hours and hours of time wasted on the internet (a first half of a sentence which could begin any story of modern youth), Teddy came up with the ridiculous plan of costuming himself like a monster in the hope that Swampy would feel some camaraderie and be less likely to kill him.

More than likely, he would die. He realized that. But he also didn't want to live without Lindsay. So it made no difference.

Teddy carried his costume in a Macy's bag he had stolen from his mother's closet. He wanted to blend in with the other shoppers, which required not changing into his monster gear until he was safely beyond closed doors. (After all, the authorities were technically looking for a "costumed" killer and he did not wish to be mistaken for the murderer).

He may not yet have stood out visually, but he certainly did nasally. Worried that the monster might sniff out his humanness even if his dangling eyes couldn't see it, Teddy had pre-"bathed" himself in mud and garbage until he reeked so bad that squirrels went into cardiac arrest when he passed by. He used moldy bread and rotting banana peels as deodorant and ran around vigorously, following his stank bath, so that his sweat would mingle with the other noxious odors. Shoppers parted like the red sea as he passed, their dinners quavered back up to their throats.

It took Teddy about twenty minutes of wandering (during which his odor set off an epidemic of teenagers wanting to know just who the HELL had farted) before he relocated the passageway he had passed through in the dark during his Lindsay stalk. Then, he snuck into the open hallway and donned his costume.

The disguise he had constructed was made from items he had found around and outside of the house. Its blank canvas was an old brown dress his mother would never be thin enough to wear again (perhaps thankfully, because it was from the 80s and quite hideous). Teddy didn't particularly want to cross-dress but the outfit's frumpiness leant itself his desired effect of monstrosity. On top of the dress he had poured out three bottle of Elmer's glue. Then he had piled on loads of leaves, twigs, dirt, and dirty tissues. (His Dad had been suffering a cold and Teddy made use of the infection filled trash bin). To cover his face, Teddy had cut some holes in an old wash rag. He wrapped the rag around his head and twisted the end closed with an extra sturdy rubber band. He had soaked the rag in a bucket of lotion and used it to sop up dust and hair follicles from the bathroom floor. He glued on detached pieces of tree bark for added effect. Once he had donned his construction, as a final cherry on top, he poured an expired carton of milk all over himself.

All masqueraded as a monster, barely able to see out of the uneven eye holes he had provided himself, doing everything he could not to vomit from his own stench, Teddy descended into the monster's basement lair.

As he went down, he wondered both how the police had missed the part of their crime scene that looked like a giant swamp and how the mall was open and running when a basement filled with important looking mechanical equipment was submerged in three feet of sludge. His fear quickly supplanted any rational consideration.

The outer mall had been loud. The voices of shoppers all blended together into a steady hum which Teddy only now realized was a source of comfort. In the basement swamp lair everything was quiet except for the occasional gelatinous drip.

"Grello?" Teddy said in his best English/monster speech meld. He wanted to sound gruff, but actually he sounded like Scooby-Doo.

There was no answer. He tenuously inched further and further into the room, well past the point that Lindsay had stopped when he had followed her.

"Grello? Ranyone rere?" he said, thoroughly ridiculously.

Farther and farther he passed in his outfit of do it yourself ugliness, each step taking him farther away from a bright door and a quick escape.

He searched for fifteen minutes but the Swamp Monster was nowhere in sight.

Finally, he sat down next to a heater in exhausted frustration. Anticipation and fear take a lot out of you. He felt like an improperly trained marathon runner who reaches mile sixteen and suddenly feels all hope of finishing drain away.

"Gruhhhh," said someone next to him.

"Tell me about it," said Teddy, too wrapped up in his emotional exhaustion to find anything odd about this exchange. Seconds later he realized that someone else talking to him in this lair was hardly something to be blasé about. He whisked his head around to the source of the voice.

There was the Swamp Monster, casually sitting right next to him, eating a rat like it was Popsicle.

"AHHH," Teddy screamed and fell back completely into the water. He splished and splashed and pushed himself out of the submersion, then ran backwards three or four steps, fell down again, splished and splashed some more, pushed himself up again, backed up a few steps a little more carefully, then realized that Swampy wasn't actually chasing him and stopped the whole slapstick process.

The monster looked at him like he was an insect he didn't need to bother crushing.

Teddy took a long moment to compose his demeanor and remind himself why he was there. He silenced all his fearful urges to run away and recalled that he was doing this for Lindsay.

He did his best impersonation of someone cool, calm, and casual who just happened to be outfitted in a garbage bedazzled dress and walked over towards the Swamp Monster.

"Sure is noisy up there," he said. "Glad to find some nice peace and quiet down here."

Swampy looked at him quizzically.

Teddy continued, inching closer with each word. "Name's Teddy. It's nice to meet you."

Swampy swallowed the tail of the rat he had been chomping on like it was piece of spaghetti.

"You must be Swampy," said Teddy, gaining confidence for no real reason. "I've heard tale of you." (An absurd phrasing). "Many a man has spoken of you over the years. Your massive frame. Your spectacular constitution. You are a much admired marvel." (He was not entirely sure why he was talking like a nineteenth century Earl but it was what was coming out, so he went with it.)

"May I?" he gestured at the spot next to the monster, inquiring as to whether he could sit down. Swampy didn't seem to care one way or the other.

Teddy sat down and the swamp water came up to his armpits. He looked way way up into Swampy's dangling eyes and saw just how large the monster truly was.

"I tell ya Swampy, there just ain't no winnin' anymore, you know what'a'mean?" (Now he was ghetto for some reason.) "Those folks out there, they think they know you – but they don't *know you*!" (Now transitioning to "drunk guy at a party" speak.) "But you'll show them. You'll show them you're not the monster they think you are. You are not a monster! You are a human being!" (This familiar quote was actually from "The Elephant Man," but had become so entrenched in the culture that Teddy didn't know where he had heard it, only that it applied to this situation.) "Although, I guess, you're not human. I mean, unless you consider yourself human. Whatever you are, that's what you are, I guess that's what I'm trying to say." (Okay, he was officially going off the rails here. He needed to focus.)

Teddy stood up. In a bellowing timber he said, "Swampy the swamp monster – I am here today to commit myself to you, so that you may find LOVE."

Swampy was uninterested.

"Lindsay Morpletopple loves you," continued Teddy. "And I love her. And I will do anything in my power to make sure she gets what will make her happy."

Swampy picked his nose. Several worms came out.

"Goddammit Swampy!" yelled Teddy (fired up now). "Pay attention! Don't just sit there like a lump of poop with eyes!" (Really, his resemblance to fecal matter with pupils was uncanny). "A beautiful girl is in love with you! You! You have a chance for something that I will never have! You think anyone is ever going to love me! No! No one will ever love me!" Tears of anger and exasperation began to pour down Teddy's face. "Why won't anyone love me?! Why won't LINDSAY love me?! How could she possibly choose something like you over me?! HUH?! Goddammit I hate life! But let me tell you something you slimy son of a bitch. You will let Lindsay love you, and that's all there is to it. Are you LISTENING?!"

Teddy pushed Swampy in the torso. Or tried to. His hands just submerged several inches into Swampy's "chest."

He quickly pulled them out, but this physical action finally seemed to grab the monster's attention.

Swampy's attached eye widened and his hanging eye sprang up. His soggy frame unfurled itself as he stood up. He grew inch by inch, until he cast a shadow over Teddy, although they were in a room with nary a light source.

A deep, guttural grumble escaped him. If indigestion could directly express anger, then this was what the sound resembled.

Teddy took a few steps back. What was that old saying about "awakening the sleeping giant?" It came to mind at the present. Goosebumps paid a visit to Teddy's skin. His heart did jumping jacks. His spine contracted like a slinky at the bottom of the stairs.

The monster's glare burned red. His rotted teeth grinded together. He slid forward, ever more threateningly.

"So," said Teddy, foolishly optimistically, "does this mean you're accepting my offer?"

All at once, the monster's gelatinous body broke like a wave. Teddy did not wait to be submerged. He turned and high tailed it towards the door.

The monster followed.

Teddy ran as fast as he could. All his well thought out intentions vanished in the face of first hand fear. He made for the door.

Swampy was close on his heels. The water splashed every which way as he raced through it. He gained distance.

Teddy was just able to escape the basement before he was grasped. Swampy departed his lair to pursue his pray.

And so, once again, the shoppers of the just opened (or in this case, reopened) Bluford Springs Mall had their acquisition of new items halted by a race through the downstairs corridor. Once more, people on the second and third floors looked down and heard the screams below (this time of a male variety, though Teddy's high pitched squeals might have been easily mistaken for a girl's). A few voices throughout the mall were even heard declaring: "NOT AGAIN," as if they were in a trailer for an action movie sequel.

The main difference in this déjà vu, was that this time the security forces (about three times as large as at the original grand opening) were ready for the disturbance.

The extra two thirds of security, who had been hired in from out of town and believed the news reports of a costumed killer rather than the local guards' ridiculous claims of a creature from the deep, initially swarmed on Teddy, fooled by his smelly outfit.

A few ex-jocks in uniform threw Teddy viscously to the ground, enacting some serious sternum damage, then high fived, screaming obscenities at their capture. They briefly imagined glory – the praise of the media, the seduction of beautiful girls worldwide looking to sleep with heroes, handshakes from the president himself – until their deluded egos were awakened from their satisfying daydreams by the ever louder screams of the public. They looked around to see what all the fuss was about and noticed Swampy barreling towards them.

They barely had time to scream "Oh shit!" before arms of acid flesh struck them and pulled them into an unfriendly hug. One by one the monster stuffed the front line of security guards into his many orifices, grinding them into nothing as if he was a radioactive wood chipper.

The mall's crowd of shoppers pushed and pulled and raced to be the first ones out the door. Swarms of backup police teemed into the parking lot. They had been prepared for the possibility of such a call and were ready to spring to action at the first dials of 911.

Not far behind, an FBI SWAT team dropped onto the scene in screaming helicopters and armored tanks. The federal government had also kept a close eye on the mall's hasty reopening, hoping to gain some points with the incredibly dissatisfied public which had repeatedly given them dismal approval ratings in recent polls.

Shoppers flooded out of every open door, screaming for their lives. All of the television coverage of the first incident maximized the hysteria that occurred upon what, really, should have been an unsurprising repetition of events. Some, on the second and third floors, jumped out of windows, afraid they would be unable to make their way down the escalators unscathed. A few of these free fallers even survived.

Inside, things were at a standstill. Swampy was the reluctant center of a growing sphere of policeman and SWAT soldiers. All manner of weapons were pointed at him. So many shouted at him to freeze that their voices became muddled together into grimy sound static. This noise quickly became absorbed into a deafening boom when the first gun was fired. Once one gun was fired, a second quickly followed suit, and then they all went off until it looked and sounded like the mall was inside of a firecracker hurricane.

Teddy, momentarily, was completely forgotten about. He remained on the ground, trapped in a maze of feet. From his hands and knees he watched Swampy absorb bullet after screaming bullet. The fact that he was clearly not dying, or even phased by the attack, didn't prevent the societal protectors from firing away clip after clip. Not even when their own men in the inner part of the circle were hit in the back and collapsed to the ground, in agony or death.

And yet…Teddy saw something surprising in the monster's scrambled egg face. Not exactly fear. Not exactly sadness. More like a kind of weariness. Emotional exhaustion, perhaps. Teddy felt for him. The poor bloke had been innocently minding his own business in his swamp when humans came by, tore up the place, built a shopping mall, and destroyed the only home he'd ever known. Teddy would probably have wanted to kill somebody in that situation too. It wouldn't do. It simply wouldn't do.

Teddy noticed that while the monster's toxic saliva melted bones and his body wide teeth tore into flesh, his dangly eye scanned the floor, looking for an escape route. He wanted to help the fella out.

Teddy crawled through the forest of feet to get closer to Swampy. Limb deforestation caused by bullets in the back made the journey treacherous. Policeman collapsed all around him but he swerved this way (and that) and avoided being trampled.

"Swampy," he screeched, trying to get the eye's attention. But the pupily strand did not see him and slithered off in another direction. "Dammit," said Teddy.

The rain of hot metallic bullet shells was quite painful and Teddy doubled his speed. He reverted back to his time as a one year old, when speedy crawling was second nature, and raced down the marble tiled floor.

Finally, as the eye whipped around a pair of filthy black boots, Teddy was able to grab hold of the extended nerve. It wiggled like a panicked worm in the mouth of a Red Breasted Robin, but could not escape Teddy's tight hold. Teddy placed his thumb and index finger around the eyeball and forced it look into his own.

"Swampy!" he said, "I want to help you!"

The eyeball continued to shimmy in his grasp.

"Please," Teddy pleaded. "I know what it's like to not be seen for what who you really are. We're the same you and me," He didn't fully believe his own inspirational words, but they still felt good rolling off his tongue. "Let me help you," he said.

The eye blinked.

Could it be? Some recognition? Understanding?

The vein relaxed. It stopped struggling. Teddy took the sudden limpness as approval.

"Okay," he said. "Here's what I want to do."

Teddy described his plan. He crossed his fingers that the monster would somehow comprehend what he said.

"Ready?" he asked, after outlining the details. The eye stared at him blankly. Teddy supposed he would take that as a yes. "Not until I say go," he said.

Teddy weaved his way throughout the still firing police squad, pulling Swampy's eye along. The vein became tauter as it neared the end of its possible extension length.

"Just a little farther," said Teddy. The eye looked pained, but pushed itself to stay with Teddy, inch for inch.

Teddy slid into the open gateway of the mattress store. The place was empty except for one devoted salesman named Rick, who was waiting for a theoretical customer who might want to purchase a bed during a bloody gun fight.

"How can I help you?" Rick asked Teddy through a big toothy salesman's grin.

Teddy ignored him. He looked deeply into Swampy's eye. "NOW!" he said.

In the middle of the mall, Swampy abruptly ceased his acidic attack on those trying unsuccessfully to kill him and bubbled up vibrantly. His gooey body contracted until he was only a thin cylindrical geyser. Then, rapidly, he melted into a puddle.

Before the policeman and soldiers could register what happened (they were still firing away relentlessly), Swampy's body traveled across the floor like rain water making its way to a storm drain. He reassembled himself to normal form once he was safely inside the mattress store.

Was Rick deterred? Not one bit! Rick came from a long line of salesman. His father had sold cars for fifty years. His grandfather had sold gramophones for sixty years. His great great grandfather had sold slaves for seventy years. (They didn't talk about his great great grandfather so much). If there was one rule in his family it was "SELL! SELL! SELL!" (That and always keep the toilet seat down). Rick would not be deterred by something as silly as being in the middle of a war zone. This was an excellent opportunity to convince a boy and his monster friend of the benefits of the new line of "Air-soft" mattresses and he would take full advantage of it.

Sadly, there was no time for Rick to do his admirable work. Because before he could say, "I've got just the mattress for you!" Teddy had led the monster underneath the air vent and indicated to Swampy that they needed to blow through it. Somehow, Swampy understood his indication. He wrapped his slimy arm around Teddy and shot up into the vents like an erupted volcano.

While the massive attack force chaotically broke down, ending any shred of organization they still maintained, Teddy and Swampy slid along the vents. Swampy liquidized himself and pulled Teddy along, turning the entire tunnel of metal work into one giant slip & slide. While the soldiers fired blindly into store windows, causing terrified owners and managers to retract into panic contortion balls under their register counters, Teddy and Swampy burst out onto the empty roof and weaved their way to the edge, avoiding the bright spotlights of helicopters circling overhead. While the inner mall was ravaged and turned into a convincing recreation of 1945 Berlin, Swampy and Teddy slid down a tree and ran off into the night, undetected.

Safely alone in a small patch of woods, about two and half miles from the mall, Teddy stopped running.

"Wait," he said, holding his chest and catching his breath.

Swampy turned and stopped. He looked down at his partner in crime. It was hard for Teddy to tell what might be going on in the monster's brain – if he even had one. Swampy had been able to follow his plan, which was pretty remarkable and unexpected. Was it possible that something intelligent lurked inside that rotten shell after all?

Teddy's thought process was interrupted when he saw Swampy pick up some dried up dog poop from the ground and chew on it like bubble gum. He even blew a couple bubbles with it, which, in turn, made Teddy blow some chunks.

"Swampy," he said, his eyes averted, "can you understand me? Can you understand what I say?"

There was no verbal response so he reluctantly looked at his turd chewing companion. "Do you understand me?" he repeated.

Swampy showed no signs of recognition.

"I know there's something inside of you. There must be," he said. "And whatever it is… we're going to use to win Lindsay's love."

5

Sam Bristolnoon calmly ceased flipping through the channels and placed the remote down on his night table at the sight of the girl on the television.

She was shown only in brief video glimpses which the news network played on a repeated loop. Her face peaked through a window curtain to see the caravan of paparazzi camped out on her front lawn. She briskly walked down her front walkway, shielded by her mother's coat as the pair pushed and shoved their way into a car so the girl could go to school. She left her high school building and when she thought no one was watching, she smiled at some unknown pleasure.

He learned her name was Lindsay Morpletopple. She was the sole survivor of some freakish mall killing spree. She was beautiful, Sam couldn't help but notice. Likely her beauty was why the media was so fixated on her, the poor girl. Bloodthirsty journalists preferred, as a rule, to report on people who were either attractive or powerful. Both if possible, though they made do with what was available.

Speaking of bloodthirsty…, Sam looked over at the clock. It was time.

He stood up and closed his eyes. He searched his mind for apprehensiveness. He located none. He was ready.

He picked up the remote to shut off the TV. His thumb wouldn't listen to his instruction to press down on the power. It hovered over the red button hesitantly.

He looked once more at the girl on the tube. He watched her mysterious smile. He smiled himself. He felt a brief, intense connection to her that he did not fully understand.

Then he forced his thumb into submission. There were more important things to attend to than human girls thousands of miles away.

...

Sam had been a vampire for exactly two hundred and thirty two days. And by all accounts he was kicking ass at it.

Sam had always been a winner. He was a huge fan of the famous quote: "Winning isn't everything, but it's what I'm going to do." Or something like that. He couldn't remember the specific wording.

From his earliest age, being the best took top priority over any other concern. In pre-school, as the other toddlers scribbled abstract crayon squiggles outside the lines in their cartoon coloring books, Sam noticed the blocked in shapes of the pictures and decided that was where the colors belonged. The teachers were delighted. When Sam was told to nap he fell asleep swiftly and fully. When he was told to clean up, his corner of the toy carpet was clear before any other child even deposited their first block in the toy bin. He was the star of the class.

It was the disappointment of the other children which really addicted him to winning. Being praised and lauded was satisfying in its own right, sure, but it was the frustrated look on the faces of those who could never hope to match up which drove the thrill home. Sam was not just *great*. He was *better*. He was *the best*.

As he got older he excelled in every activity in which he realized that he had competitors. He was a straight A student. Top of his class. He always knew the answers and always convinced the teachers to call on him before anyone else. He was a star athlete. Shortstop on the baseball team with a .560 average. Quarterback on the football team, leading the league in touchdowns, both passing and running.

He went out with the hottest girl in school. He didn't like her very much, but that was beside the point. Everyone else was jealous of his conquest. They all wished they were him. *That* was the point.

At home, Sam was easily the favorite child of his dull parents, though it wasn't much of a contest. His younger brother Gabe, perhaps in advance submission to his take-no-prisoners brother, had formed a personality as couch potato and a general lump. He was chubby and lazy and felt it was a major effort to reach for the remote sitting two feet away from him on the coffee table.

Yes, Sam was the best. He knew he was the best. And so he didn't blame the vampire couple who scouted him out and turned him into one of their kind. If he had been in their position, he would have chosen himself too.

...

Sam joined the other pledges around the blunt edge of a centuries old wooden table. The Nosferat University symbol of a fanged "N" was engraved in the middle of the table.

The cold undead skin of all of the pledges shivered with excited anticipation. They were members of an elite group, selected for an honor many vampires would (and sometimes did) kill for.

Nosferat University (renamed as such about a hundred and fifty years before as part of a rebranding campaign by the school's board of trustees from its previous name: Likijesklskulsibernn, which the board determined, after a lengthy discussion, did not mean anything in any language) rested in the hills of barren Alaska and had been there for thousands of years, since long before the territory became the fiftieth state of the good old U.S. of A. It was the perfect location. For the half of the year that school was in session the area experienced nights of epic length (including total darkness for almost three months), allowing its vampire population free safe reign of the land both day and night without the risk of brutal sun death. Its surrounding area was permanently frigid, which had no effect on creatures who had no blood flowing in their veins, but was a major detraction to humans who complained when the temperature dipped below 45 degrees.

The school was created with the intention of training newly turned vampires as to the long and convoluted ways of their kind. It was a hefty task. The record keepers lorded over at least fifty tomes of sometimes contradictory traditions and often outdated rules, each complete with thousands of pages of footnotes in ancient languages. In recent years the educational focus had shifted more to physical training. Classes taught undead newbies to harness and control their suddenly acquired powers and perfect them, both for their own benefit and in the goal of maintaining their secrecy from the human race. Though they were powerful, they were few compared to the outrageous numbers of the living and they preferred that one incompetent asshole not ruin the whole thing.

Pacing in front of the pledge group was Nicholast Jarbeque, current Master at Arms of the NosferatU Fraternity. As Master at Arms, it was Nicholast's job to arrange and conduct a series of tasks that the new recruits would have to perform if they wished to be accepted into the exclusive club.

"Welcome, members of the class of 2015, to the NosferatU Fraternity trials," said Nicholast. "You should all be honored that you have even made it this far. But this is only the beginning. Over the next year we will conduct a series of nine competitions, each of which will culminate in the release of a one pledge. We will keep track of the results on the big board—" (Nicholast pointed to the big board: a finely chiseled stone frame of bloodthirsty gargoyles surrounding a chalk board in which each of the pledge's names had been inscribed) "—and when all is said and done only one of you will be invited to join our brotherhood. The road will be long and arduous. By the end we shall see who among you has what it takes to join our elite club."

The NosferatU Fraternity had been in existence since the mid 1400s. Only one new member was ultimately invited to join each year (out of a group of ten accepted pledges) and if you were lucky enough to be that new member, you were rewarded with a lifetime of brotherly protection and safe harbor. As well as access to a full service spa, with pedicures and hot stone massages.

More than anything else though, acceptance into the NosferatU fraternity was a matter of esteem. Each progressive year's newly accepted pledge had received more and more coverage in the vampress and become a bigger and bigger celebrity. In the distant past, fraternity pledges were selected from a pool of University applicants with little ado, but in modern times, the vampublic's interest in the results had substantially upped the ante. Respectable members of the worldwide vampire community now treated the pledge trials like a high stakes cock fight. They searched far and wide in the world for right aged male humans of intelligence and physical prowess who might represent them loyally and impressively. Then they turned them into their own personal undead children.

This was precisely what happened to Sam.

He had been making his way to the locker room after setting a county record for fastest mile run at a high school track meet, when he had been tackled, bitten repeatedly in the neck, and shoved into a coffin. When he woke up he was shackled in an icy dungeon, all human spark drained out of him.

For a moment he was upset. Not because of his imprisonment, or the separation from the comforts of home and family, or even his apparent death, but rather because all signs pointed to him having suffered a massive defeat. Someone had beaten him and no thought was more depressing.

However, his worries were quickly assuaged. The two vampires who had attacked him revealed themselves and explained the situation. As it turned out, they were a loving vampire couple (Both relative newbies in the thousands of years old Vampire community: She – a former flapper turned in 1920s Chicago; He – a former pilgrim turned by a Native American vampire just after the first Thanksgiving) and they selected Sam as both their new son and entry into the 2012-2013 Nosferat U frat trials.

They had wanted to "adopt" a kid for quite some time, and they figured they might as well play a hand in the trials while at it. After scouting American high schools for months, they had finally settled on Sam as their optimum candidate for a chance at the crown. Sam was relieved. He had not been defeated at all. He had been selected for his greatness. He was a winner, as always.

Needless to say, not every human handpicked for such a purpose readily accepted their new fate. Whether because they had loved their human lives or because the vampires who turned them were socially (and sometimes mentally) challenged hard asses who unreasonably expected their victims' full allegiance without any understanding of why such a dramatic transition in lifestyle might produce some conflicted emotions, many who were turned to be star cocks in the fight did not actually survive their first month or two as a vampire. If they were unwilling to compete for the honor of those who had turned them, then they were considered useless. They were set aflame and stabbed repeatedly in the heart with the first piece of wood that could be located.

None of this was a concern for Sam. He quickly came to love his new vamparents. They were loving and nurturing and most important of all, they believed he was the best with all their (unbeating) heart. And he quickly accepted his fate not with surrender, but with glee at the new challenge.

Here was a new competition. Here was a brand new chance to show everyone he was the best.

His vamparents expected it to take about four years of training before Sam would be invited to the frat trials. To even be accepted *as a pledge* required a grueling 5,000 word application and a series of strenuous physical tests. It was rare for anyone but NosferatU seniors to receive that lucky, blood sealed letter, with only the occasional overachieving junior sneaking in.

Sam got in as a freshman. He quickly became the talk of vampires worldwide.

...

The camera lights shined painfully into Sam's eyes as he waited for the competition to begin. This year, for the first time, the vampublic's thirst would be quenched with video footage of the entire pledge trials, to be live streamed over a secure internet site that supposedly only vampires would be able to find. (The technological advancement had been vigorously demanded for years by post industrial revolution vampires who had miraculously obtained approval from ancient councils that were still transitioning from handwritten scrolls to the printing press.)

"Your first task is a rather classic one," said Nicholast, keeping the handsomer right side of his face towards the camera. "We've borrowed it from the thick headed dull tooths at their own universities but adapted it to our own particular specifications. Herrick, would you do the honors?"

Herrick Illingstation, one of the other trial conductors, placed a shot glass in front of each of the pledges. He then walked across the room and popped open a wooden crate. It was filled with cans of Wiggly Lite – a cheap brand of pig's blood.

"Herrick here will be filling the shot glasses in front of you with Wiggly Lite. The task is simple. You keep taking blood shots. The first person to stop drinking loses."

Herrick filled all of the glasses from an initial pair of cans. He took out several more to be ready for the refill.

"Ready. Set. Drink!"

Sam let loose a cocky grin as he licked his lips of droplet run-off, following the first shot. Sam, having forseen such a task in the competition, had trained himself in the previous weeks to have an amazingly high blood consumption tolerance. Sure, he preferred monkey or elephant blood to cheap bland garbage like Wiggly Lite, but he could still guzzle vial after vial of the stuff without so much as a feeling of light headedness. (Sam hadn't actually tasted human blood – the prices in the blood stores were exorbitant and he had yet to go "hunting," as the vampires called it, for live flesh).

For the first twenty shots or so, none of the twelve participants showed any sign of wear. Rather, they all seemed to be enjoying themselves. None more than Kelvish Evelhard, dressed in his popped collar and his straight brim Cleveland Indians baseball cap. Surely a total douchebag when he had been a human, and no less of one now, Kelv felt the need to taunt all of his fellow pledges after every shot, saying things like – "I bet you'd get that in your mouth faster if it was his penis," and "You fellas better get ready to DracaLOSE, if you know what I'm SAYIN!" The rest, enjoying the lightheaded buzz that comes from rapid excessive blood consumption, did their best to ignore him.

As the contest continued on and their lifeless organs were splattered with more and more thick red life juice, some of the participants began to slow down. The grins dissolved off their pale faces. Their hands gripped the glasses with less of a bone breaking clamp. Not Sam, who felt as fresh as if he'd just turned rightside up at sunset after a long day's sleep, and not Kelv who had started to moon people for some reason, but many of the others were visibly woozy from so much rapid intake.

As the night continued, shot after shot after shot was poured down the pledges' gullets by increasingly unsteady hands. The weaker among them buckled their knees and took deep breaths (even though vampire lungs didn't respond to oxygen with the same enthusiasm as their human counterparts). They battled forward. No one wanted the shame of being the first elimination.

As vulnerability clouded over several pairs of eyes, Nicholast embraced his position as Taunter-In-Chief and let fly a string of quite mean verbal abuses. He screamed right in people's faces. Vampires don't have saliva but they do sometimes sweat inside their mouths and as he yelled, his mouth sweat moisturized the future failures like a morning dew.

Lodged in the middle of the pack was a short pot-bellied vampire named Herbins Ghoulash, who had a boatload of brains but a fairly testy constitution. He wasn't the typical stud sought out by the fraternity but the search committee invited him on the strength of his essay. Herbins had been bitten by a rather ugly female vamp desperate for a child after centuries of solitude; and though he was certainly cold blooded, his body had never kicked a couple of unpleasant human habits: Namely, vomiting and defecating. Of course, he kept this shameful flaw in the most secure of secret vaults. If his skeleton ever got released from its closet he would be the laughing stock of the creatures of the night for the remainder of his immortal days. Problem was, this kick-off challenge was threatening to release his shame on the world – from both ends.

Sam noticed Herbins slowing and felt pity for the poor sap. Sam was possessed with the extremely useful ability to recognize fear. Always had been, even in his human days. And now, the subtlest shift in eye direction or movement of skin flaps alerted him to a prey's apprehensiveness. In this particular situation, his oversensitivity to others' dread told him that chubby Herbins was about to go down for the count.

"What's the matter fatty?" Kelvish declared – also apparently noticing that Herbins was teetering on the edge of failure.

"Shut your mouth Evelhard," said Nicholast, who nonetheless ventured directly in front of Herbins so he could lambast the victim himself. "Drink that blood boy. You think we have slots open for pussys who can't even drink a few gallons of Wiggly Lite. Are you a vampire or a just a walking corpse? Is that what you are? A mindless zombie with no feeling in your dick! Huh?"

Herbins sensed all the eyes of the room bearing down on him. He reached deep inside himself and looked for the strength to carry on. He brought the shot glass closer to his face, inch by inch, though it seemed to repel from him like a same poled magnet. The glass touched his lips.

"Drink it Ghoulash! I know it's not the human piss you really like, but it ain't so bad."

Everyone laughed. Everyone but Sam anyway. He found all this bodily function inspired taunting to be painfully immature.

On the border of humiliation no matter which direction he turned in – Herbins forced the blood down his gullet.

Then he immediately puked out all that he had consumed in a single projected explosion. He fell to the floor and defecated in his pants.

"Herbins Ghoulash," said Nicholast, while holding his nose with one hand. "We ask you to gather your things and leave immediately. You are eliminated from contention and will never be allowed again in our sacred halls."

The cameras zoomed in on Herbins' mortified face. At their castles and in their coffins and in their suburban townhomes, vampires of the world watched their live internet feed and laughed until their sternums hurt.

The other pledges ran from the smell, giggling like little girls. Sam backed away as well, for the scent really was quite horrendous. But his lips did not curve upward by any measurement. He didn't find such a pathetic display to be funny. He found it sad.

Sam believed firmly in survival of the fittest. And ultimately, those who were weak deserved their fate, even if he did pity them. Only the strong survived in this world. And Sam was determined to be the strongest of all.

...

As the year went on, the competitions at Nosferat U continued and the number of pledges steadily dwindled.

There were nine left and they had to race up Mt. McKinley. Yuri Crovitch slipped on a snow owl and tumbled down the mountain and then there were eight.

There were six left and they had to build a castle out of the concrete rubble of recent human ruins. Architecturally challenged Eric Lockenstock's tower tumbled as he was being judged and then there were five.

There were four left and they had to read James Joyce's Ulysses and write an essay about the notoriously hard to read novel's style and themes. Tall, bulky, Gregor Dinequellsheeva who had made it this far on the stamina of his denseness was left choking on the dust of literacy. And there were three.

The final trio consisted of Sam, a wild card named Jacoby Loonersoloart, who had an acne splattered face and didn't say much, and Kelvish Evelhard, who had been obnoxiously tooting his own horn on his twitter account after each subsequent advancement. (He had over 200 followers).

They were gathered together in an Anchorage suburb at the beginning of February. Nicholast had told them to meet him on the corner of a residential street at three in the morning. He was waiting for them in a Toyota Camry. Sam and Jacoby were already in the back when Kelv strolled up and leisurely entered the passenger seat at 3:09.

"Where've you been?" asked Nicholast.

"What do you mean?" said Kelv.

"You're late."

"I don't think so."

"Yeah. You are."

"I'm really not so sure about that."

"You arrived after the time I said you should be here."

"So?"

"So that's the definition of lateness!"

"Whatever bro."

"Don't call me bro."

"Whatever you say machismo."

"Don't call me—" Nicholast let loose an exasperated grunt. "You know what, let's just get down to it."

"That's what I'm talking bout bro," said Kelv.

Nicholast gave Kelv the evil eye, and took a deep breath.

"I gathered you here today for the second to last of our nine competitions," he said. "This one is fairly simple. To our right is a house that one of our frat brothers managed to… acquire for us. Tonight all three of you will enter the house and—"

Nicholast was distracted from his thought by Kelv, whose thumbs were typing away on his smart phone.

"Would you get off your phone!"

"Oh. Sorry. Just had to retweet this killer meme my buddy Rolph posted."

Nicholast grabbed Kelv's phone from his hand and smashed it to pieces against the Camry's dashboard.

"Hey!"

"There'll be no phone use during this competition! I swear to God, vampires on twitter, I never thought I'd see the day."

"Totally not cool—"

"Not another word out of you, you hear!" said Nicholast.

Kelv reluctantly closed his mouth after a full axis eye roll.

"Good," continued Nicholast. "Now. As I was saying. Tonight all three of you will enter this house. And you will stay there. The first person to leave is eliminated. Simple as that."

"What about blood?" asked Kelv.

"The fridge is fully stocked," said Nicholast, and we'll be keeping an eye on you, so if you run out, we'll refill it." He paused, looked at Sam and Jacboy. "Any questions?"

"No sir," said Sam. Jacoby remained quiet.

"Alright then. Get to it."

Sam and Jacoby filed out of the backseat. Kelv took one more nasty look at his broken phone, then followed.

The house was fully furnished with comfortable couches, plush carpets, and a mantelpiece covered with a pictures of a loving family who were conspicuously absent from the abode.

Within seconds of entry Jacoby whizzed by his competitors at two hundred miles per hour. He passed in a blur up the staircase. They heard a door slam shut with hostile force.

"I guess he didn't feel like talking," said Kelv.

"God knows why. You're so charming," said Sam sarcastically.

"Can't believe that dick broke my phone."

"There's a Best Buy about a mile down the road."

"Yeah, good try bro. You're not gettin' rid of me that easy."

Kelv threw himself over the back of the leather couch and plopped down. He grabbed the remote and turned on the HDTV. The program he chose to watch was "Toddlers in Tiaras."

"Yo look at this shit," he said.

"I think I'll pass," said Sam, who seriously hoped that this particular competition wouldn't drag on. The thought of having to share a residence with Kelvish for any length of time made his insides cringe.

Since Jacoby had run upstairs and Kelv had anchored himself in the main floor, Sam decided to take a trip to the basement.

The subfloor was cold, dank, and unfinished. It was mostly empty except for a series of tables, covered with what looked like high school chemistry equipment. (Also a ping pong table). The room smelled horrible. Like rotten eggs. Or maybe cat urine. Either way it certainly wasn't somewhere that Sam desired to spend any time, so he went back upstairs.

He wandered up to the top floor, past the shut room that Jacoby had barricaded himself in (where he swore he heard some sort of growling), through the two remaining bedrooms, hoping to find something of interest. The first room he came across had apparently belonged to a little girl. It was filled with dolls and children's books and every surface was lathered in oppressive pink.

Sam stared into the room for a long moment, without letting his toes cross the threshold. An intense guilt unexpectedly flushed through him. Had the fraternity killed this child? He wondered. He imagined that they had. His tear ducts were now dried up relics, but for a second, before he remembered the inner drought that vampirage caused, he thought he was about to cry. The emotional inburst really caught him off guard. He staggered back a few steps and nearly tripped over his own feet. Downstairs he heard Kelv laughing gutturally at the two year old beauty pageant queens, which helped smack him out of his haze.

Sam had thought his sympathy glands had been surgically removed with his loss of life. To feel this intense concern for the preservation of human life made him feel weak and vulnerable. He continued down the hall and came to the master bedroom. He shut himself inside and sat down on the bed. He wanted to regain composure.

"I am a creature of the undead," he said aloud. "I am a dark shadow in the night. I am the reason that folks lock their doors at night. I…am…terror."

Somehow, the off-white walls, the yellow bed spread, and the tan ikea drawers did not compliment his speech of evil affirmation. He glanced over towards the master bathroom and wished that he could still feel the pleasures of a hot shower; which made him miss the pleasure of a hot meal; which made him long for a day of basking in the sun on the hot beach. Everything about being a vampire was cold, cold, cold. It was kind of depressing when you really took a moment to think about it.

"This is my destiny," he said. But for the first time in a long time – he felt doubt.

…

Things in the house quickly settled into a routine. Kelvish remained planted in front of the TV and watched an ungodly amount of reality programming. He watched shows about teenage mothers and teenage drug addicts and adult drug addicts and people addicted to drinking their own urine and people addicted to having sex with balloons and people addicted to shopping and people whose houses looked like landfills and shows about crab fisherman and shrimp fisherman and guys who drove on particularly icy roads and rich twenty somethings who contributed nothing to society; and amazingly he didn't want to shoot himself after subjecting himself to hours of viewing that could be a very useful method for prying information out of terrorists ("Please, waterboard me again, just no more shows about housewives!").

Meanwhile, Jacoby stayed locked in his room and Sam, for the first time, felt scared that he would not be the new frat brother to emerge from the pledge trials.

He saw how content Kelvish was to occupy himself with trash TV and imagined how determined that bizarre Jacoby was to stay locked in his room, not moving an inch for as long as it took, and Sam seriously suspected that he would probably break first. The only things he could find to read in the house were housewife magazines, chick lit, and children's books. Slim pickens, though he still tried to use them to pass the time. Unfortunately he found he couldn't focus because of his sudden, ultra annoying, feelings of guilt.

What was it about that little girl's bedroom that had made him forget all his hardness? Whatever the reason, he knew he had better shake this fragility soon or more would be at risk than just the frat spot; his entire eternal life as a vampire depended on it.

Yet things did not get better. They just got worse. Sam lay in the empty bathtub and wallowed for hours, full of shame and disgust.

Sam had yet to actually kill anyone and he now doubted whether he ever could. He tried to convince himself he did not need to feel bad about his predatory status above others in the food chain. After all, humans killed thousands of other animals – like cows and pigs and chickens – every day to feed themselves. (Not to mention the hunters who killed animals purely for the fun of it!). So really he had no reason to feel bad about the concept of draining a living person of their blood. But he did.

Somehow, a single emotional brick had cracked when he saw that little girl's room and his entire house of confidence had crumbled accordingly. Perhaps the architect had not done a great job in the design if the place could be destroyed so easily, he thought. Perhaps he wasn't as strong as he had always believed.

It was terrible. All he wanted to do was run home to his mother – his real mother, the human one – and say how sorry he was and let her hug him and tell him everything was going to be okay.

He was pathetic. He locked the bathroom door. He could not let the others see him like this.

...

Luckily, on the third day Sam saw something which turned his head back in the right direction. Outside the window he spotted an American flag waving in the wind. Some honorable local had attached it to a telephone pole.

Intense love for his country inflated inside him like a moon bounce before a carnival. American was number one after all. Just like him. He thought of the revolutionaries. They were the ultimate winners. Did they sit around and mope when it looked like the redcoats would smother them with their experienced militia? No. George Washington and his fellow heroes went out there and strategized and figured out a way to beat the more powerful army.

What Sam needed was a *strategy*.

Blindly, purposely waiting at this terrible house and hoping that one of the others would leave before he had a complete breakdown was no way to attack this situation. He needed a plan. He needed to use his intelligence to combat the boredom stamina these drone competitors possessed. As soon as he allotted himself to action instead of idleness, he immediately felt much better about himself. (He would just have to avoid that little girl's room. That place was some sort of trigger.)

Sam saluted the stars and stripes, sung a quick rendition of "My Country,

Tis of Thee," and got to work thinking.

His strategy needed to be offensive, not defensive. What he needed to do was convince one of the others to leave. The best thing to do first, he supposed, was figure out which of his opponents would be easier to get rid of. And in order to do *that*, he would have to learn something about the elusive Jacoby. He already knew plenty about Kelv from visiting his twitter feed (like that fact that he was "mad tryin' to bang the chick from modrrn famly"), but he knew almost nothing about Jacoby. He had kept himself secluded from everyone else throughout the competition.

Jacoby seemed determined to spend the entirety of his visit in a locked room. Sam could just kick down the door, but such a violation of courtesy seemed very much the wrong foot to start on when trying to get to know someone. Luckily, he had a better idea.

Eventually Jacoby would need to take a small break from the room to get some bloody sustenance from the fridge. And when he did, Sam would be waiting.

Sam removed the doors from every non occupied room in the house, so Jacoby would have nowhere else to hide. Then he planted himself in the kitchen. He waited.

...

When it happened, it happened quickly. Sam was picturing a particularly delicious scene of Thomas Jefferson curb stomping King George when a blur whizzed into the kitchen and threw open the refrigerator door.

Jacoby moved at sound shattering speed. He clearly intended to collect his blood and get back to his safe haven before the others could so much as say "hello."

But Sam was quicker. While the flicker of light that was Jacoby collected his blood bottles, Sam rocketed himself up the stairs and in to Jacoby's unlocked room.

Just as soon as Sam settled into a desk chair, Jacoby's movement stream fluttered back into the room.

Jacoby took one long look at his uninvited guest then raced out – into the next room. Sam followed. Jacoby looked for a door to close but Sam's door removal preparation immediately foiled his aim. Sam smiled.

Jacoby was wary, but he did not accept defeat so easily. He raced into the next room. And the next. At each turn Sam was right behind him and at each turn there was no door to shut himself inside. The acne covered vamp became more and more exasperated but at no point did he slow down. From laundry room to bathrooms to closets, he tried everywhere, but Sam would not be resisted. Finally he ceased his momentum in the little girl's bedroom and collapsed to the floor.

Sam was prepared for this moment. Chills ran down his spine as he stood on the threshold of that menacing pink chamber, but he gathered his strength and walked right in.

"Hey Jacoby," he said. "How's it going?"

It probably shouldn't have surprised Sam that his reclusive competitor wasn't one for common courtesies, especially after being chased around a townhome.

Rather than say hello back, Jacoby responded by baring his teeth and leaping at Sam with intent to kill.

Sam's instincts kicked in at the attack. He grabbed Jacoby's extended arms and flung him full force through the wall. Jacoby sprang right back up through the rubble and plowed into Sam's midsection like a linebacker, driving him into the floor.

They fell one flight into the kitchen. They collapsed on top of a wooden table, shattering its legs.

"Why won't you leave me alone!" said Jacoby as he grabbed Sam's head and slammed it repeatedly into the floor.

Sam kicked Jacoby off him, sending him soaring into the fridge. He grabbed Jacoby by the hair and swung him around like a shot putter heaving his metallic sphere.

"I just want to get to know you!" Sam declared. He threw Jacoby into the drawers above the counter top. "I've spent all this time with you and I know nothing about you."

Jacoby dropkicked Sam in the face. "What could you possibly want to know!"

Sam punched Jacoby five or six times, sending him careening into the stove. "Anything! Like where you're from!"

Jacoby pulled Sam's arms in opposite directions until they were close to ripping out of his sockets. "Orlando! But who cares!"

Sam kneed Jacoby repeatedly in the groin. "I care! Did you go to Disney World a lot?!"

Jacoby bit Sam in the thigh. "I hate that place! My aunt used to take me there all the time. Then I ripped the head off some brat's Mickey doll and the park rangers kicked me out!"

Sam spun Jacoby around and put him in a strangling headlock. "You more of a Donald fan?!"

Jacoby stood up. Sam locked onto his back. Jacoby ran around in a circle at 200 miles an hour to try to shake Sam off. "What?!"

Sam held on tight through the high speeds. "It was… aa… a.a.a… jjj ..jj .. ooo … ooo … o….ke…!!!!"

Sam threw himself backwards, did a somersault, and pinned Jacoby to the floor.

"I don't get it," said Jacoby.

"You said you ripped the head off a Mickey doll so I asked if you were more of a Donald fan. You know, like obviously you just hated the whole scene but I was joking that you preferred one character over another."

Jacoby stared at him blankly.

"It's not as funny if you have to explain it," said Sam sheepishly.

Jacoby tried to wiggle loose and Sam held him to the ground. He realized Sam's pin was too tight and stopped struggling. For an awkward moment Sam just lay on top of Jacoby and they stared at each other.

"Hey," said Jacoby, "do you smell something?"

"Nice try," said Sam.

"No really."

Sam sniffed the air. Actually he did smell something. It was that same rotten egg/cat piss stench he had smelled in the basement. It was a lot stronger than when he had been down there before. He wasn't sure how he had missed it until now but he supposed that the fighting had distracted his senses.

"Oh yeah," he said. "That's disgusting."

Sam stood up and walked over to the basement door. He put his ear up to it. He could hear the low grumble of voices.

"There are people down there," he said.

Sam marched into the living room where Kelv was watching the third Transformers movie with surround sound, at an ear drum shattering volume. Jacoby clumsily followed.

"Hey Kelv."

Kelv of course couldn't hear because he was listening to alien robotic destruction as loud as the TV would go.

He tried again. "KELV!" he yelled as he slapped Kelv across the face.

"WHAT THE FUCK!" said Kelv. He stood up, ready to fight.

"Did you know that there are people in the basement?"

"WHAT?"

"THERE ARE PEOPLE IN THE BASEMENT!"

"REALLY?"

"Yeah. Did you see them come through here?"

"WHAT?"

"DID YOU SEE THEM COME THROUGH HERE!"

"NO, I WAS WATCHING TRANSFORMERS!"

"Jesus Christ."

"WHAT?"

"JUST COME WITH ME," said Sam. "Fucking moron."

Sam walked to the basement door. He fraternity competitors followed.

"WHAT IS THAT SMELL?" said Kelv.

Sam kicked the door in and ran down the stairs at full speed. Jacoby followed. Kelv walked after them at a casual pace.

At the tables Sam had spied on his first day in the house were three human teenagers. They wore gas masks and were cooking chemicals together to produce Crystal Meth.

They jumped at the sudden arrival of the dead eyed others.

"Who the fuck are you?" said the leader, a wife beater wearing, tattooed, bald buffoon.

"I'd ask you the same thing," said Sam.

The leader pulled out a gun and pointed it at Sam. The second teen pulled out his own pistol. The last of the gang hid behind the others.

"Big Steve ain't gonna like a couple pussys messin up his batch cook," said the leader.

Just then, Kelv arrived downstairs.

"WHAT IS THIS!" he said.

Already frightened, the second teen was shocked enough by Kelv's loud voice to start shooting. After one bullet was fired, there was no preventing both of the gun toting meth cooks from firing off their entire clips.

Once all of the commotion stopped, Sam, filled with bullet holes but still standing motionless, shook his head at the teens in condescension.

"Nice try boys," he said.

Kelv did not take being shot at with as much nonchalance.

"MOTHER FUCKERS!" he said and leaped at one of the teens. He sunk his teeth into the boy's neck and greedily slurped up his blood.

The other two screamed like little girls and ran for the door. Jacoby grabbed one and tore him to shreds. He bit his neck and drained his veins.

The teenager who had hidden behind his gun toting friends escaped out of the basement. Sam chased him down. He grabbed him just before he made of the house and threw him to the floor.

"Please. Please don't hurt me. I didn't shoot at you. That was the other guys. Please…please!"

Kelv and Jacoby ran up the stairs up with the action.

"Beg all you want bro," said Kelv, laughing. "Won't do you no good."

For a minute they all just stood there, waiting for something to happen. Finally Kelv's inexhaustible impatience broke the silence.

"Well!" he said to Sam. "Are you gonna fuckin' drain him or what?"

Sam paused. He thought. He knew he sheouldsuck his fangs into the boy's neck but he couldn't convince himself to do it.

"This one didn't do anything," he finally said.

"So fuckin' what! He's a free meal!"

Sam glanced over at Jacoby to see if he would take sides, but he was standing still, leery, curious to see how events unfolded without getting involved.

"If you don't want him, I'll take him!" said Kelv.

He grabbed the boy's ankle.

The empathetic instinct Sam had tried so hard to bury the last several days came roaring back with a vengeance. He grabbed Kelv's head and yanked him back by the hair, just as he was about to bite into the boy's leg.

"Let him go," said Sam.

"What the fuck!" said Kelv.

Sam threw Kelv back into the house. Then, with his other hand, he threw the boy into the front yard.

Kelv immediately jumped back up and ran for Sam. He grabbed him by the shirt and pushed him up against the wall.

"Fuck you!" said Kelv.

"I'm sorry Kelv. You're right. I'm acting stupid. The kid's all yours. Go and get him."

"You're fuckin' right I will."

The boy was writhing in the grass in pain. His back had slammed against the ground extremely hard. Kelv nearly walked right out the door, but stopped himself at the last moment, while still in the door frame.

He turned his head back towards Sam, sporting an evil grin.

"I see what you're doing Mutha' fucka. I ain't gonna leave the house the bro. Nice fuckin' try."

Kelv walked back into the house. He passed by Sam and bumped him hard with shoulder. "You best watch your back," he added.

Kelv retreated to the living room, where he continued watching the third film in the Transformers series. He didn't rewind the footage, but missed no pertinent information.

Sam looked out at the kid. He was crawling away as fast as his injured body would carry him – which was not very fast.

"Hey!" said Sam.

"Yeah?" said the frightened teen, hesitantly.

"Who lives here?"

"What?"

"There are pictures of a family everywhere."

"Oh. Yeah, I think they all died in a car accident or something. I don't know. I just know the boss said it was a good place to cook."

Sam paused. He wasn't sure if the kid was lying or not but he supposed it made no difference. "Get out of here," he said. "And don't tell anyone we're here."

Sam slammed the door shut with a vengeance. He turned around and noticed Jacoby staring at him.

"What?" he said aggressively, no longer in the mood to make friends with his socially inept housemate.

"Was that really strategy?"

"Was what strategy?"

"Throwing the kid out of the house so Kelvish would go after him. Was that just a way to eliminate him or did you let that kid go for...other reasons."

Sam paused for a moment, angry with himself that he couldn't answer truthfully the way he wanted to.

"What difference does it make?"

Sam marched off to the master bedroom. He was concerned that Jacoby might follow him, since he had removed all the doors, but, for the time being, his competitor graciously left him alone.

...

The next day, Jacoby found Sam in the bath tub, staring out into space, looking quite forlorn.

"What are you doing?" he said.

"What does it look like I'm doing?" said Sam.

"It looks like you're moping in a bath tub."

Sam looked his body over. "I suppose that is what I'm doing." He immediately felt disgusted with himself and stood up. "Goddammit!" he screamed.

"What's up with you? You don't seem like yourself?" said Jacoby.

"What's that supposed to mean? You don't know me."

"No. But during every challenge up until this one you seemed like the toughest, strongest player in the competition. I was really intimidated by you. Now all the sudden you seem...kind of weak and pathetic."

"Oh. Well thanks."

"I meant it as an insult."

"Are we insulting each other now? Okay. How about this? You're awkward and weird looking and probably couldn't buy a friend if you tried."

Jacoby glared at Sam angrily and turned to leave.

"Wait!" said Sam, already feeling guilty. "Come back. I didn't mean it."

"A-ha!" said Jacoby, whipping himself around. There was a big grin on his face.

"What?"

"I was just pretending to be hurt. I knew you'd apologize."

"I don't understand."

"Something's happened to you man. You're losing your edge. I know I shouldn't be helping you by telling you, but it just makes me kind of sad. It's pathetic."

Sam thought about arguing back for a moment, then slumped back into the bathtub, resigned to the truth of Jacoby's words.

"You're right. I'm in a funk. It's this house. It's that little girl's room. It did something to me. It made me...sympathetic or something. I can't seem to shake it.

"Well snap out of it! I can't stand the thought that Kelvish could win this thing. That guy is the worst."

"No kidding."

"And I don't really know if I can compete with either of you guys for the last challenge."

"Hey you made it this far. Besides, we don't even know what the last challenge is yet."

Jacoby stayed silent, but there was a knowing look in his eyes.

"Wait," said Sam, "do you know what the last challenge is?"

Jacoby looked warily at the camera in the corner of the room, which was filming them. "I may have...snuck a peak at some files..."

"What is it?"

"Well..." Jacoby paused. "No. I'm not going to tell you. You're not my friend. You just said yourself; I couldn't even buy a friend."

"I told you, I'm sorry about that."

"Ha! Got you again! Pathetic!"

"Motherfucker!" Sam leaped out of the bathtub and pinned Jacoby against the wall. The rage took over him without warning.

"That's more like it!" said Jacoby.

Sam dropped Jacoby, not overly gently.

"What do you want from me?" he said.

"Actually," he said, "I was thinking that maybe we could form an alliance against Kelvish."

Sam was a silent a moment. He laughed.

"What's funny?" said Jacoby.

"I wanted to form an alliance *with you* against Kelvish. That's why I ripped your door off."

"Why would you rip my door off to ask me about forming an alliance? Wouldn't it be more cordial to knock?"

"Well..." This was an extremely valid point. "I don't know. I never even heard you speak before yesterday! I didn't know what the hell to think of you."

"I've kept quiet out of strategy. I figured it was better to keep the other guys guessing. It's the only way I made it this far. I don't have the natural abilities that you do."

"Oh."

Sam looked closely at Jacoby's hard to read expression. He wasn't sure how much he could trust him.

"You're probably thinking that you're not sure how much you can trust me."

Damn, that was impressive. "No! I was thinking...about other things."

"Look, I don't blame you. This is why I brought a peace offering."

Jacoby reached into his pocked at pulled out a thin tube filled with an oily substance.

"I found this on the black market," said Jacoby. "They call it sunscreen."

"Sunscreen?"

"Yeah. It's not cheap. But it's worth every penny for what it allows us to do."

"And what's that?"

"Take a wild guess."

"Are you trying to tell me that lathering that stuff on my body will allow me to be out in the sun without dying?"

"That's exactly what I'm telling you."

"Well that's pretty convenient," said Sam.

(Yes. It is convenient. Maybe a little too convenient. But try to forgive the contrivance. It makes later chapters a lot easier.)

"I'll prove it," said Jacoby.

He poured out some of the liquid on his arm, rubbed it in thoroughly, then walked into the master bedroom. Sam followed. Jacoby popped open a window in direct contact with the sunlight. He stuck his arm right in the light beams' path.

"Wait!" said Sam, unexpectedly concerned for his competition. His worries were needless. Normally Jacoby's arm would have charred to a crisp. The oil protected him. He was completely unharmed.

Jacoby smiled cockily. He was extremely proud of his possession.

"That's amazing," said Sam.

"And it's all yours," said Jacoby.

He tossed Sam the bottle.

"What do you say?" said Jacoby. "Alliance?"

Sam pocketed the bottle and nodded. "You got yourself a deal."

"Great. First things first though. We gotta get you back into fighting conditions."

Sam furrowed his eye brows. He wondered what exactly Jacoby meant.

"Follow me," said Jacoby.

Their journey was not far. It took them only down the hall, to the little girl's bedroom.

"I thought you looked odd the first time we ended up in this room," said

Jacoby.

"What are we doing here?"

"*You* – are going to tear this room apart."

Sam looked around. The place felt like sacred ground. Sam had never been religious but he suddenly felt as if he was being closely watched by some deity, observing in a detached manner to see if Sam would make the right choice.

He also had the sudden inkling that their whole conversation was nothing more than intensely calculated strategy by Jacoby, intended to eliminate him from the competition.

It was no matter. Sam was sick of feeling weak. He battled back the encumbering whispers of conscience and lightly commenced the destruction. He pushed the girl's photos and trinkets from her drawers' tops to the floor. He opened her closet and pulled her clothes off the hangers her mother must have reached for her.

"You can do a little better than that," said Jacoby, with a wicked grin.

Right then Sam hated his new alliance partner. He wanted to smash his face in. Aware of the repercussions which that course of action would lead to, he restrained himself from expressing his anger. Instead, he reacted violently towards the room. He sped up his demolition. He powerfully smashed the drawers into wooden shards. He tore posters into shreds. He ripped the bed into nothing but twisted coils and puffy fabric guts. He destroyed every sign that this had ever been a bedroom where a little girl has slept and dreamt. Somewhere along the way he started crying (dryly – since actual tears were impossible) but this didn't slow his relentless attack. When he was finished it looked like a tornado had hit the pink room and Sam collapsed into the middle of the shattered heap. Sam clutched himself. His separation from the human world never felt so definitive.

"Good work," said Jacoby. "Tomorrow we'll talk about taking care of our housemate." He left Sam to his tears.

...

It was shortly after two in the morning when he heard the sound of smashing glass. Sam was in bed, still recovering from his emotional breakdown. He jumped up.

Sam raced to the top of the stairs to see what was happening. Jacoby, one step ahead of him, was already stationed there.

"What's going on?" asked Sam.

Jacoby merely motioned to the action unfolding below.

Fifteen to twenty Alaskan thugs had forced their broad shoulders diagonally through the doorway. At their head stood a smaller, older man. He had a goatee and was wearing a porkpie hat. He was clutching the skinny arm of the terrified teenager Sam had let live the day before.

"Where are they?" said the man in the porkpie hat.

"I don't know. They came out of nowhere."

"Find them!" said Porkpie.

"But sir, you don't understand. I'm telling you they weren't normal people. I think they were vampires!"

The mass of identical thugs laughed in unison.

"I think you've been reading too many 'Moonlight' books," said Porkpie. "Now find them! Nobody fucks with my product! Nobody fucks with my men! I'm going rip these motherfuckers' mouths open and shit down their throats!"

"Lovely image," Jacoby said quietly to Sam.

The teen shuddered. He did not move.

"They'll kill me," said the teen.

"They're not the only ones," said Porkie.

He pulled out a gun and pointed it right at the boy's head. The thugs laughed again. The leader pulled the trigger.

Sam felt rage explode in his core like a big bang of violence.

He leaped from the top of the stairs. Using his impossibly fast vampire speed he knocked the teenager out of the way before the bullet arrived. The bullet hit Sam in the head instead.

The meth thugs went quiet. They knew something was off but they weren't sure what. What their limited intelligences could not deduce was the fact that no blood had splattered from Sam's head when he was hit with the bullet.

Porkpie walked over to Sam, the curious person who had appeared out of nowhere to save his cowardly underling. Sam had collapsed briefly from the force of the bullet, but just as quickly he leaped back up. Porkpie jumped back. He looked around, making sure that none of the thugs noticed his fear in the same way most of us look around after an embarrassing stumble. Then he turned back to Sam.

"You must be the vampire," he said.

"He's one of them," said Jacoby, who had suddenly appeared on the other side of the room.

The thugs shuddered. They were a bit spooked.

"You assholes are in my territory," said Porkpie.

"I'll tell you what," said Sam, his usual confidence radiating with an extra sheen of anger, "You leave right now and we won't kill you."

Silence. Porkpie turned to his men. He held out his hands as if to say – *where's the laughter?*

Following his lead they sputtered out some dry, awkward fake laughter that convinced no one of their assurance in the situation.

"We're not going anywhere," said Porkpie. He raised his gun and pointed it at Sam.

"Wrong answer," said Sam. He nodded at Jacoby and they went to work.

Within seconds limbs were flying around the room, torn from bodies with the utmost aggression. The thugs were beaten and tortured and sheared into pieces.

Sam felt a strange disconnect during his first ever bout of murder. As a vampire, killing felt as natural as peeling a banana. It was enjoyable even, like eating that same banana after you peel it. Yet it was also so *cold*. So very very cold. He felt as though any remnants of soul he might have possessed evaporated away into nothingness. It was horrible. And wonderful. And horrible how wonderful it was. He hated it and loved it and hated himself for loving it.

He took out all of his conflicted emotions on the men he killed. It was brutal. Jacoby stopped his own killing at some point just to watch the disgusting display of Sam's mutilation.

"Dude, I think they're all dead," said Jacoby.

Sam looked up. Jacoby was right. Now he was just tearing up their corpses. He was covered in blood and guts from head to toe.

"I killed them," he said, shaking.

"I know," said Jacoby.

"Uh...." said a voice in the corner.

They looked over. Porkpie had pissed his pants.

"I think I'll go now," he said.

He ran for the door but Jacoby caught him.

"Sam, would you do the honors?"

Sam nodded. He stuck out his teeth and bit deep into porkpie's throat. He shuddered with pleasure. The other vampires had been right. There was nothing quite like human blood straight from the body.

"Hey guys, am I late to the party?" said just appearing Kelv from across the room.

Sam and Jacoby turned. Kelv was wearing pajamas and a bathrobe and drinking a blood cocktail.

"Ah, here's one left," Kelv said, standing over the still alive teenager.

"NOOOOOO!" said Sam in slow motion as Kelv bit into the teen's throat and sucked him dry.

Sam pushed Kelv off but he was too late. The boy was dead.

"What the fuck Kelv!"

"Ooooooh. Sorrrrry. I ate a humannnnnn. Big whoop."

"That one didn't deserve to die."

"They all deserve to die," said Kelv.

Kelv stepped over the dead bodies to make his way to living room couch. He flipped on the television and put on MTV2.

Sam thought of the little girl. He thought of the immense guilt he felt in destroying her room. All of the conflicted emotion he had felt in the last several days at this terrible house came to its tipping point.

I CANNOT TAKE ONE MORE MOMENT WITH THIS DOUCHEBAG, he thought.

He ran behind Kelv, threw his hands on Kelv's head and pulled.

Kelv's head popped off his neck like a Snapple cap. (But without the nifty fact underneath).

Sam dropped Kelv's dismembered head to the ground.

"What the fuck!" said Kelv's still functioning mouth.

Sam opened the front door and kicked Kelv's face out of the house like a soccer ball. He grabbed the rest of Kelv's body and tossed it out after his head.

Jacoby looked at Sam, wide eyed.

"Wow," was all he managed to say.

With that, a bell of victory sounded throughout the house. A lightshow went off in every room.

"Looks like we won," said Sam.

"I guess so," said Jacoby.

"So tell me, what's the final competition?"

Jacoby, still frightened by the beheading he had just witnessed did not play coy. He answered directly.

"We have to take a human virgin girl to her prom and take her virgin's blood. Then we have to bring her to Nosferat U council of elders so they can all engage in the pleasures of her flesh and sacrifice her to the vampire gods."

"Any human girl?" asked Sam.

"As long as she's a high school virgin," said Jacoby.

Someone immediately jumped into Sam's mind – the beautiful girl he had seen on TV whose friends had died at the shopping mall. He had been thinking about her a lot lately. Something about her strange expression in the video footage had stuck with him. He was fascinated by her.

"I think I know just the girl," said Sam.

6

Lindsay nearly had a heart attack when she saw him. And not in a usual teenage girl way, like, "OMG, I'm like, having a heart attack right now… like, really." Like, she really almost had a heart attack. A sharp pain shot down her arm. The blood momentarily stopped flowing. Her heart fluttered and took a split second break from its clockwork beating. She grabbed her chest and fell against the nearest wall of lockers.

The physical break down lasted only a half moment. Her shock at who she had just seen lasted far longer.

Either she had officially boarded the crazy train (a distinct possibility) or Swampy was wandering around the halls of her high school wearing jeans and a Chicago Cubs sweatshirt.

She forced herself away from the wall and hustled down in the direction he was heading.

And there, by Mrs. Hassenfeffer's room, he stood (waiting for class?), talking with a really familiar looking boy with mediocre looks whom she couldn't quite place.

Much stranger than the fact that a swamp monster was wondering the halls in hand-me-down clothes was that fact that no one else seemed to notice he was there. Students and teachers passed through the halls. Kids joked, bullied, fist-fought. Everyone went about their normal routines without paying Swampy a second glance.

...

"I knew this would work," Teddy said to Swampy outside of Mrs. Hassenfeffer's room. I've watched enough high school movies to know that the mildest of disguises will convince anyone someone is a student. It doesn't matter if they're 30 years old or a dead eyed vampire. Granted your looks are a little more conspicuous than the examples I'm referencing, but I think it's a mistake to ever underestimate how dense people can be when you use a little sleight of hand."

Swampy's eye fell out of his socket and onto his geometry textbook. Teddy hurriedly scooped it up and jammed it back in.

"It's okay," he said, "no one saw that."

...

Lindsay saw it. And she assumed that she had, in fact, lost her mind. It wasn't a surprise. Her strange fetish for queasy brutality was obviously a sickness, and sicknesses often spread, infecting the entirety of a person's body or brain.

...

Despite his confident assurances to his slimy friend, Teddy thought it rather amazing that his plan had worked. How could anyone in reality seriously not notice that the very monster who had the town so terrified was standing in front of them, just because he was wearing a pair of jeans and a Chicago Cubs sweatshirt? It made Teddy briefly question whether he was a real living person or just a character in some story. However, the existential implications of such a line of thought were so complicated that he abandoned the inquiry before his brain exploded.

In truth almost everyone in the school DID notice. I mean it was a giant swamp monster, whose eye kept falling out, how could you not? But the sight of him wearing that pair of jeans and Chicago Cubs sweatshirt was so bizarre that everyone questioned what they were seeing, and each individual person (not wanting to admit to their own inner insanity) decided not to point out Swampy's obvious presence unless someone else did first. You can see the vicious circle here. Everyone at the school (students and teachers alike) was so concerned about their own self-images that no one made open reference to the giant monster in front of them, which lead each one of these individuals to assume that they were in fact seeing things, since no one else said anything, which lead, in turn, to Swampy somehow being accepted as a new student in the high school with no voiced complaints or questions whatsoever.

It was quite remarkable. One administrative assistant in the school's roster office realized that no new students had been registered, but kept quiet. Lunch ladies averted their eyes when Swampy lifted up his sweatshirt and stuffed the platter of sloppy joes they served him into a mouth in his midriff. Most teachers avoided calling on their new student in class (who had been christened "Seth Manster" by Teddy) and the ones who did call on him accepted his blank stares and squishy grunts as acceptable answers.

Normally, certain overachieving A students would have questioned the unfair practice of praising subpar work when they were busting their asses to get answers right – but these academic prisses pretended Swampy was normal along with everyone else and kept their mouths shut. It was much the same with tests and homework assignments. Swampy, at Teddy's behest, turned in papers, but they were covered only with slimy goo – not pencil and pen marks, and certainly not the work the teacher assigned. Still he received C pluses and B minuses. Throughout B.S.H.S. the students said, "Hey Seth," as they passed him in the halls and had one sided conversations with him about football or school gossip while they waited with him for class to begin.

...

Anyway, Lindsay assumed she was crazy. (Sure everyone else thought they were crazy too, but she's really the one we're concerned about here. She is the protagonist after all).

With Lindsay's full acceptance of insanity came a feeling of liberation. She didn't have to worry about any of the disturbing thoughts she'd ever had because they were all the output of a loony mind. Loving William Denworth had been crazy. Loving Swampy had been crazy. Getting moist in her nether regions when she looked at pictures of the destruction that the atomic bombs had left in Hiroshima and Nagasaki had been crazy. (Oh yeah. That little detail hasn't been mentioned yet. Lindsay was sweet, but she really was disturbed.)

Lindsay now realized it was time to reenter the world of professional help. When hallucinations began, full blown nuttiness and a life spent in the mental institution with her grandmother couldn't be far behind.

That night at dinner, she decided to talk with her mom.

"I need to talk you about something," said Lindsay, in between bites of green beans.

"You can always talk to me honey," said Lindsay's mother, who was surprised but pleased that her aloof, mysterious child might want to open up to her.

"I think I might be crazy."

"Oh, honey." She put her hand on Lindsay's shoulder. "What you went through was very upsetting. It not that surprising for it to have some lingering effects."

"No. I think I was crazy even before that."

"What do you mean?"

"Well..." It wasn't easy to talk about this sort of thing with your mother. "Uh, take this chicken..." They were eating grilled chicken with the green beans. "Most people like chicken right. It's a pretty popular meat."

"Uh, yeah, I would say so I guess."

"Well what if, I said, I don't really like chicken. Or I only like chicken if it's not cooked. If it's bloody…" Lindsay's voice softened and became more seductive as she spoke. "If it's right off the body, ripped from the bones…" Lindsay reached down and touched herself under the table. Her eyes half closed.

"Lindsay?"

Her mother's voice snapped her out of the trance. She pulled her hand away from her crotch.

"Sorry. I didn't think THAT would turn me on," she said without thinking.

"Lindsay, what are you talking about?" asked her mother, with a great deal of concern.

"I'm saying that I'm not normal. I'm not…*attracted* to what normal people are attracted to."

"Are you into girls?"

"What? *No*. I'm into *monsters*."

Lindsay's mother paused to make sure she had heard right "Come again?"

"I'm in love with a swamp monster. And I'm turned on by violence. I get wet when I look at pictures of Hiroshima."

"Woah, okay. TMI."

That was Lindsay's mother's gut reaction to hearing the phrase, "I get wet," from her daughter. She immediately felt bad about sounding so harsh. Especially when she saw her daughter's shamed face. Lindsay was sharing something hard with her. She needed to be a better parent.

"Sorry," Lindsay's mother said. "That was a poor choice of words. What I meant was…I'm glad you decided to share with me."

"That's a radically different phrasing."

"Well you know, the English language has been really deluded over the years."

"Mom," Lindsay said softy.

"Yeah?"

"I think I need help. I don't want to be crazy. I don't want to end up like grandma,"

There were tears in Lindsay's eyes. All that she'd been through – all the stress of her jumbled mind – broke through.

"Oh honey," said her mother.

She wrapped Lindsay in her arms and held her tight like a mom should. Lindsay sobbed into her mother's shoulder.

"Everything's going to be okay," Lindsay's mother said. "Everything's going to be okay."

...

His name was Dr. Greshilgoff and he was recommended by the finest psychological institutions. His practice was attached to a Spanish tapas bar, which he also owned, and which had been rated 4 out of 5 stars by Zagat. As a result, he frequently smelled delicious, which probably did more for patient retention than his actual skills of analysis.

"Unfortunately," said the doctor, I was unable to obtain any of Dr. Bootstein's files on you from when you were a child. It seems that all of the poor deceased woman's documents were burned down in a horrible menorah accident a couple of Hannukahs ago. They said it was a miracle that the couple of small candles managed to burn down the entire office. In any event, we will have to start from scratch. So Lindsay, tell me, in your own words, what exactly seems to be troubling you?"

"Who else's words would I use?"

"I beg your pardon?"

"You said, 'in your own words.' Who else's words would I use?"

"It's merely an expression."

"Oh."

Lindsay felt rather tense. She probably could have delayed admitting her proclivities all day with discussion of linguistics if she wanted to, but that would just be wasting everyone's time. She told her mother she needed help and now, here she was.

"Well," she said, "You see the thing is...I've been seeing things."

The hallucinations actually seemed the least shameful of her problems. A good place to start.

"What sorts of things?"

"Swamp monsters. Well, one in particular."

"Ah. Yes. I can't pretend I haven't watched the news. This doesn't come as a huge shock. Victims of crimes often have trouble getting their perpetrators out of their minds."

"Right, but, the thing is..." *Here goes nothing.* "I'm kind of in love with him."

"Ah. Classic Stockholm syndrome."

"What?"

"The term has its derivation from a certain Swedish hostage ordeal but that's neither here nor there."

"Then where is it?"

"What?"

She was delaying with linguistics again. "Sorry, please continue."

"The term refers to a certain affection, sympathy, even love, that the captured or abused form towards their tormentors. It's a highly irrational mental compensation. A subconscious attempt to ease the suffering of a certain trauma."

Lindsay could have sworn that Dr. Greshilgoff's voice was becoming more British as he continued to speak. But *that* was neither here nor there.

"I don't know if this Stockholm thing is what I have."

"Of course it is."

She was thinking of William Denworth. And of the atomic wetness.

"But, you see, I get turned on by all sorts of disturbing things."

"I'm sorry, did you say something dear?" The doctor didn't hear her because he was too busy scribbling out pill prescriptions.

"Yeah, I..."

He interrupted her by thrusting the prescription note into her hands. Apparently his question had been rhetorical. "I'm putting you on 500 gram doses of Ghettohydronal for the Stockholm syndrome – standard dosage – and another 500 grams of Rettlepoppinettle for the hallucinations. Those should do the trick."

"Oh. Okay... It's just that I think—"

"Never fear dear, the side effects are minor." His British accent was now full-fledged. "A little itching in the ear. Some chaffing in various spots. Maybe a bit of tooth worm, but that's exceedingly rare."

"Uh. Yeah. No. Fine. It's just—"

"Just give the pills a try my dear. If they don't work, we can talk more then. Now, if you'll excuse me, I must send you on your way. I need to record the circumstances of your case into my audio diary before the next patient arrives. Have a wonderful day!"

"Well that was quick," said Lindsay's mother in the waiting room.

"Yes. It was, wasn't it?" said Lindsay. "I'm not sure about that guy."

Lindsay's lack of faith in Dr. Greshilgoff's judgement didn't stop her from retrieving the pills he assigned her and popping them as soon as possible.

...

Meanwhile, across town, Teddy snuck away from his parents to pay a visit to the Bigshartz family tree house.

Swampy had, for the moment, taken up residence in the crooked jumble of wood that Teddy's dad had broken both legs building ten years before. It wasn't as murky an abode as he was used to but he had made it his own. The floors were now covered with slime and somehow an eternal fog had formed.

Teddy prayed that his parents wouldn't look outside and notice this constant cloud. As it happened, his father had noticed. But he merely assumed that Teddy and his friends had been smoking pot. It was a hobby which, as a child of the late 60s, Teddy's pop had done more than his fair share of (if fair share was defined as smoking four times a day). He considered it a rite of passage. He was plenty aware, however, that Teddy's somewhat prudish mother would not feel as proud of her son for smoking the ganja. Wishing to be a loyal Dad, Teddy's father had done his duty and made sure to spin Teddy's mother around for a passionate kiss every time her eye direction turned towards the backyard. As it turned out, this physical form of distraction had reinvigorated what had for the last several years been a rather dry sex life. While Teddy made his nightly visits to his new friend, his parents ran to their bedroom and engaged in wild lovemaking.

Teddy climbed the (still rather unsafe) ladder and slid into Swampy's impromptu treetop lair. Nightly he brought packets of raw meat he purchased at the local mini mart on the way home from school. Teddy wasn't sure whether Swampy even *had* to eat for survival. There certainly didn't seem to be any evidence of a proper stomach or any other vital organs. There was no question, however, that the monster enjoyed consumption and Teddy wished to keep him satisfied. At first Teddy had cut the meats out of their Styrofoam containers before tossing them towards one of Swampy's several mouths. But one night, an unexpected mouth that emerged from Swampy's backside suckled on the remaining trash and absorbed it with great satisfaction. Ever since, Teddy had just been tossing the whole package to his eager companion.

"Evening, Swampy," he said.

Swampy gurgled.

"I've got dinner!"

Teddy opened up his backpack and heaved over a couple of packages of pork. Swampy sucked them up readily.

It had been almost two weeks since the shootout at the Bluford Springs

Mall. The ill-fated shopping facility was shut down once more for an indefinite period of time while construction crews repaired the significant bullet damage. Once again, the incident had made national news, and once again it was reported that a costumed psychopath had caused the disruption. It was reported that he was responsible for the deaths of at least thirteen police officers (all of whom, in reality, had been shot in the backs by their own trigger happy comrades). Apparently someone with a cell phone camera had stuck around to take some shots, but no footage of the actual monster was released. (The video footage of Swampy had been censored by the government who didn't want the larger public to know that there were supernatural monsters running around). Instead, what had been shown on TV was a picture of Teddy in his mother's tree bark encrusted dress. Thankfully, his face was completely unrecognizable, but it had given Teddy quite a shock to see his image on the nightly news. It had given just as great a shock to his mother who declared, "I have a dress just like that!" Teddy hoped she wouldn't enter her closet to verify the similarity.

"How was your day at school?" said Teddy.

Swampy belched. The smell was horrendous.

"Mine too. Damn Mrs. Jacobs and her pop quizzes."

Teddy looked through the tree house's unintentionally rhombus shaped window and gazed up at the stars. As a mild science fiction geek, peering at those far away suns had been a form of momentary escape his entire life. He wondered what was out there. He wondered if somewhere, far far away, there was an alien kid like him, sitting in an alien tree house, with his own alien swamp monster.

"Pretty unlikely I guess," he said out loud.

Teddy had been killing time – delaying from his actual task. He was well aware of it. The first phase of his plan (bringing Swampy to school and minimally disguising him as a student) had been so reckless and poorly planned that Teddy wondered in retrospect if he had wanted the whole thing to fall apart so he wouldn't have to go through with it. The astonishing fact that it had worked didn't really make him feel any better.

It was amazing. Even Teddy's friends Henry and Tom hadn't noticed anything amiss. They stood right there as Teddy introduced an eight foot tall swamp monster as a new kid named Seth Manster and they hadn't batted an eye. (Inside, of course, both of them just waited for the other to point out what was obviously in front of them but since neither of them did, they ended up performing the same bit of perceptual make-believe that everyone else in the school did.) Nevertheless, neither Henry nor Tom had wanted to hang out much lately. Teddy might have been more bothered by this if his mind wasn't so consumed with other matters.

Teddy reminded himself of the only reason he had saved Swampy in the first place: So that he might provide Lindsay with the love she deserved. And so that he might love her vicariously.

Teddy had seen Lindsay glancing at Swampy in the halls on the few occasions they had passed directly by her. He was sure that at least *she* recognized him for what he was. He could see it in the fire of her lovely eyes. However, she likely still felt so rejected by his rejection of her declaration of love at the mall and she was understandably wary of approaching him.

Swampy would have to make the first step. Which meant that Teddy had to make the first step.

Teddy had been running over meet cute scenarios in his head. (For those not familiar a "meet-cute scene" is the term used by Hollywood types to describe the scene in a romantic comedy where the couple of narrative destiny first comes in contact with each other in an adorable, flirtatious, coincidental moment, causing lovelorn audience members to grin from ear to ear. In other words, one of the many types of moments that happen all the time in movies and almost never in real life). Teddy had several pretty solid ideas of ways to get Swampy back in Lindsay's good graces and set her extremely weird crush on a path to culmination. Provided of course, that Swampy continued to listen to Teddy and do as he asked.

The holdup on phase two initiation was not practical difficulty. It was Teddy's own feelings for Lindsay. Now that push was coming to shove, he was having a hard time with the idea of willingly sending the love of his life into the arms of another man (or creature, we should say).

Teddy looked over at Swampy, who was playing with his shoulder snot. Teddy had been spending almost all of his time with the monster and he still had no idea what to think of him. Swampy was able to comprehend an amazing amount of what Teddy said to him and yet he still seemed as mentally blank as a piece of plywood. He was obviously capable of the most brutal, meaningless destruction, yet there was also something innocent about him. Teddy had the sense that Swampy only destroyed and killed because he didn't know any better.

Teddy thought Swampy liked him but it was hard to tell because the monster didn't *do* much of anything. He wasn't excactly a communicator. The situation was probably as simple as: Teddy had saved him and Swampy now felt loyalty or the necessity of servitude towards him. When Teddy told Swampy to put on his old Umbro shirts, he put them on. When Teddy told the monster not to eat any of the other high school students, Swampy's whole body salivated, but he kept his distance from the human morsels.

And when Teddy told Swampy to win over Lindsay, he was sure he would do as told.

But could Teddy endure the result?

Just then a thought entered his head. A devious, evil thought. A new plan of sorts. It was cruel, but it just might work.

The question: Was Teddy willing to sink himself to that level?

...

Lindsay was in a haze. The medication had spread its chemicals throughout her nervous system, passed from node to node into the metropolis of activity in her brain, then taken up lazy residence on her frontal lobe's couch.

It felt like she was trapped in the sunlight on an extremely hot day and also had the chills. It felt like her vision was blinded by gauze but was also crisp as a just toasted roll. More important than the bizarre physical side effects were the mental ones. She felt dull. Unenthusiastic, but not unsatisfied. Lustless, passionless, careless, but unconcerned about any of these conditions. She felt like a blank piece of paper.

Somewhere inside her she knew this was not how someone should feel. There was some homeless notion of improperness wandering around her mind, begging for change, but none of the other thoughts would give it the time of day.

In normal past circumstances her teachers might have spotted her glazed look and asked if she was okay, but ever since the murders at the mall everyone saw her as nothing but a strange specimen anyway. Odd behavior from Lindsay was expected even if it had been, to this point, unspotted. Folks had assumed she was damaged goods from the get go and, now that her eyes looked deadened, they considered it a confirmation of their assumptions rather than any noteworthy or worrisome change.

In the lunchroom Lindsay sat alone (as she had most days since the incident; at first not wishing to be bothered by questions, then not wishing to be woken up from her pornographic daydreams of Swampy) and attempted to eat. Not an easy task. Her hands were quite numb and it was difficult to get any firm grasp on her sandwich. She tried to scoop it up from its underside, using her hand as a shovel. This was not any more successful. Using both hands as a kind of hammock she managed to prop the sandwich up for long enough for a single bite before it dropped back to the table. She repeated this process until too small of a portion remained for any traction.

Across the lunchroom Teddy and Swampy ate their own lunches. (Peanut butter & jelly and raw pork, respectively.) Teddy shook. He was rather nervous but he was determined to summon his courage and begin phase 1 of plan B, a.k.a. phase 2 of plan A. (There was some crossover between his original plan and his new one).

When Teddy saw Lindsay get up to throw out her trash (also not easy for her – she put her brown paper bag in her mouth) he knew that the moment had come.

"Come on, Swampy. It's time."

Teddy erected himself like a skyscraper. (Thought that metaphor was going in a different direction, didn't you?) He clenched his fists and led the way.

Except, he noticed immediately that Swampy wasn't following. He turned his head around and saw Swampy eating the lunch room table. A room full of people watched through their peripheral vision, pretending not to notice.

"Swam—I mean Seth! Stop that!—I mean come here!"

Swampy reluctantly disengaged himself from the table and slithered over to Teddy, leaving behind his usual trail of slime. (The custodian liked to pretend it was spilled milk).

Oblivious to the mutual fright and fascination of their peers, everyone resumed conversing and ignored the elephant (or in this case swamp monster) in the room, so as not to be caught staring at the thing they all presumed was not really there, but of course, actually was.

Atypically, the only person who genuinely didn't notice Swampy at the particular moment was Lindsay. She was too busy walking like a zombie over to the trash can, her clarity blended into mush by the medication.

As they approached, Teddy got behind Swampy and told his oozy friend to lead the way.

The students in their path parted like the biblical red sea, diving out of the way of the monster that they "didn't notice." Swampy's path zigged and zagged since he didn't have any sense of where he was going (or possibly any sense of anything), but Teddy quietly repeated "right" or "left" and his verbal joystick seemed to do the trick. There was definitively some unconscious recognition of language within the monster even if he had no self-consciousness or abilities of intention.

"Stop," whispered Teddy. Swampy did as instructed.

Teddy waited for Lindsay to notice her crush looming over her, but her haze made her a little slow on the uptake. At the moment, she peered into the trashcan, worried that it was a bottomless pit she might fall into.

A little extra effort on Teddy's part was required.

"Rello Rindsay," he said ridiculously, reverting once again to his terribly conceived Scooby-Doo monster voice.

As it turned out, Teddy had chosen an inconvenient time to initiate phase 2 of plan A (a.k.a. phase 1 of plan B). Because at the moment phase 2 of Lindsay's prescription drug's side effects was also commencing. One of these effects was a ringing in the ears loud enough to block out Teddy's voice completely.

"Rindsay?" he repeated.

Lindsay threw up all over the cafeteria floor. (Phase 2 of the side effects also consisted of heavy nausea and probable vomiting.) The custodian, still busy wiping up Swampy's slimy residue, gave a deep, "I-can't-take-much-more-of-this-life" sigh. Though at least one thing went right in that poor, balding, moneyless, twice divorced, custodian's day. Before he had a chance to transfer his mop over to Lindsay's puddle of vomit, Swampy collapsed to the floor and sucked it up like a toddler drinking a milkshake.

Imaginary or not (it wasn't), this sight turned enough stomachs to send the rest of the student population running from the lunchroom.

And it was only then that Lindsay finally noticed him. Her dreamboat. Licking up her rejection of today's lunch with three different tongues. Her heart shifted gears into a frenetic beat.

"I thought these drugs were supposed to stop the hallucinations," she said.

She whipped her head around and Teddy, the only other remaining student in the room, dove behind the trash can to avoid being spotted.

"I know it's not really you," said Lindsay.

"Rut it is me. Res, it really is," said Teddy, hidden safely by the garbage.

Swampy's face was still flattened on the throw up, licking up any last scrap. Thus, Lindsay would have found it unlikely that his voice was the one responding if she had been able to hear. However, the ringing was getting louder and louder and at that moment she wouldn't have heard a Boeing 747 fly by ten feet above her head.

"Of course, it's not you," she said. (Really loudly – the ringing disguised her perception of her own volume). "It's not you because I'm not sane. I'm insane. I'm FUCKING CRAZY!"

Lindsay, disgusted with herself, angrily kicked over the trashcan. It hit Teddy hard in the face. He fell to the ground and most of the trash spilled out on him.

Lindsay stormed out of the room.

"Well that didn't work," said a rather smelly Teddy.

...

Down the hall Lindsay burst into the girl's bathroom. The swinging door hit some poor unsuspecting freshman in the face. The girl wailed, but again Lindsay couldn't hear a thing and that made it twice in less than two minutes that Lindsay smashed someone in the face and remained unaware of it.

Lindsay looked into the mirror and the tears began to flow. *Oh life. Oh horrible life*, she thought. *Oh epically horrible life*. Lindsay didn't care what adults said about teenagers having it good. This was hell. This was unbearable. She wanted to die.

"I want to die," she said into the mirror.

Abruptly she passed out. (Due to another of the medication's side effects: "dizzy spells & possible fainting.")

She woke up a half hour later, having missed most of her European History class. She groggily pushed herself up from the disgusting, urine scented girls bathroom floor. She pulled herself up by the sink and looked in the mirror. She was not a pretty sight. Her hair was pushed every which way. Her eyes were bloodshot.

But she felt a little better. The medicine had powered through its initial volatile period and dispersed a feeling of calm within her. Her muscles were relaxed. Her mind had passed through a storm and the thought waves had settled — not completely, but enough for her suicidal notions to pass away.

"I'll get through this," she said to her reflection. "I'm better than this sickness."

...

Getting hit in the face with a garbage can and covered in trash didn't get Teddy down. He ignored the dirty looks and poorly disguised whispers about his scent for the rest of the day. (You might be wondering how kids could even notice Teddy's stink when he spent so much time next to the far more putrid odor of his buddy "Seth," but amazingly, after enough time people will get used to any smell – even one as horrible as Swampy's – and they were able to sniff out the distinct new offal that invaded their nostrils.) Later, Teddy went home, took a shower, and basked in his unexpected (and probably unwarranted) optimism.

His new plan (a.k.a. plan B) was underhanded, deceitful, dastardly, and any other appropriate synonym you'd like to use, but Teddy had a strong suspicion that it was going to work, setbacks be damned. The twisted hope he felt made him grin from ear to ear.

While still in the bathroom, after his shower, Teddy masturbated and thought of Lindsay. It was one of the most romantic meat-beating sessions of his entire life. While he tugged on his one eyed snake, he pictured kissing Lindsay passionately for the first time. Fireworks went off in the sky (in his mind) as they made out on a picturesque bridge lit with red lights. She held him and took his hand and led him back to her house. She slowly undressed him and then instructed him to rip her clothes off before — well, actually, that's as far as Teddy got, but surely the daydream would have gotten even better from there.

...

The next several days were made up of a series of botched connections, comic misinterpretations, and general unfulfilled frustration.

Things went like this:

Teddy directed his new toy Swampy around the school using simple words of direction.

Lindsay walked around the school, heavily medicated, determined to avoid human contact.

Teddy directed Swampy towards Lindsay whenever he spotted her.

Lindsay, whenever she spotted Swampy, who she believed to be a stubborn hallucination, shuffled away as quickly as possible.

Teddy, noticing Lindsay's scampering, started incorporating words like "faster," into his language joystick.

Lindsay, noticing that her hallucination was getting more aggressive, started waiting to journey through the halls until just before the class bell rang – making her trip in an all-out sprint.

Lindsay tripped on her own feet on one such sprint and fell down the stairs. (Loss of equilibrium was another side effect of the medication).

Lindsay was forced to wear an ankle boot for two weeks and hobbled around the school on crutches.

Teddy, taking advantage of Lindsay's speed impediment, approached her, hiding behind Swampy.

"Rello Rindsay," he said.

"I'm not talking to you," she said. "You're not there."

"I am rere. I want to ralk to you."

"You're a figment of my imagination," she insisted. She hobbled away as quickly as she could. Not seeing Teddy behind Swampy, she planted her crutch directly on his foot as she passed by. This hurt tremendously and he grabbed his foot with his hand. Standing on one foot, he lost his balance and crashed towards the floor. He stuck out his hand to break his fall.

Later that day, Teddy was given a cast to wear on his newly broken wrist.

And that's how the days went.

Teddy (with Swampy) would race after Lindsay and try to talk to her.

Lindsay would run.

One or both parties would suffer an injury of varying degree.

And so on.

Until one afternoon Teddy decided that the confines of the school building were limiting him and he took Swampy to Lindsay's house after school. There, Teddy planted Swampy outside her window and hid behind a tree.

"Rindsay! I need to see you!"

Teddy saw her peeking out her window. He thought she looked reluctant to open it, but tempted.

Inside, Lindsay felt reluctant to open her window, but tempted. (It was one of Teddy's better moments of perception.) The medication was clearly completely ineffective in blocking out her hallucination and it was becoming harder and harder to resist the pull of her love's image, even if was the complete fabrication of her own mind. If you keep waving crack in front of a crack addict, sooner or later they're going to smoke it.

In a burst of desire, she threw open her window.

"Rindsay!" Teddy cried out. The ventriloquism of his voice's misplaced direction was unclear to her from the distance she stood.

"I really wish you would leave me alone," she said, looking at Swampy.

"But rhy? I thought you loved me!"

"I love the real Swampy! You're not him!"

Believe it or not, this was the first point at which Teddy had an inkling of what was going on in everyone else's mind. (For an "A" student, he could be a little slow). He thought: *Does everyone think Swampy's just some sort of delusion? It would explain his really quite unreasonably easy acceptance at the school.*

"I am real! I prove it. If I wasn't really Swampy, how would I know about the night rhat rou came to risit me? At the mall. In my basement room. When rou said rou loved me?"

Lindsay paused momentarily while she examined this logic.

"Because," she said, "I made you up so you would know everything I know."

Oh yeah, thought Teddy, *that makes sense actually.*

"And if you're real," said Lindsay "How come no one else at school can see you?"

Teddy was just catching on to the crazy logic of that particular scenario himself, so he decided to forgo the actual answer and respond with a fictional romantic one.

"Only someone who truly loves me can see me routside of the swamp. Everyone else sees a magically hidden kid."

This seemed like a serious stretch to Lindsay but she wanted so badly for it to be true.

"Really?" she asked with hesitation.

"I reak only the ruth."

"You reek the ruth? Is that what that smell is?"

"No. I SPEAK only the TRUTH."

"Oh. I gotcha."

Teddy regretted his Scooby Doo voice choice now that he had to use it so much. It wasn't easy to keep up. He decided he would have to slowly phase it out.

"I don't know," said Lindsay. Her mind was a flutter with a million disparate thoughts: Belief in her own madness. Lust for Swampy. Self-hatred over her lust. Passion. Guilt. Purpose. Shame.

"If you are Swampy," she blurted out, not yet willing to concede the point but no longer turning a blind eye to the possibility, "then why wouldn't you talk to me that night I came to see you? I bared my heart to you and you just stood there." She started to cry again. She was a real mess lately. "And then you left. You left me there all alone."

"I know," said Teddy. "I was scared. I'm a disgusting Swamp Monster who sends people running away screaming, and rou are a beautiful girl who could be with any man rou choose. I couldn't believe it was true."

"But it is true!" she said. "I love you more than anything in the world!"

"But why? Why do you love a revolting creature like me?" This was a question that Teddy desperately wanted to know the answer to.

"You can't ask why about love," she replied, unhelpfully. (She had picked up this line from the trailer to the movie "Anna Karenina" but didn't realize her plagiarism.) "I just love you. That's all that I know." Actually, she had a great sense of *why*. She knew she was turned on by violence, as she had told her mother and her therapist. But in the grips of such a dramatic scene she believed her own words about love's ambiguous, impossible to define, quality. It was so much more romantic that way.

"No one's ever loved me before," he said.

"I love you. You're the only one I've ever loved," she said, forgetting about fictional vampire William Denworth. "I'll always love you," she added, because she was on a roll now and why not go all the way with it?

Teddy noticed at this moment that Swampy had gotten distracted from his order to stand still, straight, and motionless. He was hunched over, sucking worms out of the ground with his brown, wart covered tongue.

"Swampy," Teddy whispered angrily. "Stand up. *Stand up.*"

"What are you saying?" asked Lindsay, anxiously.

"Uh, nothing my sweet," said Teddy tentatively. Lindsay's eyes were wide open and rapturous. She didn't notice Swampy's distraction. "Just how much I love you."

"Is is true? Do you really?"

"I love you with everything I am," said Teddy as Swampy continued to slurp up worms. "I love your golden hair and smooth symmetrical face. I love your intelligence and your grace." Teddy's words were getting slower. He forgot momentarily that he was playing the part of the monster and relished being able to tell Lindsay exactly how he felt. "I love everything about you Lindsay. You are so beautiful. And so kind. And pure. I would do anything to be with you."

Swampy puked up some dirt and then ate his own puke.

"I love you too Swampy," said Lindsay, her heart aglow. It was the happiest moment of her life. She didn't care if he was a figment of her imagination. If this bliss was what it felt like to be crazy, then she never wanted to be sane again. "Wait there," she said. "I'm coming down."

This took several minutes as she had to use her crutches to safely descend each step in the stair case and her body was sore from the various injuries she had sustained over the previous week, but eventually she made her way outside.

While she was out of sight Teddy ran over to Swampy. "Stand up. *Please*," he begged.

Swampy did as he was told. Worms were hanging out of all of his mouths. Teddy did his best to wipe them away with his shirt sleeve. He heard the front door opening and dove back behind the tree before Lindsay could spot him. He landed on his bad wrist. He yelped.

"What is it my love?" said Lindsay. "Is something wrong?"

"No, no," said Teddy, holding in the pain. "That was a scream of joy."

"Oh," she said. She paused for a moment. She looked confused. "Your voice doesn't sound like it's coming from your body."

"Yes, I know," he said. "It's a general Swamp Monster problem. We all sound like we have disembodied voices. Our mouths don't move when we talk either."

"Oh. So it is like some sort of ESP? Are you talking only into my mind?"

Unseen, Teddy raised his eyebrows and nodded in approval of a good idea he hadn't himself thought of.

"Yeah. That sounds right," he said.

"Wow," she said. "This is really strange. I never thought this moment would actually come."

"Me neither."

There was a pause. Lindsay waited for Swampy to walk closer to her. She looked at him. His face was expressionless. She supposed he didn't have the facial muscles to outwardly display all the emotional things he was saying, the way humans did. She hoped that he would approach her and make the first move. There was no sign of this occurring so she took it upon herself to move closer. She walked right up to him.

"Hi," she said flirtatiously.

"Hi," said Teddy, so completely in love with her, but so crucially removed from the interaction.

"You really do seem real," she said.

"I am real," he replied.

She looked deep into his eyes. (One at a time of course. They were at different physical heights.)

"Well," she said. "Aren't you going to kiss me?"

For a moment Swampy just stared at her and Teddy panicked. He wasn't close enough to whisper for Swampy to kiss her without Lindsay hearing him. Then he had a brilliant idea.

Teddy reached his hand deep into the dirt. He felt around underground intently until he found what he was searching for.

"Of course I'm going to kiss you," said Teddy. "Close your eyes."

Lindsay did as told. Her stomach was in complete knots. She was nervous as all hell but ecstatically excited. The largest smile came across her face as she waited for her prince charming to wake her from her slumber. All hesitation and all thought of her own craziness had left the building. She gave into the fantasy. She submerged herself into the dream.

Never very good at sports, Teddy stood up, approached closer, and took extremely careful aim. He held the worm over his head, wound up like a starting pitcher, and tossed the slithering thing right at Lindsay's lips.

Swampy snapped into instinct. He rapidly ejected out his tongue to seize the worm. His slimy tongue suctioned onto Lindsay's lips and pulled her to his mouth as he ingested the worm. Lindsay's own tongue was pulled out of her mouth in the process. Swampy thought her tongue was another worm and tried to consume it as well, but it was, of course, attached to her body and would not depart from her so easily.

And that's how Lindsay and the Swamp Monster engaged in the most disgusting, aggressive session of tonsil hockey that has ever occurred.

Teddy spotted Swampy getting frustrated with the worm in Lindsay's mouth that would not release and became worried that Swampy's angry side was on the verge of making an appearance. If the "hook up" lasted any longer, her tongue would likely have been ripped out by force.

Panicked, Teddy ran over to Lindsay, whose eyes were still closed, and shoved her to the ground – away from Swampy. He hid behind the monster just before Lindsay opened her eyes and looked up.

"Stay," Teddy aggressively whispered to the monster. He was worried that Swampy's monstrous desires would get the better of him, but blessedly, he did as Teddy requested.

"Wow," said Lindsay, "That was amazing."

"I have to go now," said Teddy.

"What? Why?"

"Uh…I…your parents!" (Yeah, that made sense). "Your parents can't see me. I have to go before they come home."

"My mom won't be home for another hour."

"I can't take any chances. Society wants me locked up. Destroyed. Castrated. Burned up to never be seen again. They think I'm nothing but a monster."

"Who cares? I don't care about any of them. I only care about us. I love you."

Teddy spotted Swampy's tongue elongating away and slithering towards that frustrating attached worm inside Lindsay's mouth.

"Oh shit. Gotta go!" he said aloud. Then he whispered to Swampy. "Run Swampy. *Run*."

Teddy's reliable puppet took off without a moment's notice. He started his run so quick that his extended tongue lagged behind and had to catch up. Teddy did his best to follow along for a moment but the monster was so fast that he had no hope of keeping up. After fifteen feet or so, he dove behind another tree in Lindsay's yard to hide.

Lindsay probably should have seen Teddy but her eyes were so focused on Swampy that she was oblivious to all else around her.

"I'll see you soon my love!" Teddy yelled from his tree.

Swampy's sudden departure was agony to Lindsay but the echoes of all that had been said and the life affirming kiss brightened her up to heavenly levels of happiness.

"I love life," she said to the sky. "It's the most wonderful thing that anyone ever thought of."

From his tree Teddy watched Lindsay reach her hand into her pants and start to touch herself. He watched her moan with pleasure. It took all he had to leave his own pants zipped up, but he took out his smart phone and recorded the scene for later use.

7

Principal Monica J. Misgivinns sat barricaded in her office and tried to remember the tune to an old song whose name she could not recall.

Was it "ba da ba – ba ba da da da?"

Or maybe it was "da ba da – da da ba ba ba?"

Or was there a "la" in there somewhere?

The past was so elusive. Experiences were buried so long that they had decayed and been eaten up by mental maggots and now when she tried to unearth them they were unrecognizable skeletons, lacking all the details which made them the moments she once knew.

Her mind was a giant graveyard of mauseleums. So many moments of her life were buried, but with so much lavishness, it was impossible to forget that there were things she had forgotten. Every day she lived with the intrusive knowledge of remorse and lingering pain. It was only the actual context which she repressed.

Much to her current dismay, one of her most painful memories had cryogenically frozen and preserved in all its vividness. Some unknown force saw fit to fling the icy casket open and reanimate the recollection – good as new, ready for a brisk afternoon walk.

Yes, it was painful to meet that long quashed memory again. But it was also delightful. The memory was bad for her but she could not resist its charm.

She wanted to dance with it all afternoon. And for that she would have to remember the tune to that song.

All it took was seeing him. She saw him once and was sucked into a vortex that landed her right back in the past…

…

The year was 1968. The now sixty one year old Monica Misgivvens was only sixteen. She was dark haired, pale skinned, and starting a brand new high school.

She had just moved in with her befuddled Uncle Gary, who spent most of his waking hours stoned out of his mind on all manner of psychedelic drugs. He was a kind man but a hard one to hold a real conversation with. His focus was always somewhere else, or perhaps nowhere at all.

The last three years had been rather trying. Life had become an ever expanding ordeal. It had all begun on her thirteenth birthday.

Most girls at thirteen are worried about their first pimple or their first period or remembering their Torah portion for their Bat Mitzvah, but when the clock struck midnight and Monica turned that unlucky number, she found an entirely different burden awaiting her. (She *did* also get her period, though not until a couple months later and either way, her menstrual splash down was nothing next to the bigger reveal).

Monica had lived her entire life with her Grandmother Beatrice. She was a sweet old woman who seemed like she had always been more than ninety years of age. She was a four foot ten, pudgy stump of warts who mumbled to herself constantly and didn't talk much to Monica, but was quite kind whenever she did. Monica's parents died when she was very young. She was unclear of the circumstances. Granny Bea shrugged off any questions about what happened with a grimace that indicated it was too painful to talk about. Monica figured it was her grandmother's right to keep silent on the issue, even if she was intensely curious. The old woman had generously taken her in and if the repayment for this kindness was to remain in the dark about one crucial fact, well, then that's just how it would be.

Their life together was calm, quiet, and quaint. They lived in an excessively small town. In elementary school there were the same twenty-three children in Monica's class every year. She was the right angle point of an equilateral triangle of best friends with Suzie Breasthimble and Frannie Veeceeour. They held hands and skipped around the schoolyard at lunch. Life was good.

Everything changed on that thirteenth birthday.

It was a stormy night and Monica awoke from her sleep at a crash of thunder. She glanced at the clock. The time was 11:57. Her birthday was only three minutes away. She sat up against her head board and pushed back her covers. There was no reason to go back to sleep so close to her annual milestone. She listened to the violent thunder, watched the blinding flashes of light, listened to the pervasive patter of the rain drops, and watched the clock tick slowly towards midnight.

11:58…11:59…12:00ANDBOOM!!

Monica felt as though a bolt of lightning had traveled right through the roof of the house and into her body. She wiggled uncontrollably. Each of her body parts did its own individual dance, out of sync with all the others. Her fingers swirled in a manic waltz. Her legs pranced the Charleston in and out of the air. Her sternum was all disco- jazzy electro back and forth thrusts. She lost complete control of herself for a full minute.

Then, just as abruptly as it had started, he body's rhythmic rise came to a halt and she was completely still.

Monica opened the eyes she had closed out of terror, hoping that the worst was over. She was not in luck.

At first she was too disoriented to realize precisely what had happened. She knew she was in her room – but things didn't look quite as they should. Then it struck her: "Hey, what's my bed doing on the ceiling?"

But it wasn't her bed that was on the ceiling. It was *her*.

She screamed. She tried vigorously to unfasten herself from the top of the room but it was as if she was magnetically fastened to it.

She wailed for several minutes until finally her Grandmother sauntered into the room, awoken by all the commotion. Grannie Bea looked up. She was entirely unsurprised what she saw.

"What's all the screaming about?" she said.

"GRANNIE I'M STUCK TO THE CEILING!"

"You are no such thing…The ceiling is just blocking your path."

"What???"

"Why didn't you remind me it was your birthday?"

"Wha— what has that got to do with this? WHAT IS HAPPENING?"

"Would you calm down already, you're going to wake up the whole neighborhood."

"Grannie, *what is happening?*"

"It's a rite of passage. When a witch turns thirteen, she gets her powers and takes a trip to the moon."

"*Excuse me?*"

"Now if I can just find a broom or a mop long enough to push you out the window."

"GRANNIE!"

Grannie disappeared for several minutes (presumably to search the cleaning closet) and returned with a long broom.

"Later, you'll fly on this, but on your thirteenth birthday the moon does all the work," she said.

"Grannie, I'm scared."

"Nothing to be scared of my pretty."

"What did you mean when you said that I'm a witch?"

"You're a smart girl, I think you can figure that one out."

"But…how long have I been one?"

"All your life of course. You just don't get your powers until thirteen."

"Why didn't you tell me?"

"Enough questions. Grab hold of the broom."

Completely bewildered and still rather frightened, Monica did what her Grandmother asked. Grannie Bea's short stature did not allow her to lift the broom very high and Monica had to stretch out her arms as far as she could to grab hold of the broom bristles. Once she had a hold, Grannie slowly pulled the broom towards the wall and dragged Monica across the ceiling.

"Okay now. Hold tight," said Grannie. The old witch then used all the strength she had to pull Monica down to window level. "Grab onto the window," she said, completely out of breath.

Monica grabbed on as Grannie pushed open the glass and popped out the screen.

"Alright, my dear, just slide yourself out the window and you'll be on your way. Have lots of fun."

"But, Grannie—"

Before Monica could finish her sentence, the moon's pull fastened on to her. She was yanked out of the window and up through the sky like a yo-yo returning to its user's hand.

She sailed up through the stormy night. The raindrops pounded her. Lightning bolts just missed her head.

After a minute or two, she passed above the clouds and all was clear. She was still terrified but she was also overwhelmed by the beauty of the pure, star-filled sky. She had never seen the night's sparkling lights in all their unhidden glory. It truly was something to behold.

Her heart rate calmed. She thought about the spectacular revelation that had just presented itself. She was a witch. She had *magical powers*. Who knew what wonders lay before her?

As the moon approached she wondered what would occur once she landed. Was there some sort of magical training school on that celestial rock which circled earth? Was there a masterful space sorcerer who resided there who would initiate her into the sacred cult of the witches?

As it turned out, there wasn't much there at all. Just fifty to a hundred thirteen year old girls of various other nations huddled next to moon rocks, shivering in the cold dark of space. Not one of them – even those who had known they were witches since birth – had any explanation for why the moon trip occurred.

A nice girl named Brittany from Oregon told Monica she heard it had something to do with the alien origins of witches.

The story went like this:

"The first witches were aliens from another world somewhere deep in out space. It was a hermaphroditic planet where everyone had both male and female parts. The ones who crash landed on our planet were the planet's equivalent of teenagers, out for a joy ride. The ancient paintings interpreted them as wart covered hags because they were both male and female and covered with zits from adolescence. It was the middle ages when they landed.

"At first they showed off their powers to the earthlings without any thought of hiding them. To them, these magical abilities weren't special powers, they were perfectly normal. They were characteristic of everyone. So you can imagine the tremendous surprise when all the earth people were so FRIGHTENED of them. And started calling them DEVILS. And then started BURNING them to DEATH!

"So our ancestors quickly hid themselves, pretending to be nothing other than normal peasants. They used their magic to shrink their penis parts into nothing other than a typical clitoris so that they could pass as women, although very ugly ones. They married the least attractive peasant youths they could find just to save their skins. And they pumped out babies left and right when those peasants treated them as their own personal humping stations.

"A couple of them rebelled. A couple of them refused to hide who they really were. They found brooms to fly around on. I hear, by the way, that we can fly on any long vertical aerodynamic apparatus. The broom is just the classic. Anyway, these rebels flew around and made spells in giant cauldrons and cast those spells on their oppressors and cackled in delight as they got revenge against folks who were burning their friends alive. It was those two rebels on whom most of the earth stories about witches are based. And they were never caught. They escaped off into the wilderness and nobody knows what happened to them.

"But it's the assimilators who are our ancestors. Their genetics were passed down. For some unknown reason, the witch gene was only active in females. Males carried it but they never had any magical abilities."

"Wow. So was the moon part of their old planet or something?" asked Monica.

"Beats me," said Brittany. "The whole story might be made up for all I know. But it's what my mom used to tell me. And it would explain my bi-sexuality and gender confusion. Hey – do you want to make out by the way?"

Monica politely declined the make out-session.

She was on the moon for twenty-four hours. She and the other girls exchanged some polite small talk but mostly huddled themselves and waited for their day in outer space to end. Monica never would have thought a day spent on the moon would be so *boring*. But that it was. Just dull. Nothing much to do at all. When eventually her body hovered back to earth she flushed with relief.

...

As you might imagine, everything changed for Monica after learning she was a witch. It was difficult to maintain her old friendships with Suzie and Frannie, having such a gargantuan secret that she could never share with them. The girls interpreted Monica's inner confusion and unsocial soul searching as bitchiness and, feeling affronted, stopped including her. Thus the threesome became a twosome and Monica was left standing out in the rain. (Quite literally, on one occasion).

She did not realize until later in life just what a great effect the loss of her crew had on her. At the time her mind was consumed with excitement over her new abilities.

Grannie Bea owned withered old copies of classic spell manuals. Monica wasted no time studying the ancient tomes.

Within weeks she learned to shrink and enlarge household objects, change the color of foods, make things invisible, and empty the bladder in her body without ever having to urinate.

And so went the next three years. Monica's social life vanished but she was happy being alone and learning spells.

Then one night, something occurred which may have been even more monumental in Monica's life than discovering that she was a witch.

Grannie Bea passed away.

Monica found her collapsed in the kitchen. She was breathing her last breaths. Monica frantically searched through her books for a spell to prevent someone from dying but even witches had no such power.

Grannie Bea whispered to her to stop such nonsense. "Death is a part of life," she said. "One must accept it when it comes."

"Oh, Grannie," said Monica, crying, holding her grandmother's hand. Then she thought of something. "Grandmom," she said, "How did my parents die? Were they fighting some witch battle? Is that why you never could tell me what happened?"

"No. The truth is…I'm your mother. And your father was a male whore. I never told you because I didn't want you to be embarrassed."

"Oh."

"And now I must go my child. Be strong."

Grannie…or…Mother Bea then passed along into the dark night.

Monica wept until her tear ducts were raw.

...

Which brings us back to September of 1968. Monica has just been taken in by Bea's much younger brother, eternal hippie Uncle Gary. Despite signing the guardian papers, Gary was routinely so stoned out of his mind that he often forgot a foster child had been passed into his care.

"Hey, there's a chick in my house," said Gary, after he turned his head and noticed Monica on the other couch cushion of his love seat. He raised his arm and not very subtly put it around her. "What can I do for you, honey?"

Monica calmly brushed his hand aside.

"It's Monica, Uncle Gary. I'm your niece. I moved in two weeks ago. We've had several conversations."

"Oh yeah? Far out."

It had been a long, drug filled, last twenty years for Uncle Gary. His mind wasn't all there, but he was at least friendly. Gary was happy to meet her each and every time he introduced himself. After a little while, she stopped correcting him as to the fact that they had already met. She just shook his hand and smiled and before he could hit on her, she said, "I'm your niece, Monica." And he said "far out" and offered her some pot or some LSD and sometimes she said no and sometimes she said yes and that was that.

It was tough starting a brand new school so late in the game. Everyone already had their own groups of friends and no one seemed interested in taking on a new member.

Monica said hello here or there to students in the hall who she recognized from her classes, but the friendliest only responded with polite nods and the least neighborly achieved the difficult balance of completely ignoring her while also being directly nasty. Ever since she had returned from the moon, she intuited that normal kids sensed something different about her. Their distaste for her presence wasn't something they could particularly explain or were necessarily conscious of, but it was there. Their molecular biology picked up on the alien frequency of hers and projected warning signals which indicated she was a foreign object to be avoided.

All of this made Monica rather depressed but she didn't think there was much she could do about it. Thus her depression was resigned, rather than agonizing. It was a fact of life, rather than a condition to be overcome. And sometimes Uncle Gary's pot helped.

Those first weeks at Bluford Springs High School Monica spent most of her time as she had the past three years – studying Bea's spell books every chance she got, memorizing tongue twisting verbal resuscitations and investigating where she might be able to find magical ingredients like "ear of newt" or "semen of yak," which were essential for performing some of the more complex spells. After school, she half-assed her homework and got to work practicing witchcraft in her backyard.

She accepted her solitude. She accepted that from there on out she would always be an outsider in the normal world of people. She had some vague hopes of one day using her witchcraft to do some good, but if what she was told on the moon was true, there wasn't much reason for witches to be witches in the modern world. Sorcery was a skill without real use. Kind of like an English degree. She practiced it because she liked it and because she was good at it. She had no storybook evil villain to fight and she was too good of a person to use her spells maliciously on the other students in her school, even if they *were* rather cold towards her.

She expected very little out of life.

Life must have taken her condescension personally because it was right then that the most unexpected thing happened: She fell in love.

His name was James and it happened like this.

One day during lunch Monica leaned against the wall, lost in thought, trying to figure out why the testicle shrinking spell she had attempted to use on a squirrel had gone so horribly wrong. (Instead of shrinking the squirrel's testicles, the spell had multiplied them, until the poor creature looked like an all testicle soccer ball). It was then that she was approached by a gorgeous, chestnut haired male.

"Excuse me?" he said with a friendly grin.

Monica slipped out of her squirrel testicle stupor and looked blankly at the beautiful specimen before her. Her heart raced. Music soared in her mind. *Is he talking to me?*

The boy's smile faded. He seemed confused by her lack of response. "*Excuse* me," he said again, more forcefully.

"Yes?" squeaked out Monica.

"You're blocking the soda machine," he said, this time annoyed.

"What?"

The music in Monica's mind abruptly halted. She turned her head around and noticed that she *was*, in fact, leaning against the soda machine.

"Oh," she said. "Sorry." She awkwardly shimmied out of the way.

The boy put two quarters in the machine and bought a can of Coke.

Monica didn't know what was happening to her. She felt all swollen up inside. If she hadn't been sure that only females were witches, she would have sworn that the boy had cast a sort of spell on her.

The boy opened his Coke and took a refreshing gulp. He was about to return to his cafeteria table when a force beyond her control urged Monica to speak.

"I'm Monica," she blurted out.

He looked at her. He seemed suspicious.

"James," he said.

"Sorry, I, uh, didn't move out of the way quicker. I was thinking about…" She paused for a second and remembered what she was thinking about, realizing that would not make for a proper topic of conversation. "…I was lost in thought."

"It's fine," he said, lowering his guard. "It happens." He smiled his perfect smile. "Say," he said, "I don't think I've ever seen you before."

"I just moved here," she said. "I've only been at the school for a month."

"Huh," he said. The wheels turned in his mind. "Are you sitting with anybody?"

"No."

"Do you want to come join my table?"

"Yeah!" she said, too enthusiastically. "I mean… yeah, that might be nice."

"Alright then, follow me."

James was a senior. He was stalwart at mathematics and even better at charm. His crew was made up of high achieving students with above average attractiveness levels. They weren't the most popular kids in school – that honor, as usual, fell to the athletes and the cheerleaders –but they projected an essence of uncaring esteem that made them almost as unapproachable as those at the top of the heap.

The group, males and females alike, looked rather leery eyed as the unknown entity of Monica sat down next to James at their table.

James sliced the skepticism away with his sonorous speech. "Everybody, I'd like you to meet Monica. She's new to the school and I thought it would be nice for her to eat with us."

A number of James's friends said halfhearted "hellos" and the rest ignored her completely. Monica felt the same impression she had felt with the juniors in her own classes: James's friends sensed a difference about her. They couldn't place it, but there was something off putting. They did the best to ignore her, such that her odd aura might not destroy their mood.

But none of that mattered to Monica, because, for whatever wonderful reason, James was not afflicted with the typical aversion. Quite the opposite. All of his attention was focused on her.

He asked Monica all kinds of questions as he suavely drank his Coke. He asked where she lived before now. How she liked Bluford Springs so far. What teachers she had.

When she mentioned her science teacher Mr. Flutternick, James chuckled and rattled off a hilarious story about a time in Mr. Flutternick's class when Kevin Dunbar farted into the bunson burner. At one point, while he was talking, he touched her arm. It was just a casual, conversational touch. But it sent her heart off to the races. Monica had never felt so happy in all her life.

Towards the end of the lunch period, Monica's James only blinders were briefly lifted and she realized that a girl on the other side of the table was staring at her. Monica glanced over, because she couldn't help herself, and locked eyes with an extremely pretty blonde. The blonde's face was filled with revulsion. Monica quickly turned her glare back to James, hoping naively that the girl wouldn't realize Monica had looked at her purposely if she looked away with enough speed.

"*Hey*," said James, with the flare of a sudden brilliant idea. "Are you doing anything on May 25th?"

As it was only October and Monica's social life was dryer than the Sahara, there was absolutely no chance that she had any plans on that date. She didn't wish to sound desperate or uncool, however, so she responded: "I'll have to check my calendar, but I'm probably free."

"Great," he said, ignoring her pretend doubts about her availability. "How would you like to go to prom with me?"

The blonde across the table, who was listening to every word, slammed the table, got up, and stormed away.

Several of James's friends looked over at him. The girls looked disgusted. The guys also looked disapproving, but they smiled deviously as if James's behavior was merely some misguided prank.

"Well?" James said to Monica, who was so overcome with joy that she had failed to respond to James's question.

"Of course," she whispered, because she was too affected to manage any higher volume. "I'd love to."

...

Monica didn't speak to James for two weeks after that. She passed him a couple of times in the hallway but he didn't seem to notice her, even when she called out to him. He was always with a group of friends and she supposed that she just hadn't said his name loud enough to attract his attention. (Although she had said it pretty loud.)

It was no matter. They were going to prom together and nothing would ruin that.

At home, Monica's spell casting went the best it had since she first learned she was a witch. She had successfully turned her backyard into an ice palace and turned a bird's eyes into nipples. Her passion for James infused her magic with an extra bit of oomph. Things were going great.

Then they got even better. On a Friday afternoon, out of the blue, as she was getting her books out of her locker, a riled up James marched up to her.

"What are you doing tonight?" he said. His stance was determined. His jaw was resolute.

"Nothing," she said, meekly.

"Do you want to go see a movie with me at the drive in?"

"Yeah. Sure…of course. Why not?"

"Great. I live at 154 Woodley. Meet me there at 7."

He was all business.

"Okay. I look forward to—"

James marched away before she was done speaking. She paid his early exit no mind. She couldn't have been more excited. Or nervous.

After school Monica stopped at the local convenience store to buy make-up. She was determined to look as beautiful as possible for her date. Never having had a mother to guide her on this particular feminine expertise, she had no idea where to begin. She went down the aisle and threw one item from every category into her cart.

Back at home, she tried, purely through intuition, to figure out which cosmetic item was used where. When her facial artistry was finished she looked somewhere in between a clown and Jackson Pollock painting.

She stared in the mirror and nodded her head in approval of her own artistry.

On the way out she passed by Uncle Gary who was smoking a bong in the lotus position on the living room floor.

"I'm going out Uncle Gary," she said.

He looked up at her and screamed. He fells backwards and hit his head hard on the floor.

She rushed over to him. "Are you alright?" she said.

"Dude must have sold me a bad batch," he said. "You look like a circus creature."

Monica, in one of the densest moments of her life, assumed that it was her Uncle's drugs which had made him see her this way, not the five inch thick sedimentary layer of make up on her face.

"I'll be home before eleven," she said.

...

When James opened the door and saw Monica's Van Gogh face his eyes widened to about a twofold increase in diameter.

"Hi!" she said, never more excited in her life.

"Did you get hit in the face by a rainbow?" he said.

"What?" Her heart dropped to her calves.

"Why do you have so much make-up on?"

"Oh. I…"

"Come inside. Wash some of that off."

He grabbed her arm and dragged her in.

"The bathroom is the first door on your left," he said, turning his back to her.

"Oh sure. Okay." She had a hard time getting her words out. She was on the verge of tears.

Just before he left her to cleanse herself, James turned around and said "You're a pretty girl. You don't need that much make-up."

That comment made all the difference. Her heart soared back up to its proper resting place in her chest. She still felt like she was going to cry – but from happiness instead of shame.

"Oh. Thanks," she said, but he didn't hear her. He had already left the room.

After Monica thoroughly washed her face, James drove them over to the outdoor movie theater. As he pulled his car in to the lot, he turned his head around frantically.

"Are you looking for something?" Monica asked.

"Just for the best possible spot," he said.

"There's a good spot over there." She pointed to a nice center view of the screen.

"Uh…I don't know," he said, still whipping his head around. "There! That's the spot!"

He hit the gas and raced over to a spot all the way on the left and really close to the screen.

"James, I think that other spot had a much better view."

"It's fine," he said, making clear that would be the end of the discussion.

"Alright then. Anyway the truth is…" Monica worked up her courage. "I don't care where we watch the movie from. I'm just happy to be here with you."

James gave no response whatsoever.

"James?" she said.

"What?"

"Did you hear what I said?"

"You said something?"

Now, you readers aren't dummies. I'm sure you see what was happening here. Two cars down from James and Monica, on the other side of an elderly gentleman and his wife, was the blonde girl from the lunch table. She was with the starting tight end from the football team.

The blonde girl's name was Holly and she was James's girlfriend. Or at least, she *was* James's girlfriend. They had been together for a year but lately they were having some problems.

It all started like this: The day James met Monica at the soda machine, he had just walked over from having an argument with Holly at the lunch table. They were arguing about prom. Holly wanted them to rent a limo with the rest of their friends, while James wanted to borrow a motorcycle from his drop-out cousin Luke and have Holly nervously hang onto his back as he drove them on his first attempt at driving a dangerous two wheel vehicle.

So, when James came back to the table with Monica (who it must be said, really was somewhat pretty, even if her off-putting aura distracted most of her peers from it), talked to her the whole lunch period, and then *asked her to prom*, it was all just a childish attempt to piss off his girlfriend. And boy did it work.

Holly didn't speak to him for days. When it became clear just how upset she was, James attempted to apologize.

"Jeez, sorry," he said, "it was just a joke. I didn't *really* ask that girl to prom. Of course, I'm going to ask you."

"I wouldn't be so sure I'll say yes," said Holly.

"Oh, come on. You're blowing this all out of proportion!"

"Well that's the only thing I'm going to be blowing!"

She stormed off. James, under threat of no blow jobs, amped up his apology to near sincere levels but it did no good. She was furious at him.

For a week after that he just let her be. He figured she'd get over "all of this nonsense" on her own. Until his buddy Greg told him that Holly had a Friday night drive-in date with the starting tight-end on the football team.

That was the moment when James realized he might actually lose Holly. The thought tore him apart inside. He was often a dick, but the truth was, he did love her.

Thus, he did what any rational threatened boyfriend would do — he asked another girl to the movies so that he might make his girlfriend just as jealous as she'd made him.

(What, did you think he was going to *talk* to her and tell her how he felt?)

And that about catches us back up to where we were.

As Monica tried to make small talk during the dancing cartoon snacks commercial and the coming attractions, James kept his eyes locked two cars over. He wanted to make sure that Holly spotted him. He was having no luck. She was deep in conversation with the tight end. Finally, exasperated with her poor peripheral vision, James forcefully struck his car horn.

That did the trick. Holly looked over. As did everyone else at the drive-in.

"Is everything alright?" asked Monica, who nearly jumped out of her pants at the unexpected blast of noise.

"Everything's just fine," said James, sounding slightly like a crazy person. He looked at Holly who finally noticed him. She stared back nastily.

(In between the cars, the elderly couple thought that James and Holly were staring at them and felt extremely threatened).

Holly wiped the unpleasantness from her expression with the snap of a finger and turned back to the tight end with a giant smile. She put her hands on his cheeks and pulled him in for a kiss.

"So," said Monica, blissfully oblivious to James's true attention, "what kind of food do you like—?"

James cut Monica off with a kiss. He jammed his tongue in her mouth and she felt ecstatic as it probed around like a jackhammer breaking apart a concrete sidewalk. The experience was physically unpleasant but probably the most emotionally satisfying moment of her entire life. Up until that point or ever after.

James looked back at Holly. She looked back at him. An unspoken war was declared through the angry angles of their eye brows.

(The elderly couple quivered from fear.)

Holly pulled the tight end close and made out with him.

James jumped into Monica's lap and writhed up against her.

"Oh, James," she said, trying to sound sexual although his aggressive dry hump was quite painful.

James looked at Holly with a cocky grin that said, "Let's see you outdo this."

Holly saw him. She was utterly disgusted. And extremely hurt. She pulled away from the surprised tight end, threw open the car door, and ran off on foot.

Instead of chasing after Holly and perhaps salvaging some scrap of honor from the junkyard of juvenile one-upmanship he'd been piling up all evening, James stayed in Monica's lap, feeling satisfied that he had won the competition.

He was about to dismount back to his own seat when his aroused penis sent a message up to his brain and said, "hey, you've started the job, might as well finish it."

Far be it for any teenage male to argue with that sort of logic, so he writhed on Monica a minute longer until he reached, ahem, his, uh, point of destination. Then, he returned to his own seat.

"Thus movie sucks. Wanna get out of here?" he said to Monica.

(The movie had, for the record, only begun one minute and forty five seconds before earlier).

"Sure," she said, her face all aglow.

As they drove away a song came on the radio. It was the song Monica was trying to remember when this chapter began. In present day she could no longer recall the lyrics and even had a hard time grasping on to the tune, but at that moment in time the song on the radio represented all of the intense joy she felt. The music crept inside her and cuddled with her like a sleeping puppy.

As it turned out, their next destination for the evening was Monica's house, where James dropped her off.

"Well good night," he said.

"Oh." She was disappointed that the night was ending so soon, but was far too elated by all that had happened to question it. "Good night," she said.

She leaned over and kissed James intensely on the lips. Her kiss took him by surprise and he liked it more than expected. Unfortunately, his heart was completely focused on Holly. Monica was a pawn to him and nothing more.

Monica got out of the car and strutted away. James pulled away and forgot about her immediately, wondering where he might find Holly. Feeling suddenly sad and alone, he thought for the first time: *Maybe I should have run after Holly when she left the tight end's car instead of staying around to ejaculate in my pants.* (Gee, you think?)

As for Monica, she strutted inside to her house, collapsed on her bed and spent about three hours thanking God and the heavens and the moon and her ancestral witches and anyone else she could think of for bringing love into her life and making her the happiest girl in the world.

She fantasized about her and James's future wedding. She would cast some spell on her wedding dress to make it sparkle delightfully. Handsome James would lift her up and kiss her after they said their vows. He would declare that he would never let her go for the rest of his days.

"I just can't believe I have a boyfriend," Monica said to her pal, the mirror.

Oh, poor Monica. Youths can be so blind to the truth.

...

That Monday Monica spotted James walking down the hall.

She followed him. She wanted to surprise him by putting her hands over his eyes. Then she would flirtatiously declare "guess who?" like cute girlfriends were supposed to.

Sadly, her plan was cut short. For when Monica turned the corner of the hall, she saw James walk right into the hands of another girl — Holly.

Monica watched him kiss her passionately.

(After James dropped Monica off that Friday night he had gone over to Holly's house and begged her on his knees to come back to him. Holly, a remarkably irrational teenager herself, thought she was just as in love with James as he thought he was with her. She always wanted to get back together with him. She just wanted to see him grovel first. Overcome with love at the sight of his submission, she took his hand and led her into his house where they had sex for hours.)

Monica lurked in the shadows that day. She bid her time as she waited for a moment when James was alone. It took a while. He and Holly, closer than ever following their reconciliation, were bound to each other like glue. Each time they held hands Monica felt an intense sting. Each time they kissed Monica's stomach wailed in distress. But she held firm in her stalk. She skipped all of her classes and later received a week's worth of detention. This did not concern her. She needed to speak to James. She needed to talk to the boy who had stolen her heart.

Finally, just before seventh period, she watched him kiss Holly goodbye as she entered room 108 for an English exam she could not miss. He turned away, intending to attend his own class that period, but he was impeded by a road block named Monica.

"Hi," she said, quivering inside but determined to appear strong on the outside.

"Oh, hey," he said casually. In truth he was surprised to see Monica because he had entirely forgotten about her existence.

"Who is that girl?" she asked.

"What girl?"

"The one whose tongue had been in your mouth all day."

"Oh. You mean Holly."

"If that's her name, then yeah, that's who I mean."

"She's my girlfriend."

Monica felt like she had just been embalmed. Her performance of exterior strength crumbled.

"Your...girl...friend?" She could barely get the word out.

"Yeah, she's my girlfriend," said James, who seemed already exhausted with the conversation. Reminded that Monica was a person, he did feel guilty at having used her as a pawn to get back at Holly, but his discomfort with the interaction outweighed any thoughts of conscience which might have made him do something reasonable – like apologize. "I really gotta get to class," he said.

He shuffled off.

"Then why did you ask me out on a date?" asked Monica, heartbroken, as he walked away.

Without fully turning around his body (or fully turning on his brain) he blurted out, "I don't know kid. People do all sorts of stupid things." Then he walked away.

...

At home Monica cried for hours and pitied herself.

She smoked up with Uncle Gary and got the munchies and ate an entire box of Chips Ahoy! cookies. And then an entire box of Ritz Crackers.

It was a tough night. In the morning, however, she woke up feeling fresh, relaxed, and determined.

"I will not be a victim," Monica declared to herself, just as many women who have been shit on by douchebag men have over the years.

Unluckily for James, unlike most of those newly empowered women, Monica had magical powers.

She broke out her spell books and patiently flipped through the yellowed pages of spells and curses and hexes and enchantments. She looked for that perfect something that would be the proper revenge.

She didn't find what she was looking for that morning. Or that evening. Or the next morning or evening. Something as important as this could not be rushed. She knew she would know the right spell when she saw it.

Then, Wednesday morning, on page 783 in the tome of "Spells of the Farthest Reachings of Bulgaria," there it was. The punishment she was waiting for.

It took her another month to learn it. Many a squirrel was horribly disfigured in the process but certain sacrifices had to be made so that James would receive his proper comeuppance.

With each incremental increase in confidence Monica seethed. Her blood boiled. And when she was finally sure she was ready, she let out an ear piercing cackle that would have made her ancestors proud.

...

On Saturday November 16th, 1968 Monica donned an all black dress. She topped her head with a pointed black witch hat that she found in a costume store. She painted her face green. She attached fake boils to her cheeks.

She grabbed an old splintered broom from Uncle Gary's closet and flew off into the night, laughing deliriously. (Many a child's lifetime nightmare was formed that night when they looked out their windows to see what all the noise was about).

She was, for sure, fulfilling her own stereotype. If any progressive, twentieth century feminist witches had spotted her they would have been thoroughly disgusted.

Monica delighted in playing the villain. She'd had enough of being nice. She's had enough of trying to be a heroine. She was never going to be the damsel in distress. It was time to embrace what she was meant to be. *WICKED*.

She probably wasn't in a right state of mind. In fact, later on in life, she was sure she must have been overtaken by some kind of madness during that night.

In the moment, though, her theatrical display felt so deliciously *right*.

She brought her broom to a hovering halt outside James's bedroom window. She looked in.

Her brief former paramour lay in bed with Holly, smooching intensely. His hand slithered its way down into her pants as Monica looked on.

Just as he engaged Holly's nether-regions, Monica burst through the window. Glass shards flew everywhere. Several pieces lodged in Monica's face, but she was impervious to the pain in her delirious state. The blood that now ran down her green makeup made her look all the more terrifying. She cackled wildly.

Holly screamed in terror.

James also screeched from freight. (Probably more high pitched than he would have liked).

"Hello there, my pretties!" said Monica in a nails on a chalkboard voice. (Admittedly, she was borrowing pretty heavily from the Wizard of Oz, but give her a break – what young squad of musicians doesn't play other bands' songs until they come up with their own material?)

"Who the fuck are you?" said James.

"I am justice. I am what you deserve."

"What are you going to do to us?" asked quivering Holly.

"Not you. Just him," said Monica, her eyes piercing deep into James.

"I didn't do anything," he squeaked.

"Whine all you want my pretty, but you cannot escape a witch's WRATH! BwahaHAHA!"

Monica swirled her broom in the air and the lights in the room violently flickered. All of James's things were caught in a gust of wind, which swirled aggressively around the room. Monica inched closer and closer to her victim. Her eyes glowed with madness, as a tornado of baseball cards and tee shirts surrounded them.

"VLARHEM SNENESQUA VIQUA HO," she said in a deep demonic drawl.

"What?" said James, who had a feeling that nothing good was about to happen.

"JUSSLE TREEHAREN MEENA LO."

Holly clutched onto James. Monica did not like that at all and with a flick of the wrist she sent Holly into the rotating whirlwind.

"KAPQUA CRYJADA KOONA RO!"

"Please...please," said James.

"SASQUA PENTA RINISHA SWO!"

And then it happened. James screamed out in agony as his entire body glowed yellow. His chest ripped apart like there was an earthquake in his lungs. Through the cracks, a green slime leaked out. His eyes vibrated erratically. His left socket exploded and the sphere of his eye popped out like a cannonball. It remained attached only by a tenuous strand of veins. All of his leg hair leaked to the floor, pushed out by a pestilent pus coming out of every pore.

"WHAT IS HAPPENING TO ME?" he cried.

The only answer Monica had for him was a delighted cackle.

What remained of James's skin melted off as he moaned. Holly wailed and wailed as she rotated around the room in the devilish merry go round. James's body quivered in a fit of shakes as his organs vomited up more and more slime and pus. He transformed into something horrendous. Into something... MONSTROUS.

I'm sure you can see it by now readers. Oh, yes, you see what occurred. For it was that night that James became...

THE BLUFORD SPRINGS SWAMP MONSTER.

As his body burned away, so did his mind. James's memory and his sense of self dissolved into nothing more than a bubbling shame and an unquenchable appetite.

He roared. The power of the noise surprised Monica and snapped her out of her villainous delirium. The monster pounded his bed and tore it to shreds. Then he marched toward Monica. She was scared.

Her loss of focus halted the tornado. Poor, convulsing Holly fell to the floor along with all of James's possessions. As soon as she landed, Holly's feet instinctively took control and carried her from the room. She ran all the way home.

Swampy got closer and closer to Monica. His acidic saliva dribbled out of his multiple mouths and melted away patches of the floor. He was almost upon her when Monica grabbed her broom and flew out the window. She saved her hide just in time.

She watched as James, in his new incarnation, tore his house apart. She watched as he burst through the front door and, at the street, fell into the sewer grate, not used to his less than solid body.

She imagined him washing away, never to be seen again.

She started to cry.

"What have I done?" she said. It was only then that she felt a murderer's guilt. He wouldn't die. His new "body" was too strong to be destroyed by any natural means. He was, however, as good as dead. She had robbed him of anything worth living for.

Even worse though, she had, because of petty jealousy, taken away any chance of being with the man she loved.

Just then the song from their car ride home abruptly popped back into her head. It sounded the same but it carried a different meaning. The first time she had heard it, she felt intense joy. Now the song made her feel remorse and deep sadness.

"What have I done?" she said.

...

It finally came to her without any warning. Sixty-one year old Monica J. Missgivens remembered the tune to the song. She closed her eyes and felt the bliss.

Life was giving her a second chance. The universe, after all this time, had finally decided to forgive her for her crime.

For years and years she had suffered from ravaging guilt for what she had done. She had deprived a family of a child. She had deprived a boy of his life. She had created a monster who murdered teenagers.

And worst of all... she had deprived herself of the only great love she had ever known.

It made no difference that he had acted like an asshole. Everyone has good inside them. The ensuing years might have brought maturity. It's impossible to know what might have happened because she castrated history before it had a chance to grow.

Perhaps she would have forgotten the whole incident if she had ever found love elsewhere, but life had not been generous in this regard. She often thought that she'd been excluded from romance as a punishment for her sins and she didn't blame the universe for its judgment. There was no excuse for her terrible actions.

Not a day went by that she didn't wish she could take it all back.

Then, out of nowhere, the most amazing miracle had happened. A month ago James, or Swampy, as everyone now called him, had just walked into her school and enrolled as a student. If that wasn't miraculous enough itself, then how about the incredibly bizarre fact that everyone else seemed to see him as a regular student!

Things like this didn't just happen. The universe was providing her with a chance to make amends. It was too late to take back the curse. That, unfortunately, was irreversible. But it was not too late for her and James to share the love that she had cut so terribly short.

She hummed the song.

She thought of James.

She thought of love.

8

Sam was amazed by how little verification it took to get him enrolled in Bluford Springs High School. He barely had to use any of the paperwork he had forged in preparation. The administrative staff accepted his claim of being new to the neighborhood at face value and asked him a minimal amount of questions. *Anybody could get enrolled in this school,* he thought.

His thought was confirmed a little later that day when he first saw Swampy.

"What the fuck is that?" he said to his camera man, Chuck.

"Looks like some sort of Swamp Monster," said Chuck nonchalantly. Chuck had been a vampire for three thousand years and had seen some shit *you wouldn't believe*, so he hardly thought the sight of a swamp monster was something to make a fuss about.

(The school had also taken no issue with the fact that an adult with a camera was going to follow Sam around every day and record any interactions he had with teachers or other students. Sam told them it was for a reality show, which was technically the truth. The administrators took no issue. They asked nothing about release forms for people in the school or privacy laws regarding filming inside of a classroom. It was flabbergasting how little security existed at BSHS in this day and age.)

"Why is no one reacting to the fact that a swamp monster is wandering around?" said Sam.

"Looks like he's a student," said Chuck. "He's got that Cubs sweatshirt on."

"Bizarre."

Sam was completely baffled and wondered momentarily what sort of strange place he had entered – but there was no time to get off track. He was here with a singular purpose: To find the beautiful girl he had seen on television and make her his.

Covered in the daylight protecting "sunscreen," he had been gifted by Jacoby, Sam took the day to get the lay of the land at the high school. He wanted a thorough knowledge of the areas where students congregated in between classes. He wanted to know where various cliques might station themselves, so that he might learn where to find The Girl.

As he walked the halls, he noticed that he received stares from two very distinct groups of people.

One group of stares – not so unwelcome – came from semi-attractive, heavily made up, moderately stylish girls. They traded glances at him and giggled as he passed, presumably because they found him attractive. Sam found it flattering.

The other group of stares – less welcome – came from a group of poorly dressed, pimply, body odor smelling boys. They looked upon with an uncomfortable resonance, half way between admiration and hunger.

He hoped that if one of these two incredibly varied social strata starers was going to approach him it would be the girls, but as far as those hopes went, he was shit out of luck.

Just outside of the science labs, a gawky freshman with thick glasses and a jewfro approached him, the designated speaker for his nearby crew of dweebs needing deodorant.

"Sam? Sam Bristolnoon?"

Sam stood stiff. As unthreatening as the geeks looked, it was disconcerting that their leader knew his name.

"Who's asking?" he said, impressively gruff.

"I'm Lawrence. That's Alexi, Greg, and Marvin. We're big fans."

"Of what?"

"Of you! We watch your show all the time."

"My show?"

"Sorry for calling you Sam by the way. But there's no credits on the show so we don't what your real name is."

"What are you talking about?" Sam was extremely confused.

"You play Sam Bristolnoon, don't you? On that internet show about the Vampire frat competition?"

"Oh." Sam understood. The supposedly secret web link that could only be accessed by Vampires wasn't so secret after all. "You've seen the show?"

"We watch it all the time. It's the next generation of television man. No commercials. No corporate sponsorship. Just you know, free, awesome, visceral content, right on the internet."

"Right."

"Are you filming something here for the show?" Lawrence motioned to Chuck who was recording the interaction.

"Uh yeah. We are."

"I knew it! The last challenge involves you taking some high school girl's virginity and you're using our school as the school!"

"You got me," said Sam dryly.

"Fuckin A man," said Marvin.

"Hey. I don't know what kinda sway you have," said Lawrence, "But if you need any extras or side characters or anything, we'd love to be on the show."

"Yeah, I have a feeling you might end up on it."

"Fuck yeah, man." Lawrence pulled Sam's hand into one of those awkward 'not quite a handshake/not quite a high five' hand interactions that people for some reason think is cool.

"Yep," said Sam, eager to be done with the conversation.

...

Meanwhile...

Phase one of Teddy's plan B (a.k.a. phase two of plan A) was in full effect.

Every day at school for the past week, Lindsay and Swampy had walked together down the halls, holding hands as Teddy followed, hiding around corners, behind doorways, and in any patches of shadow he could find.

Teddy had an ingenious idea after his initial Romeo & Juliet style love serenade. He ordered several packs of cheap walkie talkies off the internet (you really can't find those things in stores anymore – it's probably eight year olds having cell phones which killed sales). He fast tracked the shipping. Then, he jammed one walkie from a pair into Swampy's head, and kept the other in his hand so he could dictate both Swampy's actions (in a very quiet voice) and his speech (in a very loud voice). As it turned out, the walkie talkie end in Swampy's head melted from his acid saliva after about a day, so Teddy put in an order for twenty more pairs. He figured that would be enough to get him to phase two (of plan B).

As the incredibly odd trio paraded down the school, all of their peers did the best they could to ignore the situation entirely. They all figured their delusions had boarded the bus on a one way trip to crazy town and they were determined not to pay their fare in the hope that they might get kicked off.

One brave individual who decided to face the situation head on and not be sucked into the self-doubt vortex was Teddy's friend Henry.

Henry approached Teddy at the end of the day on Friday afternoon. Teddy was hiding in a particularly dark shadow outside the auditorium, whispering into his walkie talkie.

"Hey Teddy."

"Henry." Teddy quickly snapped the walkie talkie away from his mouth. Across the hall Lindsay asked Swampy: "Who's Henry?" Teddy quickly brought the walkie talkie back to his mouth and said in his Swampy voice: "No one.

Nothing. Let's be quiet for a few minutes." "O…kay," said Lindsay, not really bothered by the oddness of such an exchange because, for heaven's sake, she was going out with a Swamp Monster and all that was bizarre was now her life.

"Who are you talking to?" asked Henry.

"Uh…buddy of mine at another school," said Teddy.

"Do those things carry that far?"

"Sure."

"What buddy?"

"Uh. A...dw…adwardo. My buddy Adwardo."

"You have a friend named Eduardo?"

"Adwardo. With an A." (For some reason, Teddy insisted on preserving this less believable detail of his lie. Probably because most of his focus was still on Lindsay and Swampy. He watched them stand quietly together and wanted to be sure nothing went wrong).

"Who's this ADwardo? With an A?"

"Just some guy I know."

"Teddy, what the hell's going on?"

"What do you mean?"

"We've barely talked for the last month. Something's up with you man. Something weird is going on around here. Hey… does that thing over there look like a swamp monster to you?"

That got Teddy's attention.

"What?" he said nervously.

"Everybody's pretending it's not there, but I could swear it's real. And I feel like YOU know something about it."

"I don't know what you're talking about," said Teddy, entirely unbelievably.

"Look," said Henry. "We've been friends for a really long time. I care about you man. I just want to make sure you're okay."

"I'm fine. Fine."

"I'm always here if you need someone talk to."

"Yeah, I know."

Henry could tell that Teddy was severely distracted. He started to turn away, disappointed. He missed his friend.

"Hey Teddy," Henry said before he departed.

"Yeah?" said Teddy, who quickly threw down the walkie talkie he had already brought back to his mouth.

Henry looked over at Swampy and then back at Teddy. "Just be careful, alright?"

"Of course," said Teddy.

Henry walked away.

...

As for Lindsay – she was in heaven.

Years of unrequited love, first for fictional characters, then recently for a non-fictional monster, had finally come to an end. She had a real boyfriend who she was in love with and it was all she ever dreamed of.

Lindsay didn't notice the concerned or disturbed looks of the students around her – all trying to pretend Swampy's presence was a bad dream – because she was one hundred percent focused on her man (if you could call him that).

At home, Lindsay's mother noticed the abrupt change in her daughter's demeanor. The cloud of gloom that had hovered over Lindsay's face for weeks had dissipated and been replaced by a glow halfway between ecstasy and madness.

"You look much better," Lindsay's mother said tentatively at dinner.

"I am," said Linsday, too lost in her love haze to consider lying.

"I guess those pills must be working."

"I stopped taking them," said Lindsay. She didn't see the point now that she had given in to her desires.

"Oh. Why? Did something happen?"

"Not something. *Someone*," Lindsay said in the tone only used by those in the throes of first love.

"Oh," Lindsay's mother was surprised, but not displeased. "Can I ask who he is?"

"Someone wonderful," said Lindsay, unhelpfully.

"I gather." Lindsay's mother chuckled. "I meant, what's his name?"

Lindsay took off her rose colored glasses for a moment to be sure her happiness didn't lead her off a dangerous conversational cliff's edge. Swampy had specifically asked her not to tell anyone about their relationship. She didn't see why it would be such a big deal since everyone at school already saw them together, but she didn't want to break his trust.

"Seth," she said. "His name's Seth."

"Tell me about this Seth."

"He's the most wonderful person in the world. He's strong and giving and loving."

"He sounds like quite a catch."

"He really is."

"I'd love to meet him."

"Oh." At the moment Lindsay wouldn't have cared if the whole world saw her and Swampy together but she figured he would feel differently. "Well…I'd have to ask him about that," she said.

"That's fine," said Lindsay's mother.

Lindsay brought the idea up with Swampy the next day at school, after the final bell. The whole day she had coached herself to work up the nerve to ask.

"So… My mom was asking about meeting you."

"What? You told her about me?" Teddy said, concerned, through the walkie talkie lodged in Swampy's head.

"No. I didn't say who you were. I just told her I was dating a guy named Seth. I told her you were absolutely wonderful." Lindsay leaned over and kissed him on the "cheek."

"I don't know, Lindsay. I don't think it's a good idea."

"C'mon! I want to show the whole world how in love we are!"

"Henry," he said.

"Who's Henry?"

"No one. Nothing. Let's be quiet for a few minutes."

"O...kay."

Lindsay waited patiently for Swampy to speak again.

"Sorry about that," he finally said.

"That's okay," she said. "Is something the matter?"

"Nope. Everything's fine. I just don't think I'm ready to meet your mom is all."

"Oh." Lindsay paused. "That's fine honey. You know all I care about is being with you." She kissed him on the mouth. She took his hand and led him down the hallway. She thought she might have heard him mumble "walk down the hallway," but she figured she imagined it. Swampy claimed that his tummy made all sorts of grumbled noises which sometimes sounded like declarative directions.

As they continued to walk, Lindsay realized she felt slightly disappointed. She didn't want to hide her love from her mother. But if that was what it took to make her romance work, she would accept it. *After all,* she thought, *people always say that relationships require compromise.*

...

Sam finally spotted her at the end of the day, while freshmen with thirty pound book bags ran at full speed for their buses and seniors clogged up the hallways with conversation, school staff members trying to clear the hallways like those little balloons that clear out the gunk in arteries during bypass surgery. Lindsay was at her locker, dumping off the books she wouldn't need for that night's homework.

"Do me a favor," he said to Chuck. "Just stay back a little bit. I don't want to creep her out."

Sam walked over to her.

"Hi there."

She looked up at him. It had been a long while since anyone had approached her and Lindsay was slightly wary. Boys used to try to talk to her all the time but that was before the massacre at the mall. Plus, now she had Swampy. She was supposed to meet him in a few minutes and she didn't want him to spot her chatting with another guy.

"Do I know you?" she said.

"I'm new to the school. My name's Sam."

Sam held out his hand. She shook it cautiously.

"Lindsay."

"I believe I saw you on the news," he said.

"Oh."

"It's okay. You don't need to be embarrassed. I'm sure you don't want to talk about it and I don't want to burden you with remembering such a horrible day. I feel bad even having brought it up at all. The thing about it is, I just had to say something because when I saw your face on the TV I just couldn't help thinking how pretty you were. And when my parents told me we were moving here, I felt surprisingly excited, because I thought – I'm going to get meet that outrageously pretty girl."

Lindsay was no stranger to getting hit on. Sam was rather attractive, but obviously good looks weren't as important to Lindsay as to most girls. (Her boyfriend, after all, was practically made of boogers. A literal boogie man, if you will). As usual in these situations, she was mildly flattered. She was also appreciative of someone making an effort to talk to her when most of the school treated her like she was contagious. Nevertheless, she was uninterested.

"I'm sorry. I have a boyfriend," she said.

"Ah," said Sam. He had prepared himself for this possibility and was not discouraged. "Well then I guess we'll just have to be friends."

"Sure," she said, anxious to exit the interaction so she could see Swampy. "See you around then."

"You bet."

She shut her locker and walked off.

Sam followed. He wanted to get a good look at his competition. Sam preferred the idea of winning Lindsay over the traditional way but if her beau was too imposing of a male specimen, Sam wasn't going to rule out the possibility of tracking him down at night and letting certain "accidents" happen.

He turned a hallway corner and watched Lindsay run up to her...*swamp monster?*

Sam spun his head back and forth to see if any other students in the school found this strange. He was shocked to see that everyone ignored it completely.

"You see this, right?" Sam said to Chuck.

"Yeah, the girl's hugging that swamp monster."

"*THAT* is her boyfriend?"

"It certainly appears that way."

Sam took a moment to try to make sense of the situation but no explanation was forthcoming. He heard Lindsay talking to the monster. She said: "So... my mom was asking about meeting you." Apparently, he was not only in a place where pretty girls dated swamp monsters, but he was also in a place where those girls brought these monsters home to meet their mothers.

"What the fuck is going on at this school?" he said.

...

Weeks of research – perusing her spell books day and night, getting less than two hours of sleep a night – did nothing to prove wrong Monica's original presumption that the swamp monster spell was completely irreversible.

She could no more turn James back to a human than she could reverse time itself.

Monica didn't care. She was prepared to love him anyway. She *did* love him, even in his current revolting form. The truth was, she always had.

There was even the possibility that he loved her too. After all, why else would he have come to B.S.H.S. disguised as a student in that old Cubs sweatshirt? He was wanted for murders at the mall. Yet instead of fleeing town completely he had holed up at the town's only high school, hiding out in the open, barely disguised. Why take such a risky course of action except to give her another chance?

She had made a point of chatting with him in the hallway at least once a day since he came to the school. He never gave a response. Her efforts were clearly falling short. He was waiting for something more. He was waiting for her to apologize and tell her how he felt. She had delayed long enough. It was time.

At the Thursday afternoon faculty meeting Monica was cripplingly distracted. She responded to a question about budget cuts with an answer related to the cafeteria pizza. She followed up the Vice Principal's speech about upcoming state testing with an assurance that the baseball team would get new groin protective cups as soon as the old ones were no longer usable. The staff looked at her like she was some sort of maniac. No matter. Monica didn't care at that moment if the school board fired her for institutional incompetence. Her true life purpose had returned to her and she wasn't about to make the same mistake twice.

Her concentration wasn't any better all day Friday. She signed a detention slip with her phone number and made a morning announcement of her grocery list.

(Behind her back, the Vice Principal, a somewhat sociopathic, power hungry, thirty year old named Brett Denninsson took advantage of her mental breakdown to initiate a long planned coup de tat for control of the school.

He slipped notes to the series of teachers he had strategically won over to his side during his two short years as B.S.H.S. veep. "It has begun," the notes said. These socially influential teachers spread the word to meeker, potentially manipulable members of the staff that Principal Missgivens had lost a step and it might be time for a change. Denninsson's plan was to win over the most popular teachers and have them win over the weakest teachers, at which point the loyalists in the middle would crumble from the pressure on all sides. "Soon the school will be mine!" he said out loud to himself in his office, laughing maniacally.")

The day crawled as Monica waited for the weekend bell. She squeezed the stress ball in her office until it burst and the little beads inside it scattered everywhere. She didn't bother to clean them up.

When the bell finally rang she left a trail of dust behind her as she sailed out of her office. She burst out the front door and stood in the staff parking lot so that she would have the best view of all the doors as the students poured out, giddily entering the weekend.

She looked at the awkward retainer wearing nerds and the slutty pregnant girls and the pot heads and the greasers (hard to believe, but Bluford Springs High School really still had greasers), and finally she spotted the person she was looking for.

But something was very wrong. He was not alone. He was with…a girl.

Monica suddenly felt lightheaded. She tripped on the curb and would have fallen right to the ground if she hadn't been caught by Derrick Squishell, a linebacker on the football team.

"You a'ight Miss Missgivens?" asked Derrick, a sweet but stupid stump of a boy.

"Just fine. Thanks Derrick."

Derrick walked off and Monica looked back at Swampy. The girl was Lindsay Morpletopple. Lindsay Morpletopple, of all people, was holding his hand and laughing at…*something he had said? No that didn't make sense. After all, Swampy couldn't speak.* Lindsay, whose friends James had killed when they had the misfortune of crossing his path at the new mall, was holding Swampy's hand like he was…*her boyfriend.*

Monica could not believe her eyes. She WOULD not believe her eyes. She had not waited all these years for this second chance only to have James stolen away once again by some blonde bimbo.

She followed the couple on their walk home from school.

If her anger hadn't made her so short sighted, she might have noticed that she wasn't the only one following. On the other side of the street, Teddy raced from one increasingly outdated telephone poll to another with his walkie talkie, hiding himself just enough so Lindsay wouldn't spot him.

Teddy wasn't the only other one following either. Also following, pretty much out in the open, were Sam and Chuck. Sam noticed everyone else although no one noticed him. He saw Lindsay, too distracted by her love to see anything but Swampy. He saw Teddy, too distracted by playing with his remote control swamp monster, to see anything but the couple. He saw Monica, too distracted by her bitterness at having her affections inadvertently beaten out once again to notice the car that was about to hit her. BRAKE – SCREEEECH – SLAM! Nevermind, the driver braked just in time to avoid her and went into a telephone pole instead. (The same telephone poll that Teddy had vacated moments before.) Sam turned to Chuck and reiterated his earlier point. "What the fuck is going on with this school?" he said.

The unlikely gang of mutually oblivious walkers proceeded along the subdued suburban streets and eventually arrived at Lindsay's house.

Lindsay and Swampy stood outside silently. Teddy watched Lindsay. Lindsay watched Swampy. Monica watched Swampy and Lindsay. Sam watched everyone. Chuck watched Sam (with his camera).

"Want to come inside?" Lindsay said unconfidently. It wasn't the first time she had asked. Swampy always said no.

"I can't."

"Right." Lindsay felt discouraged. *Is this relationship going anywhere?* she wondered.

"I did want to ask you something though."

"Oh. What's that?"

"Would you want to go the diner with me on Saturday night?"

Lindsay lit up like a Christmas tree. It was the first time he had brought up the idea of them being together in any public place besides the school.

"Really?"

"Yeah. I thought it would be nice to take you out to dinner."

"I'd love that."

Swampy started to wander away, his attention sucked away by the neighbor's cat which was dashing around the front yard.

"Well, see you there at 7," Teddy said hastily through his walkie talkie. He decided not to direct Swampy back towards her again. His plan was in place and he felt no need to unnecessarily extend the conversation.

"I love you," called Lindsay.

"I love you," Teddy called back completely truthfully, with his own voice.

"The diner, eh?" Sam said cunningly to his cameraman. "Put on your suit and tails Chuck. Sounds like we're going out this weekend to the fanciest eating establishment this town has to offer."

"Why are you talking like that," said Chuck.

"I don't know," said Sam.

They walked off.

Monica stayed put, frozen. *He loves her?* She felt sick and sad and furious all at once. Was he intentionally trying to torture her? Was this all some form of elaborate revenge for the curse she has cast upon him? She shuddered. A few burning tears escaped her eyes before she angrily shut her lids, refusing to let any more pain out. She looked at Lindsay. She hated this child with everything she was. Feeling defeated, Monica retreated. To her lonely loveless home and her lonely loveless life.

...

The Platinum Platypus diner was the sad hub of nightlife for Bluford Springs residents not yet old enough to buy alcohol. Though business was booming, the store's owner, Mr. Martin Brandelhoof, felt conflicted about his restaurant's immense popularity. Sure the place was raking in the cash, but at what cost to its dignity? On Fridays, Saturdays, and even weeknights, teens from Bluford Springs and a few of the surrounding suburbs poured into the increasingly cracked cushions of the booths and let forth an unparalleled cascade of obnoxiousness. The screeching sounds of fifteen year old boys stutter-laughing after their own horrible jokes about boobs or farting hurt the waitresses' ears so terribly and so frequently that some filed for workers comp. The catty glare stares of enemy teen females and the hazing that followed summoned a dark cloud of feeling around the entire establishment. Chronic under-tipping and under-ordering (and only ordering anything at all for the sake of loitering) infuriated the staff. So did the occasional food fight in which they were powerless to broker peace. The endless assault of unfunny physical humor (kids kicking the tables or lying on the floor or abusively shaking the claw machine, trying to pry free an unwinnable soft animal) as well as general institutional meanness wore thin on everyone. The place felt cursed to Mr. Brandelhoof. Part of him wondered if in some forgotten nightmare he had made a deal with the devil that had guaranteed his continued financial success but doomed his soul.

For all that Mr. Brandelhoof had already seen, nothing would compare to the horror that would go down on Saturday March 9, 2013.

Sam and Chuck were the first to arrive. Sam didn't want to take any chances of missing the "It couple" he planned to break apart. He wasn't yet sure just what his plan of attack would be, but he had a curiously strong feeling that some opportunity would present itself.

He settled into his booth and immediately received intrigued stares from several rival gaggles of teenage girls. Not too long after, two gigglers from one of the gaggles approached him.

"Hi," they said simultaneously.

"Hi there."

"Our friend thinks you're cute," said one of the girls.

Back at the table the girls came from, a mortified sixteen year old collapsed her face in her hands.

Sam smiled. He enjoyed the attention but there was only one girl he wanted.

"Sorry ladies," he said. "I'm taken."

...

Teddy had a fairly elaborate ruse going in order to get Swampy and Lindsay to the diner.

He had "borrowed" his father's Cadillac XTS (the pride of his Dad's entire life, Teddy was sure he would be reminded when he eventually got punished for this most uncharacteristic act of rebellion). Swampy in toe in the backseat, Teddy had shielded his own face in a black hood and sunglasses, then picked up Lindsay, pretending to be a personal driver Swampy had hired to take them to dinner. It was a romantic gesture.

Lindsay was so delighted that she didn't notice the obvious fact that both Swampy and the driver's voice were coming from the same human mouth. Nor did she notice that the driver was obviously Teddy Bigshartz, the kid who had asked her to prom several months before.

All of Lindsay's worried feelings from earlier in the day about the relationship's future immediately felt like nothing more than frivolous fretting. She giddily jumped into the car and cuddled up against her love's fart-like warmth.

"Where to?" said Teddy, as the driver, once they were all inside.

"Platinum Platypus diner," said Teddy as Swampy, in response.

Not only did Lindsay not notice that both of the voices were the same, she also didn't notice that both of the voices sounded incredibly nervous.

Teddy was a jumble of stress. Tonight Phase 2 (of plan B) was finally going into effect. The strain of all the deception and conniving that led him to this point was beginning to draw him a bit thin.

That afternoon had been particularly taxing on his soul. He had finally met the intimidating men he had been communicating with on craigslist.

A week before, Teddy had placed an ad on the online message board seeking a couple of "ruffians a.k.a. tough guys" who, for a price, would be willing to "help him out with a sticky situation." He left the details intentionally vague in the public listing. He had created a fake email address (kingofwesteros45@hotmail.com) purely for the purpose of placing the ad, so that no one would trace the listing's origin. On the off chance that he was discovered to be the ad creator he didn't want any written evidence that could be used against him in a court of law, or worse, shown to Lindsay. A couple of days later he received an email from a man named Tony from the slummy suburb of Swabbleborough. Tony said that he and his bro Jimmy were just the sticky guys Teddy was looking for. In a series of emails Tony asked for the details and Teddy explained his plan.

As the conversation proceeded Teddy could feel his conscience growing grimier like a sink pipe that's been shaved over for too many consecutives days, never cleansed with some much needed Drain-O. He questioned his actions over and over again. *Is this really the type of person I am? At best a scumbag and at worst, a criminal?* Yet he continued to respond to the emails and he continued to put his plan in place because his uncontrollable desire for Lindsay burned away any blades of moral sanity that might have pierced the field of his consciousness.

The plan was as follows.

Lindsay and Swampy would settle into a booth at the diner. While they were perusing the menus, the ruffians would burst into the establishment.

They would harass Lindsay. They would threaten to sexually assault her. One of them would grab her and place his hand on her ass. (Teddy didn't like this detail but it was necessary for the performance to have its proper effect.) The other would taunt Swampy, daring him to do something about their harassment. Instead of helping her in any way, Swampy, through Teddy's voice, would say that he "didn't give a shit what they did to her." Lindsay would be devastated by Swampy's cowardice and lack of caring. They would taunt Swampy more. Teddy would instruct Swampy to grab Lindsay's ass as well, joining the ruffians instead of fighting against them. Just then, Teddy would come out of nowhere and fight off all three of Lindsay's tormentors. He would save her. She would fall into his arms. She would kiss him. Dot dot dot, they would live happily ever after.

Seemed foolproof enough, Teddy thought.

Nevertheless, he felt wary and meeting the ruffians he hired hadn't helped. They were a couple of steroid addled, thick necked dummies, covered in poorly sketched tattoos, who looked like they would just as soon stomp his face in as converse with him. One of them kept talking about grabbing "the broad's tits" and Teddy had to remind him that he only requested for them to grab her ass. The other killed a fly during the middle of their meeting, using far more violence than necessary. Teddy thought about calling the whole thing off and telling them that he didn't need to hire them after all, but he was too afraid for his own life after seeing what they did to that fly to do any such thing.

Teddy showed the men a picture of Lindsay so that they would recognize her. He told them that her date would be dressed in a swamp monster costume. Luckily, they weren't inquisitive enough to ask why.

After a seven minute drive that felt like seventy, Teddy pulled into the Platinum Platypus parking lot. He wiped his wildly perspiring forehead and felt the crumpled armpits of his undershirt stick to the sweat his body was pouring out like a shower head.

"Your destination sir," he said.

...

Lindsay caught the looks they received when they walked in the diner. The teenagers from the high school were used to seeing her together with her "monsterfriend" but the sight was entirely unexpected to the adult town locals, several of whom spit out the gulps of coffee they had just ingested.

The hostess stood slack-jawed, unable to speak when Swampy (through the walkie talkie buried in his head) asked for "a table for two, please."

Mr. Brandelhoof, just as stunned as everyone else, but not wishing to let that night's business come to a screeching halt, instinctively brushed past his stunned young hostess and grabbed two menus. "This way," he said to the girl and the monster. He led them to their seats. The situation was so surreal that he couldn't sufficiently register how disturbed he should be. He stared at them. The rest of the restaurant patrons stared right along. The whole place was way too silent. It was eerie. Mr. Brandelhoof thought he should say something. So he read them the list of specials. Clam chowder. Tilapia. Bread pudding. Then he backed away into the corner and waited for the evening's inevitable tip into chaos.

(Across the room Teddy snuck into the restaurant and hid underneath an open booth).

Lindsay looked over her menu. "The pancakes here are really good," she said to her date.

She looked up. Swampy had not yet opened his menu. "Do you eat human food?" she asked, with the sudden shock of the question.

She heard him mumble something to himself. Then he slammed his hand down upon the menu. Seconds later he lifted it up again and the sticky strands of residue lifted the cover open.

"Sure I do," said Swampy.

"Okay good. I don't want you to think you have to eat just for me."

"I'd do anything just for you."

Lindsay smiled. But she noticed something odd. Her usual swoon wasn't there. Her lust felt watered down. The feeling was very disconcerting.

Why did she feel this way? She questioned herself. After all, he was being so sweet.

Then she realized, with a jolt of distress, that this was exactly why her love felt off. *Because* he was being sweet. He had been nothing but sweet. And sweetness was not what turned her on. What turned her on was power. Violence. Aggression.

She was about to excuse herself to the bathroom to deal with her sudden surge of conflicted emotion when two large tattooed muscular men approached her table. One wore a wife beater. The other, a hoodie.

"Look at this piece of ass," said the man in the wifebeater.

"Honey why don't you leave this smelly fuck and let a real man show you how it's done?" said the man in the hoodie.

"Does the mother fucker even have a dick?" said Wifebeater.

"Fucking jokester in swamp monster costume with no dick," said Hoodie.

They both laughed hysterically.

Swampy started to get up. Then he mumbled something and sat back down.

"C'mon honey, why don't you come with us?"

"Yeah, let's get you out of those pants and onto my dick."

Despite the fact that these guys were complete cretins and likely had the combined intelligence of the average three year old, Lindsay felt perversely tempted by their lude offer.

Before she had a chance to fight her carnal cravings, Wifebeater yanked her from her booth and grabbed a hold of her. He dug his fingers into her ass and said, "If you don't give it up honey, I may just have to take it."

Hoodie looked at Swampy and said, "You gonna do anything about this shit face?"

Huddled under an unoccupied booth, Teddy said in Swampy's voice: "I don't give a shit."

Lindsay would have been more discouraged by her boyfriend's abandonment if she hadn't been preoccupied by an incomplete sexual ecstasy, inspired by the abuse of her posterior.

Hoodie taunted Swampy again: "Little fuckin' pussy swamp monster ain't gonna do a thing about us porkin' his girl. I see how it is bro. You're just a fuckin' pussy."

And...that's about when Teddy's plan fell apart.

(Rewinding the scene a couple of minutes): Present at the diner that night was a young cop named Keith Chetters. Chetters was a bright young cadet, both in the sense that he had heapings of career potential, and in that his slightly above average intelligence well outpaced most of the high school drop outs on the town police payroll. (Recent developments aside, Bluford Springs didn't expect much crime). Chetters was not so easily fooled as the majority of the suburb's dolts into thinking that Swampy must be nothing but a delusion. He didn't understand how or why the murderous monster had ended up at the Platinum Platypus that night but there could be no doubt it was him. He had seen him in person at the mall shoot out when a number of his good buddies had been killed. (He had also smelled Swampy and the horrid stank was unmistakable). However, Chetters, was *not* quite smart enough to realize that he couldn't possibly take on the beast on his own. He was by no means a genius – just comparatively smarter than most of the men on a police force of halfwits. He sat tense on his stool, one hand on his gun, and waited for the right moment.

(Okay, fast forwarding back to where we left off):

Wifebeater had Lindsay's ass in his hand and Hoodie was taunting Swampy. All was going according to Teddy's plan.

Teddy whispered to Swampy to stand up. He was about to whisper for him to grab Lindsay's ass as well but he didn't get that chance. For as soon as Swampy stood from the table, a bullet went flying through his head.

The entire restaurant of people screamed and hit the floor when Chetters's gun discharged.

"Freeze right there asshole!" Chetters yelled.

Swampy, of course, was completely unhurt by the bullet. Inconveniently for Teddy, the walkie talkie was not. His communication and mind control device was completely destroyed. And upon being attacked, Swampy's rage was released.

"RAAARGHHHAAAAAA!" he screamed.

He ripped the table he was sitting at from the wall and flung it across the restaurant.

It nearly decapitated the group of girls who had flirted with Sam but they ducked just in time to save their heads.

Chetters marched towards Swampy, firing off his clip at rapid speed. (None of the cops in the town could grasp the idea that bullets didn't hurt this monster).

Swampy spun like a tornado, flinging acidic slugs off his slimy body that hit the walls, as well as people's arms and legs. The flecks burned holes in everything they touched. The affected humans wailed in agony.

If anyone had been watching Wife Beater and Hoodie (instead of the phantasmagoric monster flipping out at the restaurant's center) they would have seen the hilarious sight of thuggish veneer vanishing at a moment's notice, replaced by a quivering panic. The two men screamed like little girls. They burst through the nearest window's glass and ran outside, hyperventilating in terror. Wifebeater took Lindsay with him, not out of any sense of chivalry, but because as soon as Swampy erupted he grabbed onto her like a stress ball and immediately forgot he was clutching her.

Teddy frantically yelled into his end of the walkie talkie. He begged Swampy to stop, but it was to no avail since the other end had been destroyed. Teddy knew he had to leave the protection of his booth shelter, get to Swampy, and stop the madness before something terrible happened. The commotion of diner customers running chaotically for an escape in the midst of Swampy's vandalistic meltdown made such an intervention difficult.

Outside, Hoodie and Wifebeater screamed like little girls as they dragged Lindsay along down the street.

"Wait right there," said a cold deep voice which stopped them in their tracks.

They reluctantly but helplessly turned their heads back. They were fearful of finding out who spoke to them, but they were powerless to not look.

Staring them down with his crystal blue eyes and his deathly white complexion was Sam. A mischievous smirk graced his face.

"Just where do you think you're going boys?" he said.

"Uh, home?" said Hoodie unhelpfully.

"No. I don't think you'll be going home," said Sam as casually as if he was pointing out the air temperature.

"We won't?" said Wifebeater.

"No. You won't."

Everything in Hoodie and Wifebeater's conscious minds told them that the teenager standing in front of them was no real threat to such physical forces of nature as themselves. Either one of them should be able to beat his ass, no problem. And the two of em' together? Fuggedaboutit. Yet they hesitated. Already shaken up by their altercation with Swampy, their unconscious instincts told them something was off with this schmuck who had the balls to tell them they weren't going home. There was something frightening about him.

Sadly for them, their better impulses rarely prevailed.

"You know what?" said Wifebeater gruffly, regaining his tough guy mentality.

"What?" said Sam, curious, but not the least bit intimidated.

"I think you should fuck off before I beat the shit out of you."

Hoodie saw the route that Wifebeater had decided to take in handling the situation and joined in. "Yeeah," he said.

Quiet during this whole exchange was Lindsay. She was bruised from being dragged outside, but the pain didn't bother our sadomasochistic heroine. Rather, she found it exhilarating. Even more exciting was the unconsummated violence now hanging in the air.

Lindsay recognized Sam from the day before at school, when he had introduced himself as an admirer. She was sure it was the same person, but there was something radically different about his demeanor at night in the moonlight. She felt as though he must have been wearing a thick layer of make-up when she had met him under the B.S.H.S. fluorescent lights. Some artistry had hidden his true appearance and she only really saw him for the first time now under the dark of night. Now that she saw him in his purest form, she could tell that there was something about him so unlike other boys. Something special. Something electrifying.

She looked deep into his eyes the whole time he talked. He finally looked down at her very briefly and smiled before he turned his attention back to the ruffians.

"I think I'll take my chances," Sam said with a level of confidence that was absolutely chilling.

Sam slowly walked towards his opponents. Wife Beater and Hoodie realized that Sam had initiated the fight. They ran towards him full force.

Lindsay held her breath and kept her eyes wide open, not wanting to miss a single detail of what was about to occur.

Wife Beater and Hoodie raised their arms, flexed their steroid addled muscles, and went for some skull crushing punches.

Sam easily eluded their hands with his super human speed. For a minute he played with his adversaries as they became increasingly frustrated by their failed attempts to land a blow or even make the most minor physical contact. He laughed.

Then, with no warning, Sam decided that the fun and games were over and he attacked. He grabbed Wifebeater's arm and ripped it clean out its socket. While Wifebeater was writhing around the ground in pain, Sam kicked Hoodie in the chest and sent him sailing fifty feet across the street. He landed with a terrible thud.

He turned to Wifebeater and pinned him to the ground with his foot.

"Would you like to apologize to the lady here for hurting her?" he said.

"I'm sorry, I'm sorry, I'm so sorry," said Wife Beater.

"That wasn't so difficult," said Sam. Then he brought his foot down with a crushing force, smashing Wife Beater's ribs into his lungs.

Sam was about to kill the bastard but he felt a moment of familiar hesitation towards murder. "Now get out of here," he said, flashing his fangs

In the midst of unbearable pain, Wifebeater ran away as fast he could. On the way he pulled Hoodie up and dragged his unconscious body along with him.

Sam wiped away thoughts of his failure once again to kill. He approached Lindsay and held out his hand.

"Did I scare you?" Sam asked, slightly concerned that he may have gone too far in revealing his true nature. Though he had a hunch that a girl who said she was in love with a swamp monster probably had a thing for the macabre.

"No," she said. She put her hand in his and he lifted her from the ground. Standing upright, she stood still. Her face was only five inches from his. They looked deeply into each other's eyes.

"You're a vampire?" she asked – having formed this hypothesis from his fangs and his superhuman strength, and the fact that he was licking the blood off Wifebeater's dismembered arm like it was a popsicle.

"I am," he admitted.

"I've always wanted to meet a vampire," she said, softly.

"Then today's your lucky day," he said.

"Thanks for saving me," said Lindsay. She leaned in and kissed him. He kissed her back. Fully and wonderfully. While they were kissing she noticed

Chuck filming them and looked over towards him curiously.

Sam noticed. "Oh. That's Chuck. He follows me around…uh, don't worry about him."

That was good enough for Lindsay. She resumed making out.

And with that, Swampy was wiped completely out of her mind.

Back inside the diner, Swampy was very much on everyone's minds. Because he was tearing the joint APART.

Teddy finally made it over to his slimy friend and was about to yell at him to stop, when he was knocked down and stampeded over by one of the gaggles of girls, screaming their collective lungs out at as they tried to escape for their lives.

Officer Chetters, now completely out of bullets, continued to fight the good fight by throwing salt and pepper shakers at the monster. This of course, did nothing but season him.

Just then, the door burst down and about twenty local policeman poured through the frame. Chetters had not been forward-thinking enough to call them, but word got back to the precinct anyway after everyone in a two mile radius had heard the screams.

The back up forces pulled out their guns and again more bullets were fired and again the bullets had no effect whatsoever (really, it was unbelievable the lack of comprehension at the fact that this did not work).

Swampy went right for his new opponents and tore through them like they were a rack of bowling pins and he was a well spun ball. (Under this metaphor, only the six and the ten pins were left standing). Before Teddy had a chance to fully crawl his way across the floor, eluding the whipping wind of bullet fire overhead, Swampy's skin bubbled out of control and he burst like a piece of well blown bubble gum. Some of his acidic flecks must have made it into the kitchen and come in contact with the gas powered stoves, because seconds later the entire place burst in a giant ball of flame.

Somehow, no one was killed in the explosion. But a number of busboys and teenagers were completely on fire. These inflamed individuals ran around what were now the ruins of the restaurant in such a panic that they forgot what they had been taught in elementary school about stopping, dropping, and rolling and were not put out until the fire trucks arrived a few minutes later.

Teddy, minorly scorched on his left arm but otherwise unharmed, stood up and looked around at the chaos. Deep in the distance he saw a re-formed Swampy racing away in the direction of the former swamp lands that were now the mall.

All around him tears were shed. Friends were clutched in hugs of pure survival. The policeman helped the wounded. People stood outside of every surrounding building, watching the scene with their hands held over their mouths.

A tremendous guilt came over Teddy like a fever. For a moment he thought he would pass out. *I caused all this*, he thought. *It's my fault for being so selfish.* He sat down and cried.

He started crying because of the destruction he had caused. He continued crying because his chance to win Lindsay might have been lost forever.

Amidst all the agony, there was one secretly happy person.

Martin Brandelhoof looked at the burned remains of the diner he had built up from nothing and felt a wild glee. The insurance check was going to be *gigantic*.

...

When they arrived at school that Monday, the students found a surprise waiting for them: Armed soldiers at every entrance and exit.

It was brought to the government and media's attentions that Swampy (or the murder who dressed in a swamp monster costume, as the news broadcasts stubbornly insisted on insisting) had been posing as a student at Bluford

Springs High School for the past several months. Already having killed several teens at the mall, the maniac had now set off a bomb and destroyed the Platinum Platypus diner. The president himself issued a state of emergency in Bluford Springs and ordered national troops to be stationed at B.S.H.S. so that no more harm might befall "the children who are America's future."

(At the school, all of the students and teachers pretended to be surprised that Swampy had been at the school *the whole time*. "Did you notice?" they asked each other, faking their shock. "Me? *Never*. Did you?" "ME? Of course not." No one wanted to admit their own stupidity in ignoring the monster even if meant everyone else was just as stupid.)

If the sight of the soldiers alone hadn't been enough to make the school feel like a dystopian police state, the removal of students from class for hard questioning on behalf of an intimidating military policeman did the trick. Gabby Delacroix would leave Social Studies looking cheery enough, but after a twenty minute inquisition about everything she knew about "Seth Manster," she would return in a fit of shakes and tears.

The whole thing was a big mood killer. It just created a really bad vibe. Even the eternally unaffected stoners of the second floor bathroom felt it.

"I just feel sad bro," Chad Oligard said to Nick Frencheska. "This whole thing's bringin' me down. It's killin' my high."

Only one student was in a state of such profound glee that she was unaffected by the proceedings. You guessed it: Lindsay Morpletopple.

Once again Lindsay's dream of love had come true. And once again, being with her new love put her in a state of ecstasy that blinded her to all outside things.

Sam was William Denworth come to life. He was everything she'd ever dreamed of.

Lindsay was one of the first students called in for questioning. Numerous sources had eyed her sitting with Swampy at the diner and even more sources said they had seen her walking around with him around the school, hand in hand, as if they were boyfriend and girlfriend.

Amazingly, when the military cop asked his first question about Swampy, Lindsay genuinely took almost a minute to comprehend who he was talking about. She had fallen so in love with Sam in a single day that her ex-love had vanished from her mind with nary a trace. Such is the fickle teenage mind. It jumps from one desire to another with little self-knowledge of its own inconsistency.

When she did eventually recall the monster she had briefly felt such passion for, she answered the inquisitor with some quiet, unconvincing lies, which implied half-heartedly that she hadn't known who he really was.

Any other student in the school would have been verbally torn to shreds for giving such stilted, incomplete answers, but Lindsay was lucky to have a built in base of sympathy. Everyone, even the hard ass military cop, knew her to be the monster's primary victim and assumed that she was a delicate flower who deserved to be shielded from any further trauma. Also, to be perfectly honest, her looks didn't hurt. Men have a way, consciously or not, of giving a break to a beautiful girl long before they will a mediocre looking one.

The inquisitor let her leave the room almost as soon as she entered it. He attributed any fucked up relationship she had with Swampy to be due to Stockholm Syndrome. (He must have read the same psychology books as Dr. Greshilgoff).

Waiting for Lindsay outside the counselor's office turned interrogation room was Sam. He pulled her close and kissed her.

"You alright?" he asked. "Did they do anything to hurt you?"

"No, they were nice," she said, well aware of the potential for violence which Sam's question implied and grateful for it, even if she did not wish him to harm anyone at the moment.

She rested her head against his shoulder.

"Lindsay, I've been meaning to ask you something," he said.

"Yeah?" she said, her eyes closed, her mind at total ease.

"Will you go to prom with me?"

She lifted her head off is shoulder. She looked deep into his beautiful blue eyes. Tears formed in her own.

"Oh Sam," she said. "Yes. Yes. A thousand times yes."

He lifted her off the ground and spun her around dramatically. She laughed deliriously. An impromptu crowd of onlookers applauded. Sam's pack of nerdy "internet tv show" admirers hooted and hollered. Desirous girls shook their heads with jealousy, but clapped anyway, helpless but to appreciate such a fulfilling romantic scene.

Across the hall watching, ghost pale, most definitely not clapping, was Teddy.

"I've lost everything," he said to himself.

To add insult to injury, he then had to brush right past the celebrating couple (his shoulder actually touched Lindsay's) to enter the counselor's office for his own interrogation.

Inside, he was aggressively reamed out for twenty five minutes. He was accused of all manner of moral crimes against humanity, spawned from his allegedly loyal service to Swampy. Teddy answered by repeating over and over in a monotone voice that he had never realized Seth was the Swamp Monster.

In any other context Teddy would have been shaken by such an open accusatory dissection of his character, but at the particular moment he felt so dead inside that he was completely unaffected. His emotional gears were frozen over and he would not feel anything unless something miraculous occurred to de-thaw them. Teddy didn't expect any miracles. What he expected was to live the rest of his life alone.

A similar thought floated around in the head of Principal Monica J. Missgivens as she moped quietly in her office.

What had looked to finally be a chance at redemption had faded away before Monica had the courage to act. For three quarters of a life time she had lived in despair from the crime of the curse she had committed. The guilt was overpowering. The longing for the boy she had lost was far worse. She was willing to love him again, even in the revolting form she had caused him to possess. But he loved another. Lindsay Morpletopple. How was she expected to compete with a young girl who looked like Lindsay Morpletopple?

Monica had been hard at work moping since the previous Friday when she had been part of the great caravan of followers on that fateful walk home and had discovered Swampy's relationship with Lindsay. She had been so devoted to her moping that she failed all weekend to turn on a television, or log on to the internet, or even switch on the radio in her car on her Monday morning drive to school, and thus she was left in the dark as to the events that had transpired over the weekend. She didn't know that Swampy had blown up the Platinum Platypus diner. She didn't know that Swampy had then retreated into the wild where no one knew his location. She didn't know that Lindsay had traded up and was now dating Sam Bristolnoon, who wasn't even officially registered as a student. She didn't even know that the school was surrounded by soldiers or that students were being interrogated like it was the 1950s and they were members of the communist party. She had walked right past the camouflaged uniformed men, gripping their assault rifles, without a second glance. That's how buried she was in her own troubled mind.

So what happened next came as a complete surprise.

Rosie, one of the office secretaries, barged into Monica's office to let her know of events transpiring in the hallway. Rosie dabbed a tissue on her face to wipe away her tears of joy.

"Sorry to interrupt Miss Misgivens. That poor girl Lindsay Morpletopple who survived those mall killings just got asked to prom! Everybody's cheering. You should really see this."

There was not the smallest part of Monica that wanted to see Lindsay and Swampy celebrating their engagement as prom dates, but her morbid, self-loathing instincts raised her out of her chair and made her follow Rosie into the hallway anyway.

When she got to the scene of the crime, she was faced with a surprising sight:

Lindsay deep in a make-out session with Sam as the crowd cheered.

"Who the hell is that boy?" she said.

"His name is Sam. He's new here," said Rosie, replacing her tear soaked Kleenex with a new a tissue.

"What happened to Swampy?"

Rosie rolled her eyes at her boss, implying that such a joke was far from appropriate.

"They're still looking for that bastard. No one's found him yet."

For Monica, it was one of those moments in life where it feels like a blindfold has been pulled off your eyes, and though, in your visual readjustment, the light is too bright to immediately see everything in all its detail, the notion of new clarity remains incredibly strong.

She zeroed in on Lindsay. The beautiful, beloved, scheming, lying, *bitch.* How could she tell Swampy she loved him on Friday only to make out in the halls with some hottie new student on Monday? *She must have just been using Swampy,* she thought. It was *unconscionable.* Monica would not stand for it.

For the second time in her life, Monica decided to have her *revenge.*

9

Todd Sooter let loose on his crossbow trigger and watched the arrow pierce the buck straight through the heart. His aim was unmatched.

He was deep in the mountains of Montana on one of his regular hunting trips. The locals at the town where he had recently replenished his supplies thought he was a few cards short of a full deck. Todd preferred it that way. He felt it was best to keep people on their toes, fearful of any action he might take at any moment. It gave him leverage.

Todd was determined to be the master of his reality, not some slave to it.

Now fifty-six years old, it had been a long life for Todd Sooter.

The death of his older brother Dirk back in 1969 was a truly devastating moment. The child of a fragile single mother who had never been able to shake the trauma of being left by her husband, Todd had looked to his brother as a father figure. (A father figure who was stoned about four fifths of the time but a father figure nonetheless). Dirk was an exceedingly pleasant individual. He was the kind of guy who could ease tension just by entering a room. He was immensely popular – the leader of a group of peace-lovin', bong-inhaling, long haired hippies. Yet he still found time to toss around a baseball with his little brother and bring him home some greasy fast food for dinner when their mother forgot she had a child to feed.

Dirk's death, piled on top of her already quite shattered being, pretty much did in Todd's mom. Todd was left, for all intents and purposes, alone in the world with no one to provide guidance.

Todd's sense of solitude increased with his discovery of the swamp monster and the idiotic refusal of the local police dolts to take what he said seriously.

Thus, from a very young age, Todd was faced with a harsh truth which seemed to him supreme above all other notions: *You only have yourself in this life. Ain't nobody else can do a thing for you but yourself.*

After the swamp monster incident Todd withdrew from others. Even the couple of friends who had accompanied him on his journey to find Swampy had trouble getting through to him. They eventually stopped trying. In school, he kept quiet. At home, he studied the art of survival.

Todd checked out every book about camping or hiking or hunting he could find from the library. He took them home, barricaded himself in his room and studied. He didn't have any immediate intention in gaining this knowledge; just a general desire to be prepared for any conditions that might arise.

As he went through middle school and high school Todd came to hate Bluford Springs more and more with each passing day. He hated the quaint Main Street with its pretentious cobblestone walkways. He hated the endless stretches of identical house cul-de-sac's. He hated the cheery attitude of the locals who thought they were living in paradise merely because they never had to drive more than two minutes in any direction to buy toothpaste or deodorant. He hated the name "Bluford Springs," which applied to nothing because there were no fucking springs anywhere around! Not even fresh water. Just mucky swamp water where a monstrous murderer lived.

At high school graduation, as a rain of square hats filled the sky above Todd, it immediately became obvious that he would get out of town as fast as he could.

The next day he packed his bags, kissed his mother goodbye, and hit the road without a car or a plan.

In 1975 hitchhiking was still an accepted practice and Todd managed to procure several lifts. His lack of a particular destination made this all the easier. He went from Bluford Springs to Jonesboro, Arkansas to Durango, Colorado to Carbondale, Illinois to Fergus Falls, Minnesota and so on and so on, with no intention of stopping. His life was made up entirely of movement. His location careened eastward and westward and northward and southward at equal turns. He cared not where his feet landed as long as they wouldn't have to rest there for long.

Todd lived like this for almost two years. He survived mainly on the kindness of the generous drivers who were nice enough to give him a lift and a meal. He traveled with groups of college grad males, driving drunk, on the prowl for a nice piece of ass; with elderly couples, preaching good Christian values of charity and chastity; with families heading for the beach or the lake, parents yelling at their kids to stay seated, the kids restless, antsy, nearly falling out the windows in anticipation; with creepy middle aged men who spent far too much time looking at Todd's thighs; and with hippies who could barely see the front window through the marijuana fog hovering gently in the car.

For some it might have been an epic youthful conquest – meant to be experienced for a short time, then stored in the memory as a story to one day tell children at the end of a hard day's work in a nice suburban home. Not for Todd. This was no jaunt through temporary independence. This was training for some great battle with life itself.

As he got older, Todd stopped for longer in single locations. He took a job here or there at a local mill, or farm, or construction site. Anything outdoors and physical. Anywhere he could work off the endless feeling of aggression that had been rumbling around inside him ever since those cops had laughed in his face when he told them about the swamp monster.

He saved up money. He bought camping equipment. He bought boxes of canned food. He bought a used AMC Gremlin to drive himself around in. And he bought guns. Lots and lots of guns.

He interspersed his periods of working with periods of living out in the complete solitude of nature. In a forest or on a mountain or in the desert, he killed animals and scavenged plants for food. He bathed (every once in a while) in a river.

All the while, he was haunted by nightmares. Every night he dreamed of the swamp monster. Those evil yellow eyes and the slimy, pus-filled body that they belonged to were seared deep in his subconscious. He sometimes stopped thinking about his brother's murderer during the day, but never at night. When he closed his eyes, the horror returned without fail.

These dreams, in great part, were what kept him moving. Whenever he suffered a particularly bad one, he would wake up drenched in sweat and immediately pack his bags. He fled to a new location, his instincts desperately trying to outrun the monster's hold on his psyche.

It was never to any avail. Swampy was with him everywhere he went.

As he got older, Todd got better and better at fending for himself without any new income. He had enough saved up to periodically buy new knives and bullets and he knew enough to get most of his food from the wild. He retreated from society for longer and longer until one day, just two weeks before his thirty-eighth birthday (not that Todd was aware of it, having lost complete track of days, months, and eventually years), he made the permanent departure into the wilderness.

And there he might have stayed had it not been for a chance snippet of audio reaching his ear on the afternoon of Sunday March 10, 2013.

Todd was in the middle of gutting a deer when he heard a car's engine off in the distance. He hadn't realized how close he was to a road.

Todd felt completely unthreatened by humans. There was only one thing in this world that scared him and that horrifying creature was thousands of miles away in Bluford Springs. So the rare sound of an automobile was nothing other than an interesting observation. He noted it, then continued to rip the intestines from his buck.

The driver must have had his windows down because Todd could hear the radio quite clearly.

As a song ended, the disc jockey went into a news break.

"*Yet more tragedy in Bluford Springs,*" the DJ said. "*Just a few months after four teenagers were murdered by a man dressed in a swamp monster costume at the town's brand new mall, and a second attack in which ten police officers were killed and many more injured, the same dangerous man is believed to have struck again. A Bluford Springs restaurant was bombed the other night and the same costumed man is the main suspect. The president has sent troops into the area...*"

The audio faded away as the car passed down the road.

Todd was frozen in place, the buck's kidney in his hand. All immediate sensory input disappeared. It felt like he had been sucked into a black hole. Only a thin pinprick of light kept him in the world. He was goo.

Then, anger. Furious, uncontainable *ANGER.*

Todd stood up, paced around, then kicked the buck into a mush of pebbled bones and blood.

He screamed at the top of his lungs. But it wasn't enough. Something needed to be done. Something big.

Tood ran back to his campsite, heaved his things into his truck, and drove into town.

...

The busy breakfast bustle of the local diner came to a halt when Todd Sooter burst through the door like a bout of diarrhea that will not wait in the anus for one more second.

He had not seen his reflection a long time, so had he bothered to really look at the patrons (which he didn't) he might have been surprised by the horrified looks on their faces. He was covered in grime from nearly head to toe. He had a beard down to his belly button that was filled with dirt and leaves and, at the moment, deer guts. Worms had made a home of his pant legs and a family of sparrows nested in hair. He was well on his way to being as disgusting as the monster he walked in the diner to find out about. (Though he would not have appreciated the irony if it had been pointed it out to him.)

"Newspaper!" he said forcefully through his dry, underused voice. "I need to see a newspaper!"

Everyone in the room looked around at each other. No one seemed to have a newspaper.

A man sitting at the counter bravely spoke up. "No one reads newspapers anymore," he said. "We all have smart phones."

Folks around the room cautiously nodded in agreement. They all held up their phones, proving his point.

Todd didn't have time to be a fish out of water in a world of technology he no longer recognized.

"I need to know about the swamp monster!" he said. "In Bluford Springs!"

"The costumed murderer that's been all over the news?" asked the man at the counter.

"I need to see a picture!"

"Okay." The man whipped out his phone, clicked with his thumbs a bunch of times, and located the fuzzy mall security camera photo that had been attached to every article and television piece related to the subject. He held it up for Todd to see.

Darkness consumed Todd. He felt frozen with terror.

He also felt the clearest sense of purpose he had ever felt in his entire life.

"It's him," he said.

He knew what he had to do.

10

The perennials in Jerry Morpletopple's garden were coming in particularly nice this spring. The Lavenders were lusciously lavender, the Coneflowers were perfectly coned, and the Chrysanthemums were doing whatever it was Chrysanthemums are supposed to do. Never in his youth would Jerry have suspected that he would ever become excited by the prospect of gardening. Tending to flowers and growing colorful plants in the dirt would have been well down his list of predicted hobbies, had he ever made such a list.

Though actually, he wasn't sure what would have even been on that list. When he was in high school he had one interest and one interest only: Lindsay's mother. He had fallen so in love with that girl that he didn't think he would ever want another thing again.

Jerry stood up and wiped the dirt off his knees. If he tracked soil into the house Marie would never let him the end of it. He scanned the five foot stretch of earth in front of his cottage, sparkling darkly in the moonlight. He felt the potential.

"My life has come to this," he said. He intended it as a sarcastic comment – a last ditch attempt to maintain his masculinity – but acceptance rang through and drowned out the cynicism. He was genuinely pleased by his garden. Less so by the woman waiting for him inside the house.

He and Marie had been together for eight years now and her nagging was wearing thin. She was still beautiful, of course (she had no reason not to be

– after all, she didn't age), and her beauty was a source of constant arousal, but with each passing day there seemed to be a new mannerism or feature of her husband with which she found fault. Jerry did his best to remain agreeable under the circumstances (although sometimes he thought the more pleasant he acted, the more inspired Marie was to go on the attack). Yet, he didn't see any better alternatives to the life he was currently living.

A month before, quietly, uncelebrated, Jerry had his ten year anniversary as vampire. 3,683 days earlier, Jerry had left a pub where he had watched his beloved football team be absolutely pummeled in the first round of the playoffs, and been blindsided by a thirsty pair of teeth. The unnamed vamp would have sucked him dry had he not stupidly chosen to launch his attack outside of a den of angry football fans, looking to take out their sports pain on anything that moved. All it took was one cigarette smoking pub mate to spot the harassment and call to his buddies, then thirty seconds later the vampire was stomped two feet into the sidewalk. Even with his super-strength, the undead man realized he was outmatched and fled into the surrounding woods. Jerry's drunken defenders pulled him up, noticed that the only wound he had sustained was a little blood on the neck, wiped the dirt off his back, and sent him on his way. They were anxious to find a fight somewhere else now that they had gotten started.

Jerry, lightheaded, trying to comprehend what had just happened, stumbled to his car. As he reached into his pocket for his keys, his vision went red and he fell to his knees. He felt the air flee his lungs.

The transition was brief, but painful. The life drained out of him like urine he could no longer hold in his bladder. A sharp sting flew up and down his spine. He lost consciousness and when his eyes opened back up, he knew in some guttural place of knowledge that he was no longer human.

He felt like a ghost, left on the earth after death to attend to some unfinished business. But he knew that assessment wasn't quite right. His sudden desire to drink the blood of his bar mates clued him in. He was not dead…he was undead. He was…a *vampire.*

It was quite a surreal realization. *Just what exactly was he supposed to tell his family?*

He returned home in a daze. Six-year-old Lindsay ran to him and gave him a bear hug when he walked through the door.

"Mommy said you would need a big hug after that game," she said.

"Mommy always knows what I need."

He smiled at the love of his life who immediately noticed the change in his appearance.

"Are you feeling okay?" said Lindsay's mother. "You look pale."

"Yeah, I think I might have a stomach bug," he said. "I'm going to go lay down."

He brushed past them into the dark bedroom and shut the door.

Unable to fall asleep (that night or ever again), Jerry was still lying awake when Lindsay's mother shuffled in a half hour later, having put their daughter to bed. She slid under the bed sheets and wrapped her soft arms around him. She pressed her face up against his neck.

"How's my man feeling?"

Her scent was overwhelming in its temptation. The blood flowing through her veins called out to him, begging him to free it of its tubular prison. He turned away from her, even as inside, his love for her screamed for her physical comfort.

"I don't want to get you sick," he said.

"Oh. Okay," she said, slightly hurt no doubt, since it was very unusual for him to turn away from her arms.

The next week was the worst of Jerry's life. Each moment was more painful than the next. Imagine dying of thirst and having glasses of water waved in front of your face which you can't consume purely for moral reasons. This was essentially Jerry's situation. No longer able to ingest normal food and drink, he had to make repeated excuses to his wife and daughter as to why he could not join them at dinner after returning home from the office. At work his increasing inability to focus on anything but the scent of blood hiding just underneath his co-workers' outer layers decreased his productivity to the point that his manager threatened him with a "talking to." (The fact that he now walked outside with an umbrella over his head on bright sunny days so that his skin would not burn off only gained him more unwanted intention). The weaker he felt, the more certain he became of the only cure for what ailed him, and the harder it became to resist sinking his teeth into someone around him. His beautiful wife, who he had to lay next to for seven and a half hours every night, was the hardest to resist. All his sexual passion for her still existed, but the more pressing biological need of his new existence overwhelmed all other urges.

As the days passed, he grew more and more distant from his wife for the sake of her own safety. He so desperately wanted to explain to her what had happened to him but he didn't think she would ever believe him. And if she did it wouldn't make any difference. There was no reason she would ever want to live with such a *monster*.

By Friday afternoon Jerry was practically convulsing in his need for blood. At five on the dot he rushed out of the office and scampered to his car before he could do anything he would regret. He was unable to make as clean a get-away as he intended because he was interrupted by his cubicle mate Len before he could open his car door.

"So what's with the umbrella?" said Len, jovially but with a hint of concern.

"This. Oh. The dermatologist told me to do it. Turns out I have this rare skin condition." Jerry had thought through this excuse in advance, in case anyone asked.

"You do look pretty pale."

"Yeah. It's the condition."

Jerry's hands shaking, he desperately tried to force his key into the lock and open the door. Over and over again in his mind he told Len: *Please go away. Please go away.*

"Are you alright Jerry? Otherwise?"

"I'm…fine."

Jerry's heightened nasal sense locked in on Len's fumes. His mouth started to salivate. His piercing canine fangs pushed through his gums. His sense of consciousness slowly dissolved.

"Look, can I be honest?" said Len. "It seems like something's troubling you and I'm your friend and I just wanted to see if there was anything I could do."

"You should really go."

"Hey, if it's none of my business all you have to do is say so. You were just really there for me when I went through my divorce last year and I thought I might be able to repay the favor."

"*Go…*," Jerry said. His voice sounded like it was falling down a long tunnel. His last control of himself receded.

"Alright, I'm going. Just know if you need somebody to talk to, Len's your man."

And with that Jerry sunk his fingers into Len's shoulders like nails into a plan of wood. Len screamed in pain.

"JESUS CHRIST!" Len said.

They were the last words he spoke. Jerry effortlessly tossed Len through his car window, shattering glass all over the pavement. He jumped in after him and sunk his teeth into Len's neck. He drank him up. It was the greatest feeling of relief Jerry had ever experienced.

Then, when he came back to his senses afterwards, it was the greatest sense of guilt.

"What have I done?"

He looked around the parking lot to see if there were any witnesses. He was lucky in that regard. No one was around. He frantically started the ignition and drove twenty minutes to a backwoods river. There he was covered by enough tree shade to throw the limp, deflated remnants of Len's body into the river without having to awkwardly clutch his umbrella over his head.

Then, shaken, distraught, not knowing what else to do, he returned home.

He walked in the door and brushed past his wife and child, barely able to mutter hello. He went in the bedroom and shut the door.

It did not remain closed for very long. Lindsay's mother entered with an uncharacteristic determination in her expression.

"Jerry, what exactly is going on?"

Jerry intended to respond but he was too shaken to spurt out any words.

Tears escaped Lindsay's mother's eyes. Her performance of strength vanished barely after it began.

"I don't understand. You look so pale. Your eyes are a million miles away. You're not acting like yourself and I just don't get it. Talk to me. *Please.*"

"The thing about it is..." Jerry started, but was unable to finish his thought. His mind was interrupted by image flashes of Len's corpse. He shuddered and gripped himself.

There was a long silence. It was finally broken by Lindsay's mother who asked, "Is there someone else?"

It was a question she had been pondering over and struggling. It was painful for her to ask. The question came as a complete surprise to Jerry.

He almost responded immediately – telling her not to be ridiculous and that she was the only girl he ever loved. But he didn't. Something made him stop before he spoke. He sat still and thought.

Life surely could not go on under these new conditions. There would be no return to normal. A new chapter began the moment that anonymous vampire sunk his teeth into Jerry's neck. Perhaps even a new book entirely.

Jerry said the words before he decided that it was the right thing to do.

"Yeah," he said. "There is someone else."

Lindsay's mother put her hands over her mouth and fell to a seated position on the bed. She took a minute to compose herself.

"Who is she?"

"Does it matter?"

"I want to know. I deserve to know."

"Okay…Her name is Sandy," he heard himself saying. "She's a med school student."

"I see. So I'm not young enough for you anymore."

"It's not that…"

"What then?"

"I…can't do this anymore."

"You can't do this anymore? So your mind is made up? You're leaving me?"

"I'm so sorry," he said.

It was incredibly hard for Jerry to force out his words. Everything he said, he wanted to take back immediately after he said it. But he forced himself to keep going. He knew he had to exit his family's life. It was the only way to protect them from his vampyric urges. He was too much of a danger to them. After killing Len he no longer had any faith in his ability to resist. The taste of blood was too sweet. He would do anything to protect the people he loved. What he now realized was required, was for him to leave them alone. If a tough lie made his departure easier, then so be it.

Jerry stood up. "I just… don't love you anymore."

It was the biggest lie he ever told.

"I'm so sorry," he said. That part was the truth. But the damage was done.

He left the bedroom, utilizing every bit of resolve he had not to hug his wife on the way out.

Jerry located Lindsay in the living room, playing with her Barbies. He lifted her into his arms. She laughed at the unexpected ride.

"I love you Lindsay. Don't ever forget it," he said. He kissed her on the cheek.

He composed a letter for his daughter, which he hoped she would be able to comprehend. In it, he expressed his deep regret in having to leave, but assured her it was for the best. He wished her "an awesome life," because she had just recently taken up the adorable habit of working the word "awesome" into her daily conversation.

He composed a letter to his wife too. He wanted to tell her he would always love her. Instead he just apologized and promised to send money on a regular basis.

He snuck out in the middle of the night and he never saw his family again.

For the next couple of years Jerry was a wanderer. They were difficult times. He did a lot of things he would rather forget. The guilt of killing was overwhelming but the thirst for blood was more powerful. There was not a day that went by that he didn't think of walking out into the sun suicidally and burning up into nothing. One time he actually tried, but the pain was so severe that he jumped back into the shade within five seconds. He was monumentally depressed. Imagining the eternal life stretched out in front of him only made it worse.

Then, one night, while camping out in a forest somewhere in Canada, Jerry heard some voices who would help turn his life around.

"I swear vampires today are afraid to get their teeth dirty. It's pitiful," said a male voice.

"Hey, I don't see why I should have to do the work if someone else is willing to do it for me," said a second voice.

"Lazy. You're so fucking lazy," said the first voice, laughing.

"Hey, I don't live in a wooden casket or wear a fucking Dracula ascot either. It's the twenty-first century. You want to live in the past, feel free," said the second voice.

Terribly lonely, Jerry took a leap of faith and ran over to the strangers.

"Hello there," he said.

The more tough talking of the vampire buds suffered a spasm of fear at the unexpected greeting. This in turn caused his friend a great spasm of laughter.

"Sorry to interrupt," said Jerry. "I couldn't help overhearing. Are you guys vampires?"

"This guy's got some serious balls," said the first, trying to regain some of his rough image. "You looking to get your blood sucked?"

"No. No. It's not like that. I'm a vampire too."

"Can't you recognize one of your own Al?" said the second. He walked over to Jerry and put out his hand. "I'm Zack. This is Al. Pleased to meet you."

Jerry shook Zack's hand. After, Al reluctantly stuck out his own hand and Jerry shook it as well. Zack appeared to be in his early twenties. Al appeared mid-forties. But when it came to vampires there was no way to know how old someone might actually be.

"Boy am I happy to meet you guys," said Jerry. "I've been wandering around for almost two years and I've never met another vampire."

"Oh man," said Zack. "That's rough pal. Well today's your lucky day. Because we're a couple of the finest lads a lonely vampire could ever hope to meet. We were just making our way to the Devil's Cremaster Pub. Why don't you come?"

Al grumbled something.

"Is there a problem Al?" asked Zack in a polite tone.

"I just…thought it was just going to be me and you tonight. You know. Guys night."

"Well Jerry's a guy. So it's still guys night."

"Thanks so much," said Jerry.

"Don't mention it," said Zack. "If you've never met another vampire then you have a whole lot that you need to learn."

The Devil's Cremaster Pub turned out to be an underground vampire bar with various types of craft bloods on tap. It was an extremely popular venue, packed with vampires of all shapes and sizes and apparent ages. Jerry was surprised by how un-gothic the décor was. The walls were brightly colored, the seats plush and comfortable. All around, various vamps laughed with their friends, drank blood, and even played darts. It could have been any human bar, except that it was buried in the ground and the stench of lifelessness was all pervading.

While Al sulked at the fact that his best friend was occupied by another for the evening, Zack told Jerry all about the rather organized vampire world. He told him about the vampire parliament and the seventeen regulations passed seventeen years prior which changed the way vampires lived. He told him about the designated hunters who gathered the blood for everyone else, even though the laws still permitted human hunting. (This explained the argument Al and Zack were having when he came across them.) Zack said that most of the vampire population lived in cold places towards the poles of the globe where the daylight length was shorter.

Jerry was amazed at how normal it all seemed. He had spent the previous two years creeping from one dark corner to another feeling like some monstrous rodent who would never be the least bit liked or wanted by anyone else ever again. And here, suddenly, was a veritable *community*. Suddenly there was hope. There might be a place for him after all.

It didn't take long for Jerry to be accepted as a full-fledged member of his new compatriots' social circle, Al's reservations aside. They were a nice crew, ten strong. They got together for pub crawls and midnight picnics and board game nights. They were male and female alike and they made Jerry feel right at home in the world of the undead. It was all very heartwarming (metaphorically of course – Vampire's hearts are as cold as a penguin's testicles).

Right from the beginning, Jerry struck up a particular bond with a vampress in the group by the name of Marie. Prior to his inclusion she was the newbie of the group, having only been turned in 1986, when she was 23. She had gotten a little too drunk at a Cyndi Lauper concert and decided to make out with a cute guy standing a row behind her. As it turned out, the cute guy was a vampire and he wasn't giving her neck a hickey, but draining her veins of a life source she needed to survive. "I know it sounds like a crazy thing to misinterpret," she said, "but I thought that he was just really into neck biting."

Jerry could tell fairly quickly that Marie was interested in him as more than a friend. (In the vampire community, Jerry learned, there was a complete feeling of sexual freedom – since female vampire wombs were incapable of producing vampire babies.) The other guys in the group noticed her affection for Jerry as well and were not reserved in expressing their jealousy. Looks wise, she was easily the pick of the litter in their social circle. They had a hard time understanding his initial hesitation.

Jerry could have told them that he was still madly in love with his wife. One or two of them might even have understood. But he didn't want to. His impossible love was a private affair that he wanted to suffer alone.

He would never love anyone the way he loved Lindsay's mother. That was certain. Nevertheless, the days went by, and Marie's advances became more aggressive, and a guy can only resist for so long.

One night Marie invited Jerry over to her apartment. She filled the abode with romantic candlelight. She bought the finest bottle of aged Belgian blood. (Who the Belgian was, we can't be sure.) She played sexually charged jazz on her Bose speakers. She curled up next to Jerry with every intent of seduction and finally, then and there, his desire got the better of him.

They made love all night. (Vampires have far fewer physical limitations than humans when it comes to sustained love making). He knew he would never feel about her the way he did about Lindsay's mother, yet he saw no reason to deny himself some small happiness which could make his circumstances easier to bare.

Soon after, they were married. It was a delightful little ceremony in a picturesque moonlit clearing in the woods. It was followed by a rollicking, earth shaking dance party. (Literally. Vampire dancing is rather intense.) At that moment, Jerry felt happy. In his own tempered way, he was quite taken with Marie.

However, eight years in, the passion in their marriage had devolved into a near comatose state, similar to the marriages of many humans, with the notable difference that vampire pledges of eternal faith were actually capable of going the immortal distance. He and Marie rarely had sex anymore. Their physical and emotional affection had waned. And she had become a supernatural force of nagging.

Which was why Jerry now spent most of his time in his gardens.

Which brings us back to the present.

Jerry double checked his clothes to be sure that he had removed every speck of dirt before entering the house. He thought he was safe so he walked in.

Marie was busy watching some sort of show on the computer in the living room. Jerry thought, with any luck, he could sneak to the kitchen for a drink of blood without her noticing that he had entered the house. However, he was distracted from walking by secretively when he heard a particular name spoken on Marie's program.

"Lindsay."

Just hearing that name spent him spinning down a rabbit hole of memory and regret.

His daughter. She was sixteen now. What would she look like? What sort of person had she aged into? He so wished he could have been there for her. He suddenly felt an overwhelming wave of depression.

Caught up in his bout of emotion, he walked into the living room and peered at the streaming video on the computer to see the Lindsay whose name had been mentioned.

You can imagine his surprise when he saw his own daughter on the screen. He watched silently in horror for several moments as he pieced the situation together. The program Marie was watching was the Nosferat U fraternity frat competition. Jerry was aware of all the hoopla surrounding the event but he hadn't watched any of the programming himself. He found the whole idea rather barbaric.

On the screen was a vampire, frozen in his teenage form, eyeing Jerry's daughter from across the hall. The teenage vampire told the camera that come prom night he would take the girl's virginity and acquire her blood. He smiled an evil grin. Jerry wanted to jump into the computer screen and rip the kid's head from his neck.

Unable to hold in his anger he actually growled out loud. This got Marie's attention. She turned around and noticed his clothes.

"You're tracking dirt in the house!" she said.

"Marie. SHUT YOUR MOUTH!" he replied.

That silenced her. In the entire time that they had known each other, he had never once responded with such aggression.

Jerry's heretofore unknown violent vampire instincts all switched into gear at once. There was no way in hell he was going to let that scumbag lay a single finger on his daughter.

He was going to be at that prom. He was going home.

11

Holly woke from her usual nightmare at five am, shaking and sweating – all par for the course.

How many more times would she have to relive that moment? How many more times would she have to watch James's body glow yellow and implode in pus, transformed chillingly into the swamp monster by the cruel witch girl?

Every night she took her pills and spoke to herself of kind dreams (as Dr. Gretmüller recommended) and every morning she woke up, in a fit of terror, kicking and screaming and waking up her hallmates. Every morning the hall guards ran to her bed and restrained her from tearing off her own skin. Every night she went to bed hoping she wouldn't wake up again and every morning she wondered how she would get through another day.

She had been medically considered crazy for forty-three years and she had never once argued with the designation. There was no question that watching James melt away into that revolting creature had shattered her beyond repair. Yet, she also knew she was different than most of the patients at St. Carl's. The cohorts with whom she "conversed" (meaning that vocal exchanges were made, even if they did not contain words strung together in any coherent order) or "played games" (meaning that board game pieces or cards were picked up but usually ended up being thrown across the room or tucked into someone's armpit rather than used in any accordance with rules) had neural irregularities which made them the way they were. The cellular wiring of their brains was faulty and a disconnect with the reality experienced by the rest of the world was the result.

This was not the case with Holly. Her brain was just fine. Her neurons fired in the same patterns as all the "sane" people who were not locked up in a mental institution.

Because the "hallucinations" the doctors told her she had experienced had been real. The witch girl and her spell and James's horrific transformation had not been delusions. They had *really* happened and she knew it, even if no one else believed her.

Still, she was crazy. And she acknowledged it. The fact that what drove her crazy was real instead of imaginary didn't make much difference. Holly couldn't so much as walk down a hallway or go to the bathroom without feeling sudden overpowering fits of terror, which incapacitated her with full body tremors.

Living in a place where she almost never had a typical conversation, she had lost her ability to speak like a normal human being. She noticed this when her daughter came to visit.

Holly's daughter would generously visit on a regular basis. She would chat and update Holly on what was happening in the life of her own daughter – Lindsay. Then Holly would try to respond and what would come out were the babblings of a nut job. Holly could hear herself and her own loony tone. Yet, she seemed incapable of doing anything about it. Her inner awareness had lost access to the control switch of her outward personality and there was nothing that could be done about it. Lindsay's mother was kind. She listened to Holly with open ears and a smile but they both understood the painful truth of the situation.

Holly saw James as the swamp monster everywhere. She knew that these images, unlike the events that spurred them, were not real. But she still spoke to them, trying to get through to the boy she once loved. The boy who fathered her daughter.

In what might have been the most painful moment in those horrible events back in 1969, Holly had learned she was pregnant. She had already been at the mental hospital for three months when one of the orderlies informed her of the news. She was carrying James's child.

She snuck into a doctor's office one night to use the telephone and call James's parents to tell them the news. She thought they deserved to know. James's father had screamed and cursed at her. He and James's mother apparently blamed her for their son's disappearance. They believed she was crazy, like everyone else did. They thought that in a fit of insanity she must have murdered their son and disposed of the body. They had no proof, but James's father said it was the only scenario which made any sense. He told Holly that he hoped she died a horrible death. Then he hung up the phone.

She couldn't take it. She screeched in agony and tore up the doctor's office in exasperation. The night orderlies found her, grabbed her, forced her onto a stretcher and strapped her in. The next day she received heavy doses of electric shock therapy. This did as much to usher her into a permanently unhinged state as anything else. She was never quite the same after that.

Six months later she had given birth to a beautiful baby girl – then she had to watch her immediately be taken away. Holly cried and cried and pleaded to let them keep her just for a little while. "I just want to hold her for a little while!" she begged. Her request went unacknowledged.

Holly's parents raised her daughter. They stopped by over the years to tell her how the little girl was doing, but they did not bring her with, despite Holly's imploring. Holly's parents never seemed to know how to react to their daughter's mental condition. Her break with reality had been so sudden that they didn't know what to make of it. She had never shown any signs of trouble before that fateful night. They stayed loyal to her but Holly could tell much of their love was gone. When they came to see her they had a perpetual look of removed disbelief on their faces. As if this was all a dream and there was no point in getting too invested, since they could wake up at any time.

At some point her parents (her only visitors – any friends she had previously had never bothered, probably too frightened to step in such a facility) stopped coming. Holly was left with no one and nothing. She considered daily trying to find a piece of glass she could slit her wrists with, but the hospital employees kept any sharp objects extremely well-guarded.

Years later she was given a small sense of purpose again. Her daughter, now eighteen and in control of her own legal rights, came to see her.

Holly recognized her immediately although she hadn't seen the girl since she was a newborn. She pulled her daughter in for a big hug. The guards watched closely but Lindsay's mother assured them it was fine. She desired the embrace as much as Holly did.

Lindsay's mother had wanted to meet Holly for a very long time but her grandparents wouldn't let her. They were frightened that whatever crazy Holly possessed might exist inside Lindsay's mother too. They thought, irrationally, that if the two women interacted the crazy gene might be immediately unlocked. Lindsay's mother took matters into her own hands once she became legal. Her grandparents could no longer stop her from discovering her origins.

Holly could tell that her daughter didn't believe her story any more than anyone else did. But she didn't care. She loved her with all her heart. And as the years went on, her daughter's regular visits were the only thing that got Holly through the days.

Eventually, on occasion, Lindsay's mother would even bring her own daughter, Lindsay. Holly thought looking at Lindsay was like looking in a mirror. The effect was pronounced by the fact that there were no mirrors at St. Carl's, since they could be too easily shattered. Holly hadn't looked at herself since she was a teenager. Now, here was a girl, a generation removed, who was her spitting image.

Lindsay saw Holly just as her "crazy grandma," and as usual, Holly's attempts at speech didn't do much good in convincing her otherwise.

Holly didn't care much care though. During the visits with Lindsay and Lindsay's mother, she was the happiest she had been since before that terrible night when the bitch witch had taken everything from her. She was so grateful to have a family again.

But she still missed James. There was not a day that went by that Holly didn't wish she could see him again just one more time. For that, she would have given anything.

12

Despite everything that had occurred, Teddy still couldn't manage to give up hope that Lindsay would one day be his. His hope persisted past the point of all reason. (For hope persists beyond all reason as consistently as rumors spread, scandal ensues, and havoc is wreaked.)

He had no new plan for how his hopes would be fulfilled. There was no phase three of plan B in the works nor any phase four of plan A. Not even a plain old plan C.

He waited patiently for his brain to be struck with some brilliant bolt of an idea of how to win Lindsay's love.

And in the meantime, he stalked her.

He followed her around school. He followed her on her walks home each day with Sam. He watched through her bedroom window, atop a ladder, peering in as she and Sam made out, seething with envy but unable to avert his eyes. He followed her to the movies on Friday nights, where he subtly seated himself behind the couple, listening closely to every crunch of popcorn her teeth made, wishing he was a puffy kernel so he could find out what the inside of her mouth was like. He followed her and her mother to the department store for prom dress shopping. The blue dress was his favorite. She went with the pink. No matter. She looked gorgeous in all of them.

Teddy was fully aware that he had stepped well over the line of decency. That didn't prevent him from continuing to follow Lindsay around every corner, to every room, night and day, in darkness and light. Until such time as he figured out how to be *with* her, being *near* her was the only thing that eased his suffering.

On May 24th 2013, the morning of prom, Teddy waited outside Lindsay's house on his bicycle, ready to follow her to her hair and make-up appointments and to anywhere else she should venture on the day. Teddy hadn't bothered asking anyone to prom despite Henry and Tom's urging that he ask Deena Voloboulos or Sandy Dinkens or any number of average to below average looking nice girls, all of whom were eventually swooped up by other unpopular males who were more willing to settle than Teddy. His buddies had then encouraged him to go solo but he considered this suggestion such an affront to his ego that he hadn't talked to them since.

Lost in his thoughts, Teddy was taken by surprise when Lindsay and her mother emerged from the house earlier than he expected. As they got into their car, Teddy readied his legs and began to pedal vigorously.

The hair appointment was first. Her blonde locks were twisted and twirled and sculpted into a series of hardened artistic loops. The make-up appointment was second. Her face was painted with mascara and blush and lipstick until she looked more portrait than human. Teddy had never seen her more beautiful. He could barely take it.

After the make-up appointment they got back in the car and Teddy followed Lindsay and her mother in a direction he was unfamiliar with. The road took them away from most of the suburban development in the area. They drove in the opposite direction of the swamps, out towards the grasslands.

...

Lindsay had no desire to see her grandmother. The mental institution where she lived gave her the creeps. (Technically these days they called the place a psychiatric care hospital, but let's be honest, it was a mental institution.

They're just lucky the term "loony bin" had fallen out of favor). Lindsay had a slight grasp on the irony of being turned on by a swamp creature who ate people through his anus and at the same time being creeped out by a well-run, clean, modern facility for those whose mental conditions were such that they could not care for themselves, but this awareness did nothing to lessen her aversion to going there.

Aggressive violent monsters were one thing. Quiet sad humans living in a skewed version of a world they couldn't comprehend were quite another.

She hadn't seen Grandma Holly in over two years. The last time her mother had forced her to visit, her grandmom had spent most of their visit nearly silent. Then, when they were getting ready to leave, she had suffered a hysterical fit. She screamed and shook and rambled on about some "witch" who had "cast a spell." The hospital workers restrained her and Lindsay had refused to accompany her mother back ever since.

Part of Lindsay's distaste for seeing her grandmother, of course, came from her own fear that she had inherited whatever crazy gene Holly possessed. She feared that those around her would one day learn of her sick desires and would throw her in St. Carl's with her grandmother.

For the past two years, Lindsay's mother had respected her daughter's desire not to visit the hospital. Today, however, no amount of arguing dissuaded her.

"I want your grandmother to see you looking so pretty. I told you it was part of the deal when I paid for you to get all gussied up."

"But MOMMMMM," said Lindsay. (A classic teenage counterargument.)

Lindsay's mother was insistent. "Lindsay, my mother has very little in her life. I know she's not all there and I know that can be frustrating. How do you think I felt as a child? Living with my grandparents, having to hide from all my classmates that my mother was locked away in some loony bin?" (See – it sounds significantly worse than "mental institution"). "Don't you think I was ashamed? Don't you think I hated going there, seeing a mother who could barely talk to me coherently without rambling on about witches and curses? Of course I did. And I understand where you're coming from. But over the years I learned that she's still a person. She needs little moments of joy to break up the pain just like everybody else."

It was a touching, revealing, heartfelt speech. Lindsay had never heard her mother speak so openly about her own childhood. She responded the only way she knew how.

"But MOMMMMMMMMMM," she said.

Her mother was not persuaded.

Lindsay, prettied up like a porcelain doll, got plenty of looks at they passed past the security desks. Beautiful and sixteen, she was plenty used to being ogled. The ogling of mental patients provided for another level of discomfort entirely. Men on the street looked like they wanted to fuck her. Men in the mental institution looked like they wanted to peel off her skin and use it as a coat.

They were led by a security guard through the various corridors of patients, organized into different living sections by important factors like gender, ailment, behavior, and how likely they were to put you in a headlock and try to choke the life out of you for no reason whatsoever. The guard kept his eyes peeled for loose wackos who might impede their progress. He led them to a visitation area filled with plush couches and harmless women patients gazing pleasantly out the windows. They were seated onto wooden chairs. After a minute, Holly was brought into the room and seated on a couch across from them. She kept her eyes downward. She would not look straight at her visitors.

"Hi mom," said Lindsay's mother.

"Hi grandmom," said Lindsay.

Holly gave no response.

"Lindsay wanted to come see you today," said Lindsay's mother. "Her junior prom is tonight. She got her hair and face done up all nice. Doesn't she look pretty?"

This statement got Holly's attention. Her eyes snapped forward. She looked around with struggling eyes. Something seemed to be on the tip of her tongue.

"P...p...pr...prom?" she sounded out.

"Yeah, she's going to prom," said Lindsay's mother.

"I was supposed to go to prom," Holly whispered, her eyes looking down once more.

"Oh yeah?" said Lindsay, curious. She never heard this story before.

"With James. Then he asked *her*."

"Who was James?" asked Lindsay. Her mother gave her a look of reprimand but it was too late.

"James was my great love. But we had a fight and he asked *her* to prom. It was only a joke. A mean joke. He should never have done it. He didn't know what he was up against."

"We don't have to talk about this," said Lindsay's mother, suddenly feeling very foolish for thinking that Holly would be pleased to see her daughter gussied up for prom. She should have known it would trigger Holly's delusions.

"She was a witch," Holly continued. "She cursed him."

"Oh," said Lindsay, realizing her grandmother was just relaying the same crazy story she had told the last time she had seen her.

"She cursed him and turned him into that *swamp monster*!" sad Holly.

"Wait, what?" said Lindsay. She didn't remember *that* detail of the story.

"She said these horrible sounding words and he transformed into the swamp monster in front of my eyes."

"Swampy?" said Lindsay.

"Yes, that's what they called him," said Holly.

"We can stop talking about this now," said Lindsay's mother forcefully, concerned for her daughter. She turned to Lindsay and whispered: "My mother is delusional. Don't take anything she says seriously."

Living in a world where she now knew there were, in fact, such things as swamp monsters and vampires, Lindsay was suddenly less likely to doubt Holly's claims about witches than she had been when she was thirteen. In fact, she was surprised she had not reached this conclusion earlier.

"Tell me the whole story, grandmom," said Lindsay. "I want to know what happened."

"I loved him," Holly said, raising her eyes to look right in her granddaughter's. "He wasn't the nicest boy but I loved him. And she turned him into something horrible..."

Lindsay's mother tried to stop the conversation again but Lindsay shushed her vigorously. Holly then related the whole story in detail. Her and James's relationship. The new girl in school. The drive-in movie theater. The terrible night at her house.

Lindsay immediately knew that every word Holly spoke was the truth.

Across the room, so did Teddy.

Teddy, more and more resourceful as his life as a stalker continued, had managed to sneak past security and make his way to the visitation area. He hid behind an obese patient who did nothing but stand still and sway from side to side, humming Neil Diamond's "Sweet Caroline." It would later take Teddy hours to get the song out of his head.

Teddy couldn't believe what he was hearing. (Not "Sweet Caroline" – Holly's story). Learning that Swampy had once been a teenage boy, much like himself, filled him with an incredible feeling of guilt. Teddy had used Swampy like a puppet and forgotten about him completely when it was no longer convenient to be around him. Now he knew that Swampy was just another lovesick teenager whose love had been thwarted by the gods. They had more in common than Teddy could ever have imagined. The whole reason Swampy had always behaved differently towards Lindsay must have been that she had reminded him of Holly. After all, Lindsay was her granddaughter.

Suddenly, Teddy was struck with an overwhelming feeling of moral obligation. He needed to make things right. If he couldn't make his own love story come true, he could at least bring about someone else's. Swampy and Holly deserved to attend that prom that was stolen from them. And Teddy was the man to make that happen.

Besides, Teddy thought, making Lindsay's grandmother's dreams come true wasn't a bad way of trying to impress Lindsay.

Enter Plan C.

All systems go on Phase 1.

As for Lindsay, she wasn't sure exactly what to make of the realization.

I was going out with my grandmom's boyfriend? was one odd thought which worked its way through her mind.

Then: *WAIT. If Swampy was my grandmom's boyfriend does that mean he was my... GRANDFATHER?*

The world was so much more topsy-turvy than she could have ever imagined it. The mythical creatures of the young adult novels she read all apparently existed in the real world. Yet, society still frowned upon pointing this out enough that her grandmother has spent the entirety of her adult life in a mental institution for her claims about seeing a swamp monster – a fact which could now be verified by two thirds of the town.

If there was anything Lindsay felt like she learned from this prom morning visit, it was to keep her mouth shut and pretend to be just as sane as everybody else.

Nonetheless she was shaken. She was shaken by the fact that her grandmother had been locked away for life for simply witnessing the swamp monster's birth. What would happen to Lindsay if people found out about her relationship with him? She was shaken by the thought that she had maybe committed some sort of incest with her grandfather. (The fact that he was made of snot and pus didn't bother her, but the fact that he might have been a family member did – go figure). She was shaken by the whole convoluted, nonsensical, madcap situation and she felt a crucial need to escape all these horrible thoughts as swiftly as possible. She needed comfort.

So she tossed the whole situation into the trash heap of her mind and she thought about Sam. She thought about Sam to calm her down and the thought of him instantaneously made her smile.

She wondered what he was doing at the present moment. Was he was getting ready for the evening yet? Boys always took so much less time than girls. He would probably throw on his tux about twenty minutes before picking her up.

She really did like him. For his violent nature, sure. But she also liked him for his non-bloodthirsty side. He was suave. He was funny. He was all that she wanted in a man.

Thinking about Sam, Lindsay graciously forgot about her grandmother, who was now blubbering away in tears, and now screaming, and now being restrained by the guards, as Lindsay's mother pleaded with them to be gentle. Lost in her daydream, Lindsay missed all of this. She was thinking about prom.

She couldn't wait for prom.

...

Sam was hard at work watching the Price is Right in the motel room he currently called his home when his cell phone rang.

Lindsay was the only person who had called him in the last three months so he was hesitant to answer when he saw an unknown number. He considered letting it go to voicemail, but his curiosity got the better of him after the third ring.

"Hello," he said.

"Hey there old buddy," said a familiar voice on the other side of the line.

"Jacoby," said Sam. "How the hell are you?"

"Not terrible. Not as good as you, I think."

"What do you mean?"

"I've been watching our show. Looks like you're primed to win."

"Oh." Sam was a little embarrassed. He hadn't bothered to keep track of Jacoby's doings at all. "Well I'm sure you're doing great too."

"Please. I finally got some girl at one school to agree to go to prom with me. But she's incredibly shy and I don't think there's any way she'll have sex with me. If we just had to kill them it would be easier, but talking a girl into bed is not my strong suit."

"I see."

"Can I admit something to you?"

"Sure."

"I'm a virgin."

"Oh."

"I never had sex when I was a human and I've been too nervous to hit on any vampire girls. They're scary."

"No kidding."

"I don't think there's anything left in the world that scares me except sex. I used to be afraid of a lot of things but not being able to die wiped away a whole host of them."

"I wouldn't work yourself up about it too much," said Sam. "It's really not that big of a thing. You just line up the parts and from there, your body sort of takes over."

"I feel pathetic," said Jacoby.

"Don't," said Sam. "You're still young. And you have thousands of years ahead of you to have as much as sex as you want."

Jacoby laughed. "That may be true. But I still doubt I'm getting laid by my prom date. So I was just calling to wish you luck and some advance congratulations."

"Well thanks pal. But it's not over until it's over."

"Trust me. It's over. Have a good time tonight. Save some blood for me back at the college."

"Thanks," said Sam.

"See you later."

"Bye."

Jacoby hung up and Sam put down his phone.

The truth was, Sam was nervous about the coming evening. Unlike Jacoby, it wasn't the sex which scared him. He was sure that would go off without a hitch.

What scared Sam, rather, was what was supposed to come after.

Sam felt extremely unconfident about his ability to turn Lindsay over to the vampire council of elders. He shook with fear and anger when he thought of the council using her as their own sexual plaything. He felt downright chilled when he thought of them sacrificing her to the vampire gods.

He reprimanded himself that he should have been prepared for these dangers from the start. He picked Lindsay as his target because her image on the news captivated him. This was the wrong strategy. He never should have picked someone who had any hold over him. He should have gone with some random dweeb who he wasn't attracted to and who he could have cast aside without a second thought. *But no! I had to go with the gorgeous girl with the great personality! STUPID SAM! STUPID!*

He was falling in love with her. How was he supposed to hurt someone he loved so much?

He picked up his cell phone and tossed it violently at the TV, shattering the screen and preventing him from ever knowing whether Tony or Marcia won the Showcase Showdown.

At that moment Chuck reentered the room from the morning blood run.

"Get in a fight with the TV?" he said.

"I just...can't watch The Price is Right without Bob Barker. Fucking Drew Carey. It's not the same."

"Riiiiiiiiight," said Chuck, not buying Sam's hasty excuse for a second.

"Give me my goddamn drink."

Chuck handed Sam the Styrofoam cup containing the squirrel blood on which they had been making due.

Sam downed it and threw the cup across the room. "I'm sick of this squirrel blood. I can't wait for this shit to be over so I have something real to drink again."

"There are humans all around. Go nuts."

Sam said nothing. He just stared forward and grimaced.

"Well tonight's the night, my boy," said Chuck. "Your princess awaits."

"Yeah. I know," said Sam, settling back into his pillows. *And she's thinks I'm a prince. But somehow or another – I've got to be a dragon.*

...

About fifteen minutes into his search, Teddy started to wonder about what exactly the point of swamps was in the ecological circle of existence. Grasslands fed the grazing creatures. Forests were a lush palace of life. Even deserts had a clean beauty which sustained certain arid creatures. As for swamps, well, they were the homes of many insects, he couldn't argue against that. Trudging through the waste high muck, he had already been stung, bitten, and sucked dry all over his torso, arms, and neck by every sort of speck-like buzzing creature he could imagine. What swamps lacked that those other ecosystems had was *grace*. If swamps wanted to be a water based environment, then they should have just been a blue-green lake or river or ocean. If they wanted to be a tree based environment they should have fully committed and become a forest. Instead they were caught in a disgusting middle . They were the overused public bathroom of nature that the custodial staff forgot to clean. Of course this place would be the home of monsters. No self-respecting non-monster would want to live in such a mess.

Teddy's particular bitterness towards swamps at the present moment probably extended from the seeming impossibility of ever locating Swampy in the endless muck. The building of the mall had destroyed a significant portion of the local swamp lands, but a giant swath of them still remained and Swampy could be hiding in any repulsive crevice. Teddy had not been searching for very long, but he was paying a down-payment of frustration for later on in the day when he would really feel exasperated and might no longer have the energy to give his exasperation the full attention it deserved.

As he trudged on, he yelled, "Swampy! It's Teddy! Swampy where are you?" The only response he received was more bug bites.

He ventured forward to spots where the swamp water got deeper. He swam and tried hard to keep his head above the stinking surface. Determined, he continued forward. He refused to look back towards the solid ground where he started.

Teddy had not swum since his last summer at Camp Wachalukenat just before ninth grade and eventually his body got tired. He turned himself vertically to see if the Swamp floor had become any shallower but after several moments of submersion his feet didn't even touch the bottom and he torpedoed himself back to the air. A sense of panic set in. It struck Teddy with a powerful force just how little physical energy he had left in the tank. He realized he might have carried himself too far from any spot of rest.

Not really imagining it would do any good, instincts kicked in and Teddy yelped: "HELP! SOMEONE HELP!"

His screams were met with silence. *I'm going to die here*, he thought, in disbelief. He tried to soothe his panic by telling himself that if he couldn't be with Lindsay he didn't want to live anyway, but at such a crucial moment his mind refused to hear his teenage whining. His thoughts shot back with the surprisingly rational: *there will be tons of girls out there if you live, none if you die.*

With bleak hope he paddled furiously, trying to keep his head above water. Unfortunately, his body could only keep going for so long before his batteries ran out. He screamed "HELP" with one last half-hearted blast of voice before his head drifted into the dirty dirty water.

As fate would have it, Teddy was not to die right then.

Three feet deep he felt the water itself coalesce around him and wrap his torso in a constricted squeeze. It felt like he had slipped into an underwater tornado. He was thrashed this way and that, yet he felt a strange sense of direction to the way in which his body was thrown around. He knew he should have been saying his final prayers, but the evidence of his imminent drowning aside, he felt an odd confidence in his survival.

Moments later, his confidence was rewarded. He went sailing into the air on top of a geyser of liquid and landed on a hard rock in a moist cave. He took a minute to catch his breath and spit out the excess liquid which had made its way into his lungs. Then he looked up.

Standing above him – with, could it be, a look of concern? – was Swampy. Swampy had saved his life.

"Thanks my friend," said Teddy.

Swampy merely huffed and slithered over to a dank pit of dead creepy crawlers – aka, Swampy's snack drawer. He opened up his many mouths and ate out of all of them.

Teddy tenuously forced himself into a standing position. He was still quite out of breath. He peered around and took in the sight of Swampy's lair. He knew this particular cave had not been the monster's home for very long. His previous home had likely been destroyed with the construction of the mall, explaining why he ended up there in the first place. This cave mostly seemed untouched but there were a few signs of fresh decoration. Most notably there were the beginnings of a cave drawing on one large wall. It appeared to be a drawing of a girl. It looked somewhat like Lindsay but Teddy now knew better.

"Is this Holly?" he said.

Swampy's entire body shivered upon hearing her name. His loose eye flung around and hovered in the air only inches away from Teddy's. The rest of his body slowly turned and slithered over towards the drawing.

The loose eye turned to the drawing, then back towards Teddy, then back to the drawing. This continued on for about two minutes.

It seemed to Teddy that the monster both knew his drawing was a representation of Holly and didn't. Some instinct inside him recognized her but the majority of whatever constituted his "mind" had painted the picture unconsciously, with no recollection that the lines even formed a human face, let alone the image of a girl he had once loved. (Also a girl he had been a huge dick to, but Teddy was unaware of that part of the story).

This tip of the tongue knowledge wore thin on Swampy after his two minutes of careful observation and he roared a terrible ear splitting noise of exasperation. He grabbed Teddy and pinned him against the wall with his slimy hand.

"It's okay," said Teddy, in the most reassuring voice he could summon. "It's not all lost yet. She still loves you."

Swampy was awash in confusion. He quivered. His loose eyeball twitched. He looked like he wanted to destroy something but was unsure what exactly deserved to be crushed. To Teddy, he appeared as an amnesia victim, just awoken to a world so familiar and yet so hidden from his knowledge – terrified to find himself on that unstable middle ground of awareness.

"It's okay," Teddy repeated. "I'll take care of you."

Teddy felt good knowing that he was about to take action which was, at least in part, unselfish. He was happy to do something for someone else for once, even if there was a destination of personal hope penciled in at the end of his itinerary.

"I've got a plan," Teddy told Swampy, with confidence.

His monstrous friend didn't understand his words but he caught onto the tone. Swampy calmed down. His greasy body became less taught. His eye looked into Teddy's with an undeniable affection.

"Swampy," said Teddy. "Will you go to prom with me?"

...

Sam arrived at Lindsay's house just before five P.M. He brought her a bouquet of blood red roses.

Lindsay's mother opened the door.

"You must be Sam," she said. Her gracious smile at his handsomeness quickly transitioned into sideways suspicion when she noticed the cameraman behind him.

"Who is this?" she inquired.

Lindsay, rushing to the door, answered before Sam could. "That's Chuck," said Lindsay. "He's Sam's cameraman. Sam's going to be on some PBS documentary about American teenagers."

"Oh," said Lindsay's mother. She was not thrilled by the possibility of her daughter's prom night being broadcast on public access television, but at least she didn't know the actual truth, which was far more disconcerting.

Sam took a long look at his date. Lindsay looked absolutely breathtaking. She typically didn't put on make-up or wear clothes that fit her fine figure as tightly as it deserved. Seeing her glammed up was a revelation. Her usual beauty was impressive but it had never indicated the full potential which lied behind the curtain of effort.

"You look beautiful," he said.

"Thanks," she said, blushing. "You look really handsome."

And so he did. Lindsay was quite overtaken in her own right with her date's attractiveness. His tall dark pale features complemented his pitch black tux to perfection.

He was William Denworth and she was Betsy Rose Gardner and it was the prom scene at the end of "Mummy Dearest", the sixth book in the Midnight series. Lindsay, breathless in eager anticipation of the evening ahead, imagined that everything was about to go exactly as it had in the young adult novel. They would dance all night in romantic loops as all of the other girls swooned with jealousy. They would be voted prom king and queen to rousing applause so enthusiastic that the hands of those clapping would start to bleed. (Lindsay didn't really like being the center of attention but if her night matched the scenes in the book, she would receive the public glory with delight). Afterwards, just like William and Betsy, they would retreat into the shadowy night before anyone noticed they were gone and they would make love in the grass as he seized her virginity with a vigorous aggression, providing her with a blinding pleasure heretofore unknown in this life.

Sam reached out and took Lindsay's hand.

"Are you ready my dear?" he said.

She was gripped by such emotional ecstasies she could not utter a word. All she could manage was a head nod of approval. He led her from the door frame.

For a long moment they looked into each other's sparkling eyes.

"Alright, everybody hop in the mini-van," Lindsay's mother said, shattering the romantic tension.

Lindsay's mother drove them to the front of Laura Wolconheimer's house where many of B.S.H.S.'s more attractive students were gathered for pictures and where Lindsay would convene with her limo crew.

If Lindsay had not been so wrapped up in her own head she might have noticed the ruthless stares she received from the junior class's most popular girls. They had recently engaged her with sympathy and pity over the murder of her friends, but they forgot their basic human kindness just as quickly when Lindsay started going out with a guy who was better looking than their own boyfriends. Also peering with jealousy were Tommy Questinghouse, Bobby Fusilage, and the other jocks with trans-fat for brains, who probably would have asked Lindsay to prom themselves (as Teddy originally suspected) if she had not been going out with a swamp monster during prime asking season and then been immediately swept up by Sam when she and Swampy went their separate ways. Really no one wanted her there at all, but she was unquestionably the talk of the town that school year and each of the popular factions thought it might one up their social strata competitors by claiming her for their own limo group. Lindsay was blind to all of it. She only had eyes for Sam.

On Laura's lawn the parental paparazzi fired off enough smart phone camera flashes to blind someone four times over. Various factions of students organized and reorganized themselves in every possibly pattern of friendship (Megan and Dee and Kelsey, okay now Megan and Kelsey and Brianna, okay now Brianna and Dee and Kelsey…). Lindsay was mostly ignored during these independent closeness groupings, but she was approached by one of the less popular girls at the gathering – a slightly overweight sweetie named Nicole.

"Would you and Sam take a picture with me and Howard?" she asked.

"We'd be happy to," said Lindsay.

They lined up next to Nicole and Howard, her date, an offensive lineman on the football team who had both the look and personality of a buttered roll. Nicole's mother, a housewife all in a titter at being in the presence of someone as famous as Lindsay, nervously held out her camera and snapped a photo.

"Let me see!" said Nicole eagerly, less than a second after the flash went off. She ripped the camera from her mom's shaking hands and her face went blank with confusion. "Huh, that's weird," she said. "Look at this Lindsay."

She showed Lindsay and Sam the photograph. There were Nicole, Howard, and Lindsay lined up against each other just as they had stood a moment before. But right in the spot where Sam should have been there was only the front lawn of the house. Sam's eyes widened for a short, hard to catch moment, then cool as an pack of frozen waffles he said, "digital cameras these days have all sorts of weird technical issues. Make sure your mom downloads the online update." He took Lindsay by the arm and led her away before any further questions were asked.

"I forgot that vampires don't show up in photos," he whispered to her when they were out of earshot.

"What about Chuck?" she asked. "Isn't he filming you with a camera?"

"I think the vampire council commissioned some special technology that picks up our quantum wavelengths or something," he said.

"Huh," she said. "That's weird."

Sam avoided the rest of the photos by hiding in the bathroom, claiming "stomach issues." These "issues" conveniently disappeared when everyone was ready to gather in the limousine.

As she prepared to board her white-stretch prom chariot, Lindsay's mother pulled her aside.

"I remember my prom. It was technically the first date I ever went on with your father. It was one of the best nights of my life." Her eyes were far away.

Lindsay threw her arms around her mother.

"I love you mom," she said. "Thanks for being there for me this year. I'm sorry I haven't said that until now." Lindsay's unadulterated joy made her want to right every wrong and spread joy throughout the whole world.

"You're very welcome," said Lindsay's mother. The affection took her by surprise but was quite wonderful. "I love you too. Have fun tonight. And be safe."

"I will," said Lindsay. She kissed her mom and hopped in the limo.

13

The Bluford Springs High School gym was decked out with small romantic lights and fluffy streamers and photographs of the years gone by. In the center of the room, just behind the DJ table, were tribute portraits of the five students who had been lost earlier that year: Chris, Dustin, Jane, Kelly, and Sean. Above those memorials hung a sign. It stated forcefully and simply: "B.S.H.S. JUNIOR PROM."

As the little hand on the gym's analog clock (the last of its kind left in a five mile radius) swung past seven, un-fashionably on time students began arriving in their over-priced, under-classy limos. The girls wore too shiny dresses and the boys wore ill-fitting tuxes. Their eyes were full of stars.

There was Mark Wushiwitz, the trumpet player who didn't like to empty his spit valve, with his date Stacy Reddenbocher, whose clam chowder recipe in home-ec had made seven and half students throw up from its smell alone.

There was Joel England, who had converted to Orthodox Judaism, with Kendra Broccolbeiber who had a verified case of Herpes Simplex 1.

There was Ivan Mussivitch with his monstrous pectoral muscles. There was Chad Oligard with a bag full of weed inconspicuously tucked into his tux.

There was Angela Waymentooth with Bobby Crumpler. She had refused to believe that he had been staring at her just because of a Pop-Tart crumb in his eyes, and he lied and said he liked her because his buddy Kevin told him that Angela put out. (This particular rumor turned out to be true).

They all filtered in. The cool kids and the nerds. The religious abstinence promoters and the venereal laden sluts of both genders. The class president James Gerling with his long term girlfriend Pamela. The D+ student Hayley Dershwin with Hank, the creepy twenty-eight year old townie who checked out underage girls' asses at the 7-eleven on Nerlens Rd.

It was the most glamorous, sophisticated, meaningful night of their entire lives. They were filled with nerves, knowing they needed to seize this once in a lifetime moment and make it special.

They were also nervous because they were surrounded by army soldiers carrying assault rifles.

The soldiers who had been occupying the school were in full force tonight. Fifty men guarded the evening closely from further attack by the unpredictable terrorist known as "swamp monster." Two hundred more waited just outside of town, ready to be summoned should any assistance be needed. The President wanted no possibility of any further tragedy in Bluford Springs. His re-elections chances couldn't stand for it. (His poll numbers dropped with each successive Swampy incident).

The soldiers were told to pay special attention to the girl who was just arriving. America's sweetheart. America's survivor.

Let's all say it together…Lindsay Morpletopple.

The national news persons on the scene went wild as Lindsay stepped out of the limo. At the sight of the flashbulbs Sam yelled, "I gotta go to the bathroom!" and ran inside in order to avoid being seen. (Or "not-seen," technically).

Lindsay forgave her vampire beau his necessary departure and took her time walking in. The rest of the year she had hated the media hounding, but tonight she didn't mind. Tonight everything was perfect. Tonight all of her worries were brushed under the rug and her dreams were reality. *Let them film me*, she thought. *I've never looked better.*

She even turned to the cameras and smiled, which made the attention starved paparazzi nearly faint from the unexpected courtesy.

"LINDSAY! LINDSAY!" They yelled excitedly.

"TELL US ABOUT SAM!"

"IS SWAMPY REAL?!

"DID YOU REALLY DATE SWAMPY!?"

"WHO ARE YOU WEARING?!"

Lindsay didn't answer any of their questions, but she waved and they swooned.

The other beautiful junior girls entering the school directed seething looks of jealousy at Lindsay, knowing they could never compete. (A couple of them would have sex with photographers before the end of the night, falsely promised that their image might make it onto the pages of some supermarket tabloid, identified as the girl falsely accused of breaking up a celebrity marriage).

Sam was waiting for Lindsay just inside the doorway.

"Hi there," she said.

"Hi, sorry. I didn't want the media wondering why your date was invisible."

"Quite alright."

She leaned in and kissed him. It was a deep, lingering kiss.

When she separated they both smiled radiantly.

"What was that for?" Sam asked.

"For making me happy," Lindsay said.

She took his hand and led him into the gym.

Despite his lack of glands, Sam swore he could feel a bead of sweat make its way down his forehead. *I love this girl. How the hell am I going to do what I'm supposed to do?* he said over and over again in his head.

Lindsay and Sam entered the room and heads turned. Even if the events of the previous year had not made her the object of scrutiny, she and Sam still would have garnered attention. They were the most attractive couple in the place. As it was, the conflation of their beauty and Lindsay's notoriety was absolutely magnetic. Every person in the place watched them.

Every person, including principal Monica J. Misgivens. She was wearing an all black dress and watching from behind the soon to be spiked punch bowl. She was completely consumed by hate.

Monica was ready to punish Lindsay for her sins.

She let out a malicious cackle, deeply frightening Alex Nucklonng, who was on the first date of his life and already walking on needles of nervousness. He dropped the cup of punch he had just poured for his date and ran straight out of the building.

It was probably a smart move. He would be the only one who would be safe that night.

...

During the day St. Carl's had looked like a harmless clinic; in the dark of night it looked like a giant medieval tomb.

Teddy got the shivers. He loosened the bowtie around his neck, suddenly feeling very tense and constricted. He looked over at Swampy. He had dressed his monstrous buddy in his own tuxedo, an XXL he found at "Thrift Shop," the local thrift shop. He looked pretty dapper for a guy who could have been mistaken for a pile of vomit that got up and started walking around.

The boys were dressed and ready prom. But they couldn't arrive at the gala until after they picked up Swampy's date.

"You ready for this James?" said Teddy.

He had taken to calling Swampy by his given name. He didn't think the monster actually remembered his former life on any conscious level, but he responded to "James," with a sense of confused recognition. Teddy wanted to ease him back into his old self as much as possible.

Swampy didn't respond to the question but he started walking towards the building. Teddy thought that maybe he could sense Holly and was pulled toward her by the magnificent force of love. Or perhaps he just smelled something he wanted to eat. It was hard to tell.

A security guard sat behind the front doors. He was an adorable old man who appeared to be half asleep. Teddy had figured they would have to break in through a side window but seeing that only a cute elderly road block stood in their way, he decided it wasn't necessary. Breaking a window was a bigger risk. They might set off an alarm. Teddy could just work his charm and convince the octogenarian up front to let them through.

"This way James," he said.

They walked through the doors.

Just as they passed into the building, a giant steroid addled security guard who could have torn people's arms off with his bared hands walked up and joined the old man at the security desk.

Teddy and Swampy froze in their tracks. Teddy thought that if they didn't move perhaps they wouldn't be noticed.

"Sheesh. That was a hell of a shit!" said the bull. "Anything happen while I was gone?"

The old man shrugged his shoulders. He said casually, "This boy and this swamp monster just walked in. That's about it though."

The bull looked up and spotted the odd duo in front of him. His eyes went panicked and he pulled out his gun.

"Freeze!" he said.

For a moment Teddy's lifelong instincts of whimpishness kicked into high gear. His armpits were soaked with flash flood perspiration and he almost bolted off into the night.

"Wait…Wait…" he pleaded to the guard. "We're just here for…" He searched his mind for a reasonable explanation.

Then – just as quick – his fear vanished. He looked to his side. There stood Swampy, twitching and bubbling and just waiting to unleash some havoc. *I have the most imposing wingman in the history of wingmen*, Teddy realized. He had no reason to be scared. He could win any fight that was thrown against him.

An enchanting, pleasurable, almost supervillain level of cool washed over Teddy as he looked at the security guard.

"Why don't you just put down the gun and let us through?" said Teddy calmly.

"Move and I'll shoot!" said the bull. He nervously lifted a walkie talkie to his face and spoke into it. "Jason, Phil, Marcus, anybody on duty, we got a situation down here, I need all hands on deck."

Teddy ignored the scratchy responses that issued through the walkie and focused his eyes on the bull with eerie precision.

(The old man guard ignored the situation entirely. He seemed bored with the whole thing).

"What's your name?" said Teddy.

"Fuck you."

"Huh. What an odd name. Okay listen Fuckyou, I really think it would be in your best interest to let us through. My buddy here, Swampy – you might have heard of him – his girl's in here and he's not going to let anyone stand in his way of seeing her. He's quite the romantic."

The guard considered Teddy's words. He seemed uncertain of what to do. He kept his gun uneasily point at Teddy.

"Put your gun down," said Teddy. "You have three seconds. One…two…"

The guard wavered. His hand shook.

"Three."

The bull man kept his gun pointed at Teddy's chest.

"Wrong decision my friend," said Teddy. "Swampy, dispose of this fleabag."

Swampy convulsed electrically like a piece of metal in a microwave. He walked towards the bull. The guard fired his gun at Swampy but, as has been well established, bullets did not hurt our beloved monster.

Just before Swampy reached out to snag his snack, the rest of the guards descended on the lobby.

"OH SHIT!" one of them called out.

"FUCKING BALLS!" another responded.

Teddy hit the ground and yelled "James, spin!"

Swampy took the instruction. He arched on his "toes" like a gold metal figure skater and threw himself into a whirlwind twirl which Scott Hamilton surely would have declared "breathtaking," had he for some reason been in the room.

As he spun, flecks of acid flew off him like horizontal hail.

One of the guards was hit in the chest. He screamed in agony as his old body turned to lava. The others ducked behind close walls. The bull dove under the old man's desk.

The melting guard ran down the hall in a frenzy, unsure of which way to turn. He collapsed onto a particularly secure locked door. His nuclear reaction of a body melted right through the five layers of chrome protection keeping the dangerous patient inside from emerging.

Manic laughter slithered out of the now open doorway. The lobby went silent. The guards, Teddy, and Swampy all waited to see what would emerge.

Through the smoke stepped a 4 foot five, cherub faced man, who would have looked more at home shooting arrows on a Valentine's Day card than locked up in a mental institution.

The cherub man looked around at the strange scene for a moment, then let out a squeal of laughter. With remarkable speed, he took off into the depths of the institution, unlocking every patient's door as he proceeded.

The guards all forgot that there was a swamp monster in their midst to deal with and, panicked about the mass jailbreak, ran after the cherub. They all went except the bull, who remained under the desk, quivering between the old man's knees.

"C'mon James, let's go," said Teddy to his monstrous friend.

They followed.

...

"Ewww, did you fart?" Fran Nickelback said to her date Juanny Tavalis.

"No!" Juanny insisted truthfully. "I do smell that though. What the hell is that?"

Fran and Juanny were making out in the school store against a shelf of rubber B.S.H.S. erasers. The sudden unappealing smell interrupted their tonsil hockey.

"C'mon I know it was you," said Fran.

"It was not! Maybe it was *you*," said Juanny.

"How dare you?!" said Fran. "It was NOT me."

"No. It was ME," said an unseen voice.

Fran and Juanny jumped in fright.

Out of the shadows of sweatshirts and spiral notebooks appeared dirty, long bearded Todd Sooter, wearing a coat so big one could probably hide five or six children inside of it.

"Hey," said Fran. "Are you that guy from Duck Dynasty?"

"Of course not," said Todd.

Todd had been out of the cultural loop for so long he had no idea what Duck Dynasty was, or even what reality TV was. If he had taken a ten minute break from his plans of revenge to catch up on the tube he would have been shocked by the trash that passes for programming these days. But there was no time for that. He had only one thing on his mind.

"Where is *he*?" he said.

"Who?" asked Juanny, who had just peed his pants in fear. An impressive feat considering he still had a raging boner from his make-out session.

"Swampy! That monstrous asshole! Where is he? I'm going to kill him."

"We don't know," said Fran. "Ask Lindsay Morpletopple. She's the one who went out with him."

"Where's she?"

"Probably out on the dance floor with the rest of the kids. Now, would you mind? We were kind of in the middle of something."

Todd grunted and left the school store. As he exited he heard Fran say, "Why are your pants all wet?"

It was the first bit of helpful information Todd had received. (The info about Lindsay – not that the fact that Juanny's pants were wet).

He had snuck into the school that afternoon, pre-prom, and he had been haranguing teenagers at various intervals, trying to find out anything he could of Swampy's whereabouts. When he first arrived he had simply tried to walk right in but he had been stopped by one of the U.S. army soldiers working security at the event.

"Can I help you?" the soldier had said.

"Just going to the prom," said Todd, who had harbored a hate of uniformed authority figures ever since those cops had laughed in his face when he was a child.

The soldier had pulled him back from walking through.

"Yeah, I don't think so. I'm not just gonna let some hick stranger wander into a high school prom so he can sell the kids meth."

"Oh," said Todd. "Okay, no problem."

He made it inside ten minutes later, tucked underneath the five foot diameter of Jeanette Durucello's poofy skirt gown. She screamed when he appeared from inside the hidden folds of her excessive dress.

"Do you know where Swampy is?" he asked, unconcerned by her feelings of violation.

Mortified, she looked at her date, Oliver Frumplesmith and said, "Aren't you going to do anything about this?"

Oliver looked at Todd and said, "Hey aren't you that guy from Duck Dynasty?"

Todd knew he had to be very careful to avoid the soldiers parading around the halls, so he moved around with stealth, hiding inside lockers and trashcans, popping out intermittently when he spotted unaccompanied teens, scaring the wits out of them and receiving no helpful information at all.

But now he had a lead. And he would risk being spotted by the authorities in order to pursue it.

As Todd made his way to the gym, using the sound of throbbing dance music as a GPS, he passed by a classroom filled with B.S.H.S. teachers.

Todd can be forgiven for not noticing. The staff gathered did not want to be noticed. All of the lights were out and they spoke in whispers. Inside, all of the desks were filled. At the front of the room stood Vice Principal Brett Denninsson. Those with him were his rebel alliance.

Denninsson was inspiring his army with a fiery speech. He spoke of the "dawn of a new era at Bluford Springs High School." He said that all of their months of covert operations had led to this night – the junior prom – when the school's tyrant leader would crumble and they would take over.

Tonight was the night. Prinicpal Missgivens would fall and the school would be theirs.

The revolution was ready. Viva la revolution!

Meanwhile in the gym, the party was just kicking into high gear and Sam and Lindsay were right at the center of it.

Lindsay was having the time of her life. Devoid of the typical teenage disconnect between hopes and reality (since she was living out her dreams), all her inhibitions crumbled away and she danced like a wild woman. Sam, with his undead stamina, kept right up with her.

No other couple could compete. Thus, Sam & Lindsay were unofficially selected as the sun of the dance floor's solar system. They would remain in the center and the other planets of dancers would rotate around them, deriving all of their energy and power from the beaming bright light at their core.

Not that Lindsay cared about those in her orbit any more than the sun gives a shit about us. She cared about one person and one person only. Sam. As one techno fused pop anthem fused into another remarkably similar techno fused pop anthem, she leaped into Sam's arms and planted a huge kiss on his lips.

"*Thank you*," she said with intense feeling.

"For what?" said Sam.

"Everything."

She dropped herself from Sam's arms, turned her back towards him and twerked her butt up against his crotch.

I love this girl, Sam thought.

As his boner grew, so did his panic.

With every moment, his will to turn her over to the Vampire council of elders grew smaller and smaller. Yet he knew he would never be accepted again in the vampire community if he didn't follow through. He was trapped in a no-win scenario and he could hear the clock in his head, ticking down towards his demise.

"I have to go to the bathroom," Lindsay said at the end of the song.

"Okay, I'll walk you," said Sam, who had no desire to remain by himself with the other students.

As they passed the gym lockers and made their way to the nearest restroom a disgusting bearded man, who looked like he might be homeless, passed them in the opposite direction. He was mumbling something familiar.

"Morpletopple…Lindsay Morpletopple…Morpletopple…"

Lindsay and Sam paused, curious.

"Yes?" she said.

Todd turned.

"What?" he grumbled.

"I'm Lindsay Morpletopple."

"Lindsay Morpletopple!"

"Yes. That's my name."

Todd became very excited, having found his lead. He rushed over to Lindsay and Sam. He was so close they could see the maggots in his beard.

"WHERE IS THE SWAMP MONSTER!" he yelled in her face, flecks of saliva sprinkling Lindsay and Sam like a front lawn.

"Woah, back up," said Sam forcefully.

Todd ignored Sam's warning. He grabbed Lindsay's shoulders.

"WHERE IS HE?!"

That was a about enough for Sam. He slammed Todd's head against a locker as hard as he could, denting the locker door severely. Todd survived thanks to his large tufts of hair, but he was knocked unconscious. Sam picked him up and stuffed him into the now open locker. He then forced the door back into a closed position.

"Are you alright?" said Sam.

"I just really have to pee," said Lindsay.

...

Back at St. Carl's, chaos was spreading quicker than the obesity epidemic among American children.

The cherub man, who had remarkable speed for a man with such stumpy legs, had unlocked every door whose knob he could reach and loons had flooded into the hallways at every turn. In one corner a man was using his toe nails as floss. In another a woman was shrieking "THE TREES STOLE MY CHILD!" Over by the window a man was walking around on all fours, mooing like a cow…and wait, was he? …yep, he was definitely trying to milk himself.

The guards were so distracted with trying to wrangle up the stampede of crazies they forgot completely about Teddy and the swamp monster. Our beloved pair walked calmly through the madness like they were on a Sunday morning stroll.

Swampy was periodically distracted by some particularly appetizing mental patient he wanted to eat, but Teddy managed to repeatedly regain his attention before he slurped someone up through one of his many mouths by saying: “Holly, James. We’re here for Holly.” At which point Swampy was hypnotized into a direct path. He did not consciously remember her, but somewhere inside him the love lived on.

Teddy kept speaking to Swampy as if they were moving forward with purpose, but in fact he was lost. Retracing his steps from the morning to Holly’s section of the hospital proved more difficult than he expected. All of the rooms and hallways looked exactly the same. Each time he turned down a hall that led to nothing but a dead end Teddy felt more and more like a rat in a maze. *If these people weren’t crazy before they arrived here, this wildly inefficient floor layout would be enough to drive them insane*, he thought.

At some point, as he passed by an inspirational kitten poster he could have sworn he had passed at least five times already, Teddy noticed that Swampy was no longer at his side. In fact, he was no where in sight.

“Shit!”

Teddy sprinted through the mental patients and the guards. He had no better sense of direction than he had moments before but he ran as if he did, knowing if he didn’t find Swampy quick something terrible might happen.

Then – there he was. Swampy wasn’t eating some schizophrenic or stuffing a guard up his anus as Teddy had feared. He was actually standing quite still. The stillest Teddy had ever seen him. It was eerie.

Swampy’s back was turned towards him. Teddy could not see what was on the other side of his large frame. He cautiously approached, afraid of what remains of destruction he might find. But there was no mangled corpse on the floor. There was only a woman, standing up straight and looking right into the monster’s eyes.

Holly.

“I never thought I’d see you again,” she said.

Swampy said nothing, but his dangling eye went wild. It whipped this way and that, stirred with feeling. It was the only part of him that moved.

“Everybody says I imagined you, but I knew I didn’t,” she said. “I guess they'll tell me that I'm imagining you now too but I know I'm not. I know the difference between dreams and reality."

The dangling eye tried to calm itself down. It would extend towards Holly, make direct visual contact with one of Holly's eye, and then lose its stationary position in a new buzz of excitement. It would flit about once more like a butterfly newly transformed from its cocoon shell.

"James. I still love you. I want you to know that. I never stopped loving you Jamcs."

Swampy's eye froze in midair. It inched closer and closer to Holly.

Teddy waited anxiously to see what was about to happen.

The eye slithered onto Holly's shoulder. And there it rested. She raised her hand and rubbed it gently.

It was the most grotesque, adorable show of affection Teddy had ever seen. He was so overcome by the beautiful horror of it that he burst out in applause.

Holly jumped back, afraid.

"Oh it's okay!" said Teddy. "I'm a friend of James."

She looked to Swampy for approval. He seemed unconcerned so she decided to believe Teddy.

"I'm Teddy," he said. "It's a pleasure to officially meet you," he said.

"Officially?"

"Uh...just meet you, I meant. I've never been here before. Certainly not this morning. Or...I just mean, James has said so much about you!"

They both looked at Swampy who was as eternally speechless as ever.

"Oh. Well it's nice to meet you Teddy," she said. She shook his hand.

He looked right into her eyes and saw Lindsay's. A rush of love poured through him. He was so happy to have reunited these teenage lovers. And now it was time for him to finally fulfill a love of his own.

"Holly," he said. "I have something for you."

"Oh?" she said.

He reached into the duffel bag he had been carrying around and pulled out a bright pink prom dress.

"If it would please you, James here would love to take you to prom tonight."

Holly's face lit up. The teenager still living inside her rose to the surface for a moment and it was like catching a glimpse of paradise.

"I would love to!" she said directly to Swampy.

She ran over to Swampy and hugged him tight. "Oh James, I'm so happy."

Swampy wrapped his eye around her back and caressed her with it. The rest of him started to move again. His shock relinquished and his love for this woman actualized. He may not have understood it, but he loved her.

"I *was* wondering why he was wearing that tux," Holly said to Teddy after she separated from the embrace.

Teddy handed her the dress. "Whenever you're ready," he said.

She changed quickly and the gang prepared to depart.

Just then, the guards, who had been running around madly stuffing patients back into their rooms, came into the hallway where Holly, Teddy, and Swampy were standing.

They pointed their guns at them. At their head stood the bull guard, who had apparently regained his composure and joined his crew in the hunt.

"Freeze motherfuckers," said the bull. "Jason, put that bitch back in her room and I'll deal with these clowns."

Jason followed orders. He ran over to Holly and grabbed her arm. This... was not the smartest move.

As soon as the guard touched Holly, Swampy's eyes lit up with a furious fire the likes of which Teddy had never seen. His body changed from its usual puke green color to deep red. He bubbled and shook and thunder farted from his ass.

Teddy looked over at the bull guard and smiled.

"Toodle-oo," he said.

The tremor of Swampy's eruption was felt three counties away and registered as a 3.8 level earthquake on the Richter scale. Someone watching from outside would have seen the guards fly through the glass of the third floor windows, saved from the pain of the fall only by the fact that they no longer had any heads.

Inside, Teddy lifted himself up off of Holly, whom he had pinned to the ground. The entire back of his tux was covered in slime and guts.

"Sorry," he said to Holly. "I didn't want your dress to get dirty."

She looked around at the scene of destruction, in a state of semi-shock.

"That's fine," she said.

Teddy looked to Swampy. "Alright!" he said, as if they had been pre-gaming with shots of Jägermeister instead of murdering guards at a mental institution. "Everybody ready to go?"

Phase one of plan C – complete. On to phase two: PROM.

...

"Is Teddy coming?" Tom asked Henry, while they and their dates waited in line to have their photographs taken. (In front of a cheesy painted beach background that was not thematically related to a single other thing at the event.)

"I don't know," said Henry. "I doubt it. I've barely talked to him lately. It's been really frustrating. I just don't know what came over him this year."

"LINDSAY MORPLETOPPLE!" shouted the photographer (a man unfortunately rocking the bald head and ponytail look that has ruined many an appetite) as Lindsay and Sam walked by the photo station. "Come take your picture! YOU don't have to wait!"

All of the couples who had been waiting practically since their arrival at prom groaned loudly.

"Thanks," said Lindsay. "But we don't want a picture."

She and Sam went back to the dance floor, from which they had only taken a momentary break so Lindsay could pee.

The other couples panicked and reconsidered their decision to have their photo taken. *If Lindsay and Sam aren't taking their pictures, maybe it isn't cool to take your picture at prom anymore.* They all supposed they could make do with the three hundred or so photographs that they and their friends would take throughout the evening on their smart phones and post immediately to Facebook and Instagram.

Tom grabbed his date's arm and started to follow the throngs to the dance floor.

"Hey, where are you going?" said Henry, whose own date had joined Tom in his departure.

"You heard Lindsay. We don't need to take our pictures."

"Does the decision of one popular girl determine what every single other person has to do?"

Tom paused. "Well yeah," he said. "This is high school."

They all walked off, leaving Henry alone.

"This year sucks," he said.

Back at the dance floor, Lindsay had no idea she had just cleared the portrait area.

She was locked in to the best night of her life. She knew, in theory, that there were other people around her and Sam, but they were mere peripheral fuzz. She caught them out of the corner of her eye, she heard the steady murmur of their voices, but she did not register them as individuals.

As is typical when the populace is completely ignored by the one they adore, their love and admiration grows ever stronger.

Thus, when it came time to announce Prom King and Queen, there was no doubt as to who the royals would be.

"Lindsay Morrpletopple and Sam Bristolnoon!!!!!!!!!!!!!!!!" squealed Ashley Lionbear, the president of the prom committee as she opened the envelope to announce the winners.

Amazingly, and much to her credit, our heroine was really surprised. She was oblivious to her new position at the top of the social food chain. The admiration of many had never appealed to her. She had always only wanted the admiration of one – that perfect one – and now she had found him. Her instinct was to turn down the award and tell them to give it to a girl who actually wanted it.

But then Sam took her hand and said, "Let's go!," all excited to be crowned king, and she could hardly deny him the pleasure. She followed him up to the podium.

The applause was overwhelming. Even the bitterly jealous girls who might have won had it not been for Lindsay's epic year of death and drama joined in the clapping. (Though they may have been slapping their hands together more as a socially disguised anger release than as an actual sign of appreciation.) Ashley topped Lindsay and Sam's heads with the cheaply made plastic crowns that were only a slight step up from the paper crowns given with a Burger King Kids' Meal. The crowd went wild. Ashley handed them bouquets of half dead flowers. The adoring fans nearly fainted with enthusiasm.

"Speech! Speech!" one stray voice chanted. The rest quickly joined in. "SPEECH! SPEECH! SPEECH!"

Ashley handed Sam the microphone.

"Thanks so much. This a great honor. I'm sure it's not me you want to hear from. Isn't that right? It's Lindsay."

The promgoers erupted. Sam passed the mic to Lindsay.

Lindsay was embarrassed. She had always had a fear of public speaking. At heart she was an introvert. And rather humble. She had no desire to be the center of attention like this. She had no desire to even acknowledge that there were other people at the prom. She wanted to continue to tune everyone else out, keeping them safely in another frequency while only she and Sam shared the same wavelength.

She felt her body shake. Her mouth went dry. This year she had been part of an assault from two trashy thugs and a murderous swamp monster rampage, yet she had at no point felt fear like she felt at this moment.

"Th…Th…Thank you," she stammered out. "You are all t…t…too kind."

Lindsay spotted the pictures of her dead friends behind the DJ table. Though they were the furthest thing from her mind, she figured she should pay them tribute.

"I lost some good friends this year. We all lost some great people." (She thought about Dustin and Chris farting in each other's face and wondered if anyone would have ever called those boys "great people" had they not died an untimely death.) "This is for them."

It was cheap pandering, but the other students loved it. They whooped and hollered. Some of the army soldiers on the edges of the room wiped their eyes of tears. Several teachers in the corner of the room screamed like banshees, apparently unable to control their enthusiasm.

The DJ hit the music. Miley Cyrus's power ballad "Wrecking Ball" barreled through the gym. Sam took Lindsay's hand and led her back towards their place at the center of the dance floor. All of the other students inched away to allow the newly crowned couple their private slow dance.

Lindsay threw her arms around Sam and leaned her head against his shoulder. They swayed gently like flowers in the wind. It was lovely. Yet… something felt wrong. Suddenly she felt the most horrible, itching, venomous doubt.

Then the lights went out.

…

(A few minutes earlier).

The corners of Monica's mouth spread apart like two shifting tectonic plates. Ostensibly she was smiling, though there was not an inkling of mirth in her grin. It was a smile of pure calculation; the kind of smile that is always supposed to precede a remorseless, intentional evil act from a self-declared villainess. She was playing her part to the fullest. She had accepted her role and she couldn't wait to spring her master plan on her unsuspecting victim.

Monica inched her way over to the Prom King and Queen ballot box. She said a simple spell to spring the lock and opened the box, prepared to slip in a card which declared Lindsay and Sam the winners. The public beat her to it. They had already been voted the winners.

This was not unexpected but it still made Monica all the angrier. Lindsay deserved punishment and everyone who treated her like a goddess deserved punishment. They ALL would pay. MUHAHAHA.

Monica slid back into the shadows while Ashley Lionbear collected the results and announced them to the junior class of Bluford Springs High School.

As the crowns were placed on Lindsay and Sam's heads Monica could feel the magic in her fingers just waiting to burst out. She took a step out of her corner, but before she could continue her path towards her victim she was stopped by a wall of teachers standing in her way.

For a moment, she worried they were on to her plan. These worries were quickly soothed as Vice Principal Brett Dennisson stepped to the head of the group and announced their purpose.

"Miss Missgivens," he said with a sneer. "Your reign of incompetence has gone on long enough. I have formed an alliance of over a third of the staff at our school. We demand that you peacefully abdicate the principal's chair to me, or else we will be forced to TAKE ACTION. That's right, I'm talking press releases and social media smearing. So just think about that before you make any quick decisions."

Denninsson's cronies all nodded their heads in approval and agreement with their leader's words.

Monica rolled her eyes. She didn't have time for these shenanigans.

"Julix Qor Alorsa," she said.

The teachers all looked at each other confused, seemingly trying to find anyone who understood what Monica's words meant.

"Huh?" said Denninson.

Monica snapped her fingers and Bret Denninnson's head flew off his body like a popped champagne cork. Blood immediately flowed out his body, much as champagne would have the bottle.

The rest of the teachers screamed like banshees. (This was the screaming Lindsay thought was from unrestrained enthusiasm at her pandering. Actually, they were screams of terror at seeing the Vice Principal's head launch away from his neck). They all wanted to run away, but they were frozen in place by shock.

Monica pushed through them and walked towards Lindsay. She was now on the dance floor, swaying with Sam to Miley Cyrus's power ballad "Wrecking Ball."

"Geersh wubba po," she said.

The lights went out. The music cut off.

An excited titter spread amongst the students. They assumed this sudden darkness was part of some spectacle on the DJ's part. They waited for the strobe lights to kick into gear and heart-pulsing electronic dance music to ignite its thumping rhythm throughout the hall. They were not in luck.

After a minute a single fiery red light ignited itself in the middle of the gym. It hovered over Lindsay and Sam. He clutched her protectively, but Lindsay seemed unconcerned. The look on her face was mere curiosity. Out of the darkness, into the small stream of menacing light, walked Monica.

The other teenagers, all hidden in the darkness chuckled when they saw their principal. Miss Missgivens was so unthreatening that they knew whatever was happening must be some cheesy prank on the part of the school's staff. They waited impatiently for Monica to perform her stupid skit so they could get back to dancing suggestively with one another.

"LINDSAY MORPLETOPPLE," Monica said in a booming voice, very unlike the timid tone the kids were used to. "You have SINNED. And tonight, you will be PUNISHED."

"What's the joke?" Tom whispered to Henry deep in the crowd.

"I don't think there is a joke," said Henry, having experienced enough of the bizarre this school year to stop expecting that anything would be normal.

"I'm sorry, what's happening right now?" asked Sam.

Monica continued monologuing. "Lindsay, you took the love of a man who could not help himself, and at the moment something better came along you CAST HIM ASIDE!"

"Who?" asked Lindsay.

"JAMES, THAT'S WHO!"

"You mean my grandfather?"

"Your grandfather?" said Monica.

"Swampy," said Lindsay.

"Your *grandfather*?" said Sam

"It's a long story," said Lindsay.

("*Her grandfather*?" said a succession of teenagers in the crowd.)

"SILENCE," said Monica.

"What do you mean Swampy was your grandfather?" said Sam.

"I only found out this morning," said Lindsay.

"SILENCE," said Monica.

"Don't you think that's the kind of huge piece of news most people would share with their boyfriend right away?" said Sam.

"I just wanted to focus on us tonight. I didn't want to think about all that right now."

"SILENCE! SILENCE! SILENCE!" said Monica, stomping her foot on the ground like a toddler having a tantrum.

She finally managed to regain their attention.

"Jeez, sorry," said Lindsay.

"I'm trying to damn you here! NO ONE EVER LISTENS TO ME," whined Monica.

"Just wait a second—" said Sam, who wanted to continue his conversation with Lindsay.

Lindsay cut him off. "Sorry," she said to Monica. "Please, continue your damning."

"*Thank you.* Now, as I was saying," she cleared her throat, "LINDSAY MORPLETOPPLE, IT IS TIME YOU GOT WHAT YOU DESERVED."

Monica swirled and twisted her arms in a herky jerky motion.

"TAQREN – HALLICK – NIMBA – CLOOOORK!"

The room rumbled. The teenagers felt a strange wind slither past their ankles. They yelped in surprise. The flashing lights the promgoers had hoped for finally started up, but there was nothing rhythmic about them. The flashes were sharp and disturbing. Everyone started to feel nauseous.

"SPIRITS!" said Monica. "I COMMAND YOU TO TAKE THE FORM OF—"

Sam cut her off. "This is fucking bullshit," he said.

It wasn't the best possible moment for him to voice his protest.

You see, Monica's spell had just summoned an army of demons from the depths of hell. The spell was designed such that the demons would take whatever form that was specified when they passed through hell's gates into the earthly realm.

Monica had planned on telling them to take the form of dragons. Unfortunately Sam's interjection made them instead look like—

"Are those giant pieces of poop?" said someone in the crowd.

"Are the giant poops having sex?" asked someone else.

In fact, both of those nameless extras' observations were correct.

Following Sam's words ("fucking bullshit"), the demons had materialized into giant fornicating turds. They had arms and legs and creepy eyes made of kernels of corn.

"NO!" shouted Monica, again stopping her foot on the ground. "NO! NO! NO! THAT WASN'T WHAT I WANTED!"

Sam whispered in Lindsay's ear. "We have to get out of here."

"No, I want to stay," she said. "This is getting interesting."

Sam was incredulous, but there wasn't much time to stew.

Monica took a deep breath and calmed herself down. One detail had gone awry but her plan was still intact. She needed to refocus.

"DEMONS!" she cried, "I HAVE SUMMONED YOU TO DESTORY LINDSAY MORPLETOPPLE AND DRAG HER BACK WITH YOU TO DEPTHS OF HELL! ATTACK!"

The turd demons paused their sexual relations and focused their corn eyes on Lindsay. They stood up straight and made their way to her.

The fact that they had a specified target did not stop them from gleefully destroying others in their path. They used their squishy poop hands to pick up students in the crowd and rip them into pieces.

This in turn caused two successive things to happen: 1) The army soldiers around the corners of the room who still, up to that point, thought this was just some extremely bizarre B.S.H.S. prom ritual, realized they were in the midst of a real threat. They threw down their smart phones (on which they had been watching either porn or checking sports scores, respectively), pulled out their guns, and ran towards the demons, shooting with reckless abandon. 2) The promgoers fled the gym in terror. The stillness of their shock and curiosity over the unfolding drama was overcome by instincts of self-preservation. About half the demons (unable to resist a continued attack on fleeing teenagers, for after all, demons from hell are not the best at following direct orders) went after them. Several of the soldiers broke from the pack to chase this group.

When they first appeared there were only eight demons (Hell couldn't exactly be expected to loan out its full supply of demons to a low level witch, now could it?) and the soldiers were able to hold their own. Unlucky for the humans, the demons' copulation, conception, and birth process was about as thousand times as rapid as that of a human. The lovemaking they had been doing when they were summoned had impregnated the female turds and within minutes they were popping out full litters of eight or nine fast-growing poop demon children.

Chaos finally unleashed to the full extent she desired it, Monica cackled with delirious joy. "YOU WILL PAY! YOU WILL ALL PAY! BUT ESPECIALLY YOU LINDSAY MORPLETOPPLE! YOU WILL PAY MOST OF ALL!" she said.

Lindsay did not seem the least bit concerned. She snapped right into her usual state during supernatural pandemonium – a near comatose level of calm; a slight smile; a feeling of beauty and pleasure.

"Lindsay we gotta get out of here!" Sam insisted once more.

"Aren't you going to fight some demons for me Sam?" she said, in a tone that a girl might usually use to convince her boyfriend to buy her a drink.

"What? Have you seen these things?"

"Of course. There's one right here," she said pleasantly.

Sam turned his head. One of the turd demons descended down up him. He yelped. Instinctively, he shuffled to the side and sunk his teeth into the demon's "neck."

"Yuchhhhkkkkkk," said Sam, his fangs covered in shit, as he took his mouth off. His vampire bite had no effect on the demon.

"I don't think that did anything," said Lindsay.

"Yeah. *I know*," said Sam, annoyed.

The turd continued its path toward unafraid Lindsay.

"Watch out!" yelled Sam. He grabbed her and used his super speed to protectively slam her against the opposite wall.

...

(Ten minutes earlier.)

Jerry Morpletopple was stuck in traffic. The highway was bumper to bumper. Congested. Crawling. Logjammed. You know…fucked.

Jerry joined the masses in pointlessly honking his horn.

“C’mon!” he yelled at unknown forces. He scrolled through the radio, trying to find a traffic report but he couldn’t locate one.

Jerry knew he could very easily get out of his rental car (a Kia Soul) and use his legs to run at speeds just as fast as the car would take him, but he didn’t want to attract attention. He always criticized other vampires for their reckless use of their powers in public places and he didn’t want to be a hypocrite.

Still…he was fifteen miles away from Bluford Springs and the traffic needed to start moving a little faster or he was going to miss the prom and that asshole was going to have his way with Lindsay.

“GAHH!” He honked his horn again several times.

The car in front of him stopped it’s barely moving crawl completely. The driver’s door opened and out stormed a burly bald man with skull and crossbones tattoos all over his head.

“You gotta fuckin’ problem?” said the man, who clearly thought he could terrorize Jerry and his skinny, bookish looks.

Jerry rolled down his window. “I was expressing general honking rage at the situation of the traffic. It was not directed at you.” he said calmly.

“You’re fuckin annoyin’. How bout that?”

“Why don’t you get back in your car?” Jerry said with a hint of force.

“Why don’t I kick your ass big talker? How about that?”

“I really think you should get back in your car.”

“I really think I should stick my foot up your ass.”

Neither as a human or a vampire had Jerry ever been one to fly off the handle or engage in silly confrontations. He was, however, wound a little tight at the moment. Thinking of that little twerp with his hands all over his daughter put him a position to snap at any moment.

Jerry leaned forward.

“Say that again. I dare you.”

The bald man leaned in close. "I'm gonna stick my foot up your ass."

Before the man knew what had happened Jerry's arm flew at the speed of a fighter jet right into the man's chest. Jerry grasped onto his heart and ripped it from his body.

"AHHHH!" Jerry yelled, letting his anger transform him into a commanding force. He jumped up, burst through the roof of the Kia, and held the man's heart in the air in the triumph.

After a moment the high of the violence settled. Jerry looked around. Hundreds of terrified faces stared at him. They all double clicked the locks on their cars, as if those factory provided seals would have made any difference if Jerry wanted to enter.

Jerry felt mildly guilty, but now the game was up and there was no more time to waste. He started the motor on his feet and raced off into the distance.

He ran through the forest, knocking down trees unfortunate enough to brush against his shoulder. He ran through parking lots, leaving foot sized craters as he stomped along. Once he got running, he covered the fifteen miles between himself and B.S.H.S. in two minutes flat.

He took a moment to catch his breath. He had run fast, even by vampire standards. (Vampire average is about a twenty second mile. Jerry had run each mile of his fifteen in about eight seconds). He was about to plunge on into the school when the front doors of the building flung open and hundreds of students in tuxes and dresses came racing out of the school. They were screaming and frantic. Something serious had spooked them. Jerry scanned them the teens as they ran by, hoping to locate Lindsay. But there was no sign of her. As the crowd thinned out, he grabbed one of the boys.

"Where's Lindsay Morpletopple?" he asked.

"She's in the gym with the demons," said the boy.

The boy tore himself from Jerry's grasp and ran on to join the others.

Demons?

Jerry's inner inquiry was answered quickly as several of the fornicating turd demons followed the last of the students out of the building.

"Well that's weird," said Jerry.

The demons were followed by soldiers, firing off their rifles with little aim, hoping to put an end to the "shit show."

Jerry shook his head at the whole thing and walked into the building as everyone else tried to get out.

Having attended Bluford Springs High School himself when he was a youth, Jerry knew the way to gym without having to question any of the terrified students or poop monsters or trigger happy soldiers passing him in the opposite direction. He was hit with a wave of nostalgia, having not walked those halls since the day of his graduation at eighteen years old, back when his body still aged along with the passing of time. He thought of his days as a high school lothario before he met Lindsay's mother. He made out with twenty five different girls in his grade over the course of freshman and sophomore year. Or roughly twenty percent of all of the girls in his year. Factor out the forty percent of unappealing females he never even tried for and it was quite the mathematical accomplishment. Of course, in retrospect, all of his conquests seemed quite empty once he fell in love with Lindsay's mother. And so they had been categorized in his memory ever since. But seeing some of the locations where many of his trysts had taken place – in the girl's bathroom with Cindy Laroux and by the no longer present payphones with Donna Oleander, to name just a couple examples – made him remember how much he really had enjoyed himself at the time. He had no desire to return to that way of being, of course. He would give anything to be with Lindsay's mother (and only Lindsay's mother) again. But it didn't erase the truth buried in these halls.

Jerry was awoken from his reminiscence by the smell of more passing poop demons.

Right, he thought. *I'm here for a reason. To save my daughter.*

Jerry picked up the pace. He ran into the gym.

A swirl of dark stars hovered at the room's ceiling. It looked like a portal to another universe. (Actually it was a portal from Hell, but Jerry was pretty close.) More demons were battling more soldiers throughout the room. In the center of the room, a woman in dark robes was cackling.

Then Jerry saw what he was looking for: Sam, that douchebag Nosferat-U contestant with Lindsay. As Jerry spotted them, Sam picked up Lindsay and slammed her into a wall.

"NOOOOOOOOO!" screamed Jerry.

He ran over, grabbed Sam, and threw him across the room.

Lindsay looked right into her father's face. He, of course, hadn't aged a day so she recognized him immediately.

"Dad?" she said.

"Hi sweetie," he replied. Then he flipped around and dropkicked Sam in the face before he had a chance to get up.

...

(One hundred and thirty-seven seconds earlier).

By the time that Swampy, Holly, and Teddy arrived at Bluford Springs High School military helicopters were flying overhead, shooting at the giant poop demons tearing the town to pieces below.

"Well this is weird," said Teddy.

He looked over at his companions – an escaped mental patient holding hands with a swamp monster – and he realized he was in no position to judge levels of weirdness.

Still, the fact that most of his fellow students were running in the opposite direction of the building was somewhat disconcerting.

In the exit race he spotted Henry.

"Henry!" he called out.

Henry was quite surprised to see Teddy. He ran over to him and almost ran away just as quickly when he spotted Swampy.

"He's fine," assured Teddy. "Don't worry."

"You sure?" said Henry.

"Absolutely. Swampy and me, we're tight." Teddy looked back at Swampy and nodded his head approvingly. "Anyway," he said to Henry, "what's happening here?"

"Well..." said Henry, trying to find the right words to describe the madness. "Lindsay Morpletopple and Sam Bristolnoon were voted prom king and queen—" (Teddy scowled) "— but then when they went out to dance, Prinicpal Missgivens came out yelling all of this crazy shit about how Lindsay needed to be punished or something and she cast some spell like she was some sort of witch and then all these giant pieces of shit came from some portal and they were having sex with each other, but Miss Missgivens told them to attack Lindsay, but some of them started to attack us and then we all just sort of ran away."

Fear drenched Teddy like an unexpected thunderstorm. "These things are trying to kill *Lindsay?!*"

"Yeah."

"WHERE IS SHE?!"

"Inside, still I guess. If she's even still alive."

Teddy slapped Henry in the face.

"What the fuck was that for!" said Henry.

"Don't you ever say that about Lindsay!" Teddy said.

Henry looked thoughtful as he rubbed his sore check.

"Wait...do you have a thing for her or something?"

Teddy sighed. He guessed there was no reason to keep secrets anymore.

"I've had a giant crush on her for three years."

"Really? Why didn't you ever tell me?"

"I don't know."

"I'm your best friend."

"I know. I'm sorry. I just have trouble expressing my inner feelings I guess."

"Dude. You can always talk to me. You know that."

"I know. I'm sorry. I should have shared things with you."

They both went quiet.

"Come here," said Henry. He opened his arms for a hug.

Teddy obliged. They wrapped one arm around each other and patted each other's backs, man-style.

"While, we're at, what's with you and the swamp monster?" said Henry when they separated.

"It's sort of long story," said Teddy. "This one night I went to Lindsay's house with a boom box—" He interrupted his own story. "Lindsay! Sorry Henry, we'll continue this later. Holly! James! We got a girl to save. Let's go!"

Teddy waved to his companions and they stormed into the school.

"James?" said Henry quizzically, as they disappeared.

Inside, Hell looked like it had set up a colony. One of the soldiers had set the turd demons aflame, hoping idiotically that creatures from Hell could be put out by fire. The demons smeared the walls with their fecal bodies. Bullet holes decorated the lockers from the soldiers' manic shooting.

"C'mon, the gym's this way," Teddy said to Holly and Swampy, who were observing the proceedings with detached curiosity. He felt surprisingly calm himself. He supposed all three of them had seen so much outlandishness that they had lost their ability to be shocked.

The trio arrived at the gym just in time to see Jerry dropkick Sam in the face.

Teddy wasn't sure what that was all about, but his only concern was Lindsay.

At the moment Monica was walking towards Lindsay at a slow villainous crawl, flanked by two of the demons. (She had magicked herself a clothespin to fasten on her nose so that she would not be weakened by the smell). Monica had officially surpassed her mental breaking point. She had been teetering on the edge of insanity for years and her commitment to Lindsay's death had finally tipped her into the endless fall down the bottomless crazy hole. The screws of all mental clarity officially loosened, Monica saw Lindsay and suddenly thought she was Holly. The perceptual swap was seamless, much like in a dream when one person is traded for another without any concern to the dreamer. Her mistake was at least somewhat understandable because Lindsay did greatly resemble her grandmother. (Little did she know that the real Holly was standing twenty feet behind her). Focused in her mind on the girl who stole James from her the first time, Monica became angrier than ever.

"DEMONS! KILL THAT BITCH! KILL THAT BITCH!" she screamed.

Teddy knew he needed to act. But how to defeat such monsters? Bullets obviously didn't do the trick. Fire clearly only made things worse. *How would I dispose of shit normally?* he thought.

Then a bright idea lit up his mind. He ran as fast as he could to the janitor's closet in the hall. He filled up one bucket with water and a second bucket with cleaning supplies. He tucked a mop under his arm.

He ran back to the gym. Luckily Monica was savoring the drama and not rushing her attack (all fictional villains tend to draw things out, usually leading to their defeat) so there was still time.

Just before the poop demons reached Lindsay and swallowed her into their fecal matter, Teddy yelled out: "Hey you pieces of shit! Look over here!"

They turned. Teddy threw the bucket of water onto them.

Immediately they became less solid. Gooey-er. They had a harder time standing straight up. Teddy sensed weakening and did not give them a chance to re-fortify their attack. He pulled out a bottle of 409 and a bottle of Lysol spray from the second bucket and ran towards them, spraying like the bottles were revolvers and he was an old west sheriff defending his town from a band of outlaws.

The turd demons screamed and wailed as the cleaning solutions hit their bodies. They spun and shrank. The dissolved into mucky shit puddles.

Teddy brought the bottle of 409 towards his mouth and blew like the cowboys used to on their gun barrells in the movies.

"NO!" screamed Monica. She trained her eyes on Teddy. She attacked.

...

Meanwhile, Swampy and Holly's entrance had not gone completely unnoticed. The first to spot them was Todd Sooter. He was dazed, suffering from a concussion, and had just forced himself out of the locker Sam had stuffed him in after a long struggle. He forgot all of his hazy pain when he spotted Swampy.

"YOU!" he said.

"Do you know him James?" Holly asked.

Swampy showed no signs of recognition.

Todd opened up his large jacket. Inside was a large bomb. Todd had constructed a rudimentary, homemade suicide vest.

"I'm going to sacrifice myself to kill you, you monster!"

Swampy ate one of his own boogers.

Todd ignited his bomb. He ran towards Swampy.

"This is for Dirk!" Todd yelled as his war cry.

"James look out!" said Holly

When Todd was just a few inches in front of Swampy, the swamp monster stuck out a tongue from his crotch and swallowed Todd Sooter whole.

Holly was extremely worried.

"James! Spit him out! He was wearing a bomb!"

Swampy licked around the area where he had swallowed Todd, wanting to taste every last bit of him.

Holly resigned herself. "Well," she said. "If you're going to die, I don't want to live any longer either." She took his hand. "We'll go out together."

She closed her eyes and waited for the explosion.

Finally it came: An ear drum shattering crack and ripple. Though she knew she would see their bodies flying apart, she couldn't help but open her eyes to get one last glimpse of the boy she loved.

When she looked, however, she was shocked at what she saw. The bomb's explosion didn't kill them after all. In fact, the only thing that the explosion did was expand Swampy's frame like a balloon for about a half second. He contracted just as quickly.

After, Swampy belched and a little fire came out.

"Excuse you," said Holly, delighted.

The bomb may not have had the effect that poor dead Todd intended, but it did attract the attention of all of the soldiers in the room, who turned to see what the loud noise was. When they did, they spotted Swampy.

"The swamp monster!" they all yelled.

Though they were in the middle of battling turd demons from Hell, the soldiers universally thought destroying Swampy was more important than anything else. They abandoned their battle and ran towards the monster.

Swampy roared. He prepared to fight.

...

Meanwhile (again), Jerry and Sam's fight raged on.

"You stay away from my daughter!" said Jerry as he kicked Sam through the refreshment table.

"I thought Lindsay's father had abandoned her!" said Sam as he grabbed Jerry and threw him into the ceiling. Jerry's head got lodged into the cork roof, but he quickly pulled himself out.

"There were extenuating circumstances," said Jerry as he flew back down and elbowed Sam in the face.

"What sort of extenuating circumstances make it okay for a father to leave his child?" said Sam as he kicked Jerry in the nuts.

"I was turned into a vampire and I wanted to protect my family from the monstrous thing I had become," said Jerry as he kicked Sam in the nuts, returning the favor.

"Isn't it a bit hypocritical for you to be worried about your daughter going out with a vampire when you're a vampire yourself?" said Sam kicking Jerry in the nuts again.

"It's not hypocritical because I left since I knew I was a danger! You don't care a thing about Lindsay. You just want to win this stupid Nosferat-U frat contest!" said Jerry, as he grabbed Sam's nuts and used them to swing Sam over his head like a lasso, then slam him to the ground.

"That's not true," said Sam. "I do care about her! I love her!"

"I will not let you hurt her," said Jerry.

"I don't want to hurt her!" said Sam truthfully.

"I don't believe you," said Jerry.

Jerry put on a latex glove, then reached into his pocket and grabbed a large clove of garlic.

Sam gasped. "You wouldn't," he said.

"I would do anything to protect my daughter," said Jerry.

Jerry lifted his hand up high, then speedily brought it down towards Sam's face. Sam kicked Jerry's hand away just in time. He knocked the fatal garlic out of Jerry's grip. It slid twenty feet away. The both looked at each other for a slow silent second, then they both ran towards the garlic.

...

There was plenty at the present moment for Lindsay to wrap her mind around: Fornicating turd demons summoned by B.S.H.S's principal who was apparently a witch with some sort of deep vendetta against Lindsay, the sudden reappearance of her father who seemed to have the same supernatural vampire abilities as Sam, and Swampy and her grandmother (a.k.a. both of her grandparents, evidently) who were standing in the corner of the room, holding hands. But despite all the madness, the only thing Lindsay could think about was the terrible sensation of doubt she felt during her last slow dance with Sam.

It had struck her without warning, the feeling of doubt. She had been having the most perfect night of her life and then this doubt dropped on her like an atom bomb, ruining everything. The demons attacking her didn't hold a candle against the unexpected doubt in terms of bringing down her mood. Actually, Monica's spell summoning the creatures from Hell to kill Lindsay was a welcome relief. It was a bit of excitement which distracted Lindsay from her own annoying mind for a little while.

What do I WANT!? Lindsay screamed at herself inside.

Then she thought, *I am so fucking tired of being ME.*

Lindsay slumped onto the floor. A rare tear escaped her eye.

What happened? She was in the middle of a nice, typical romantic moment with Sam and she suddenly felt like he could never satisfy her. She felt that all her affection for him could vanish in a moment like the pee filled water of a flushed toilet. It was like their relationship was one of those automatic flushing toilets. The flushing away of everything between them was already set in stone. It was just a matter of her wiping away the last flecks of urine (a.k.a. her affection for Sam, under this metaphor) and standing up, then the flushing (a.k.a. the death of her affection) would occur whether she liked it or not.

Lindsay's emotions were an out of control pendulum, swinging in every possible direction with no rhyme or reason and she hated it. She so desperately wished she was normal. She looked up. Through the haze of bullets and fires and fighting she spotted Jane's portrait on the memorial wall. Jane, her best friend. Her best friend had died and she had not once during the previous eight months taken a moment out of her busy schedule of violence fetishizing to miss her. Lindsay was disgusted with herself.

"I'm a horrible person," she said out loud, though there was way too much noise in the room for anyone to hear her.

The tears flowed readily then. She cried the most she had since she was a child. She cried and cried and wished to be saved from the misery of her own existence.

Several feet in front of her, Teddy spotted her tears and naturally interpreted them as fear.

"Don't worry Lindsay," he yelled out to her.

She looked up. She recognized him. *That's the guy who asked me to prom at the beginning of the year*, she thought.

"Everything is going to be okay," said Teddy. "I guarantee it."

Then Teddy was punched in the neck by Monica, who had been charging towards him.

...

Teddy was knocked to the ground. He held his tight grip on the cleaning sprays. He sprayed some 409 in Monica's eyes as she leaped on top of him.

Monica clutched her lids and yelped.

"YOU'LL PAY FOR THAT YOU LITTLE TWERP!"

Monica waved a large group of the turd demons towards Teddy.

Teddy dug deep down below his surface self and found an unknown well of coordination in his core, just waiting to be exploited for energy.

He jumped up using only his ab muscles and spun the sprays around on his index fingers.

"Go ahead. Make. My. Day." he said, ripping of Clint Eastwood.

The demons attacked from all sides but Teddy was quicker and smarter. He moved with the stealth of a ninja, slipping in between the open cracks between the turds, spraying them with the cleaning solutions from above and below. He thought of himself as Batman as he weaved his way in and out of the assault, killing demons from every angle. He thought of himself as Keanu Reeves in the Matrix. He thought of himself…as John Cusack.

"Take that you pieces of shit!" he cried out in his best John Cusack impression.

He fired off cleaning spray like there was no tomorrow.

Then he realized that his John Cusack impression just sounded like his actual voice, so he said it again, this time doing an Arnold Schwarzenegger impression.

"TAKE ZAT, YOU PECES OF SHEET!"

Much better.

...

The soldiers formed a large circle around Swampy. A contracting circle, enclosing in on him by the second. They fired off every bit of ammo they possessed. As usual, Swampy was unaffected.

Swampy threw his arms into the air. Out of the ends of his fingers came long slimy vines. They grew and grew and then fastened onto the soldiers' feet.

Swampy twirled around at a rapid speed and the soldiers went spinning like the horses on a merry-go-round.

As soon as the soldiers spotted Swampy they had radioed their companions out in Bluford Springs who were busy preventing the demons from destroying every last bit of the town. These soldiers followed the lead of the ones in the school and (despite the fact that the town was literally BURNING and CRUMBLING) they abandoned their current fight to join forces against the swamp monster. (Kids be warned – this is what the dangerous power of *reputation* is capable of).

Swampy's merry-go-round was put on halt as a helicopter full of soldiers blew through the roof and started pelting Swampy with grenades. They did not physically hurt him, but the constant explosions and the insufferable brightness distracted Swampy from fighting back. More soldiers arrived. They inched ever closer.

Holly had been watching all of this from the sidelines. She knew that James was quite powerful in his swamp monster form but she was still worried. The soldiers held weapons the likes of which Holly had never seen. She wanted to help.

Holly grabbed a machine gun that had fallen out of the hands of one of the soldiers who had been twirling around in the merry-go-round. She locked and loaded and pointed the weapon at the hole in the roof through which the soldiers were entering.

"TAKE THIS MOTHERFUCKERS!" she said.

She fired viciously. She took them out one by one.

...

Jerry and Sam raced to the fallen garlic.

Jerry was about to grab it when Sam grabbed Jerry's legs first and flung Lindsay's father across the floor.

"You don't understand!" said Sam.

"I saw the show online. I understand perfectly!" said Jerry.

Jerry tried to run around Sam but the younger vampire delivered a vicious uppercut that sent Jerry flying once again.

"I love your daughter!" he said.

"Bullshit!" said Jerry, who was starting to tire out, his physical skills having had far less recent use than Sam's. He tried to sneak through Sam's legs to the garlic. Sam snapped his feet shut around Jerry's head and held him there. He lifted his hand to smash Jerry into the ground.

"It's not bullshit! I don't want to hurt her!" said Sam. He lowered his hand. "I don't want to hurt anybody..."

Saying it out loud, Sam realized once and for all that it was true.

Sam had pretty much known for most of the last several weeks that he would never be able to do Lindsay any harm. And now, all at once, it became clear to him that he didn't want to do anybody any harm. Yes, he loved being the best. Yes, he loved winning. And yes, one cannot be a winner without others being losers. But there was a difference between besting another person in a fair competition and *murdering* people. He didn't have the stomach for it. He realized he never would. He was a failure as a vampire. He was a loser.

Jerry, held tight between Sam's ankles, managed to rotate his body around so that his face looked upward.

"I'm sorry," he said. "I can't take the chance that you're lying. That's my little girl out there."

Sam saw that Jerry would never let up. He also knew that all of the vampire viewers watching (Chuck was still in the gym filming by the way; he was completely unaffected by any of the events taking place – a true professional that Chuck) would never let him live a peaceful life again if he didn't complete the task that he set out to do. And that was fine. He didn't want to be a vampire anymore anyway. Sam looked inside himself and realized there was only one way out of his terrible bind.

Sam loosened his ankle grip on Jerry's head.

"Oh no, I lost my grip," Sam said blandly and unconvincingly.

Jerry was too caught up in his vengeance seeking to notice the falseness in Sam's voice. He slid into the garlic like a lead-off hitter stealing second.

"HA!" said Jerry.

"Oh. No. You got the garlic," said Sam, dry as New Mexico in the summertime.

Jerry leapt on Sam and drove him to the ground. He held the garlic inches from Sam's face.

Sam looked over at Lindsay one last time.

She was sitting on the floor across the room, crying. He had a last second instinct to abandon his suicidal plan and go rescue her from whatever ailed her. But he knew that his presence in her life could only end up causing her harm in the long run.

"Goodbye Lindsay," he said quietly.

Then Jerry forced the garlic down Sam's mouth and Sam fizzled up like an over-shaken soda bottle. He burned and charred and shriveled into nothing.

...

Monica's fury grew by the second as she watched some puny dweeb with a couple of bottles of cleaning solution completely dismantle her demon army. All the while, Lindsay Morpletopple sat fine, unharmed, weeping her stupid little eyes out in the corner.

"If you want something done right," said Monica, "you have to do it yourself."

She marched over to Lindsay.

"I hope you're enjoying yourself *my pretty*," she said, still covering the great Wicked Witch of the West, never having been able to find a style of her own.

"What's your problem?" said Lindsay without much emotion.

"My problem is YOU and YOUR WHOLE KIND! All your girls who think you can just do whatever you want because you're sooo hot. Well I'm here to tell YOU CAN'T GET WHATEVER YOU WANT!"

Monica raised her hand to take action.

"THOTWALD GOOBER MINKIN DROO!"

"Go ahead," said Lindsay. "I don't want to live anymore anyway."

Lindsay closed her eyes and prepared for the sweet relief of death – the only medicine for her ailment of insanity and dissatisfaction.

A ball of fire formed in Monica's hands. Blue and red, it swirled and grew until it was ready to launch.

Teddy looked away from his fighting. His attention was grabbed by the bright light in his peripheral vision. He saw Monica ready to throw a fireball at Lindsay.

"NOOOOOOOO!"

He leapt over to Lindsay as the fire sailed out of Monica's hands. He pushed her out of the way just in time. His left hand was hit by the fireball. It engulfed in flame and dissolved instantly.

"GAHHHHHHH!" he yelled in pain.

Lindsay looked up at him. Her eyes were full of shock. Both because she was still alive and because a boy she barely knew had just nearly sacrificed his own life to save her.

"Are you alright?" said Teddy, concerned about Lindsay even though he had just lost his own hand.

"I'm fine," she said. "Are *you* okay?"

"Talking to you Lindsay," he said, "I'm the happiest I've been in a long time."

Surrounded by chaos and death, his hand vanished into the magical netherworld, Teddy had no desire to hold back any longer. It was time to tell the girl of his dreams how he felt.

"Lindsay, I could survive for weeks merely from the sight of you," said Teddy. "I could survive for months from a brief conversation with you. If I ever got to kiss you, I think I could make it to old age on the happiness I'd feel from that one meeting of the lips. Lindsay Morpletopple, I am completely and totally in love with you. I think you're the most perfect person in the world."

Lindsay didn't know what to say. She looked down. She felt embarrassed. But also, intensely happy. She looked up at Teddy, right into his eyes, and smiled.

While Teddy and Lindsay shared this romantic moment, Monica once again stomped her feet like a toddler whose favorite toy had been taken away.

"NO! NO! NO! Stop ruining my plans! I…HATE…YOU!" she said to Teddy. "ROOLAN DOLISH NEVILE MANSCH!"

From Monica's hands emerged the specter of ghostly skeletal fingers. They shot towards Teddy, grabbed him by the neck, and pinned him against the wall. They choked him. He couldn't breathe.

Lindsay felt all her despair dissapear. She stood up with force.

"Let him go!" she said.

Monica cackled and laughed deliriously. She didn't even hear Lindsay. She was too delighted watching Teddy suffocate to pay attention to anything else.

Lindsay lowered her shoulders and ran full force towards Monica. She tackled her to the ground like an expert linebacker. Monica was taken completely by surprise. Perched on top of Monica, Lindsay pummeled her principal with punches to the face.

"Stop! Stop!" said Monica. She tried to wiggle away but it was to no avail. Lindsay's punches came fast and furious.

Monica tried to get a spell out. "GLLAA—" she said. Then "VLOO—" But Lindsay would not let up her brutal punches long enough for Monica to get the words out.

Lindsay looked over at the wall and saw the life draining out of Teddy as the hands choked the last breaths from him. She stood up over Monica.

"Let him go!" she said.

Monica's bloody busted face fell to the ground. She looked across the room. For the first time she noticed that Swampy was there with them – busy battling soldiers.

"James?" Monica said softly.

"I said LET HIM GO!" said Lindsay.

"James! I love you! I'm sorry!" Monica cried indecipherably through her now mostly toothless mouth.

Lindsay waited dramatically for Monica to release Teddy. The only thing Monica did was reach her hand longingly towards the other side of the room.

"Have it your way," Lindsay said.

Lindsay lifted her foot and stomped Monica's head into the ground. Monica's face cracked in half. Lindsay killed her principal with one swift kick.

With Monica's death, all of her spells immediately disappeared. The demons were sucked back into the portal to hell and then the portal itself closed with a large swoosh. The ghostly hands vanished and Teddy fell to the ground, struggling to breathe.

Lindsay ran over to him and put her arms around him.

"Are you okay?" she said, extremely concerned.

Teddy looked up at her face which was mere inches from his own. He felt delicate arms around him.

"I'm the happiest I've ever been in my entire life," he said.

He pulled her in tight with his remaining hand and kissed her forcefully.

It was unlike any of the other kisses she had ever experienced. The expression, "sparks fly," came to mind. Lindsay felt her whole body infuse with a delightful energy.

Teddy, taking control, finally felt like a man. He dipped Lindsay down and caressed her tongue with his own. He imagined that if heaven existed, this was what it must be like.

Just then Jerry ran over.

"Lindsay, are you alright!" he said.

Lindsay and Teddy separated their mouths. They kept their arms around each other.

"I'm great," she said. She was overcome. She didn't have a full grasp on what had just transpired in the last few minutes but she knew it was something special.

"I killed Sam," Jerry said.

"Who?" asked Lindsay. "Oh right Sam."

"He was a vampire," said Jerry. "He was going to take your virginity then sacrifice your body to the vampire council of elders for a contest taking place in the vampire world."

"That's nice," said Lindsay, She was still thinking about her spectacular kiss with Teddy and was having trouble paying attention.

"Lindsay dear, I'm so sorry for everything. There's something I need to tell you."

Teddy interrupted the thought. He glanced around the room and saw that Swampy and Holly were surrounded by soldiers.

"James and Holly are in trouble," he said. "We need to help them."

Lindsay looked over. She flushed with infatuation over Teddy's loyalty to her grandparents. "Let's go," she said. She took Teddy's hand and together they raced across the room. "C'mon Dad! You can help too!" she said.

"Oh…okay," said Jerry, disappointed that his big apology and revelation had been put on hold.

Teddy and Lindsay jumped on a couple of soldiers from behind and knocked them to the ground. They stole their rifles.

They joined Holly's already in progress shooting of as many soldiers as possible. Jerry ran over with his vampire speed and began throwing soldiers against the walls. Swampy tore heaps of soldiers limb from limb with his multiple mouths, eating a few for a snack during the process. They stood together, fighting the good fight. An unlikely group of allies all doing their best to vanquish the young members of the United States Military.

…

(Thirty-four minutes earlier).

Lindsay's mother flipped on the lights in her quiet living room, settled into her favorite spot on the left end of the couch, and flipped on the television.

A reality show was on in which fourteen twenty-somethings, used to fast cars and high end clubs, were forced to live together on a eighteenth century wooden ship slowly making its way across the Atlantic Ocean. The show was called "Swab the Dick."

It was pitifully dumb and there were way too many occurrences of a thick-headed male telling the camera: "I'd like to make her walk my plank, if you know what I mean." Yet Lindsay's mother could not summon the effort to change the channel and search for something better.

Her energy was depleted. Her emotional strength was spent. It had been a taxing year.

As two slutty girls debated who would raise the sails on the television, Lindsay's mother's mind drifted off and she thought about all that had happened during the past year:

Lindsay had gone to the mall with her group of friends and every one of them except for Lindsay had been killed by a swamp monster. Her only child had then become even more distant from her than she already had been. Lindsay had never been quite the same enthusiastic extroverted child since the day that Jerry left. That asshole had never so much as called his daughter on the phone afterwards. And now the poor kid, already traumatized from paternal abandonment had to face the death of *five* friends. Lindsay's mother's heart had broken for her and her heart had broken even more when she realized there wasn't a thing she could do about it. To make matters worse, Lindsay hadn't even seemed sad. Only blank. Empty. Lindsay had come to frighten her and she hated that.

But no matter what she knew she would love Lindsay and she would give everything to her. Lindsay was all she had in the world.

Then after the mall killings, things got worse. They re-opened the mall and again there was a brutal swamp monster attack in which many were killed. Then Lindsay had revealed to her that she suffered from some really disturbing fetishes and she had gone on that medicine, but then she had stopped taking it because of some ambiguous boy she was dating and Lindsay stopped talking to her about her mental issues just as quickly as she had started.

Then the monster was apparently spotted at the school where, the guidance counselor later informed Lindsay's mother, Lindsay held his hand in the hallway like they were boyfriend and girlfriend! And then the Platinum Platypus diner blew up (Swampy again) and she just knew that Lindsay was there although her daughter would never admit it!

Jesus, what the fuck was happening in this town? Nowhere was safe! *No one was safe*!

Then it hit Lindsay's mother like a sack of bricks.

Why the hell did I let my daughter go to this prom tonight after all that has happened this year? There's no way she's safe!

Not even bothering to turn off "Swab the Dick," Lindsay's mother grabbed her car keys and ran to her vehicle. She needed to get back to the prom as soon as possible, before anything terrible happened.

As soon as Lindsay's mother turned out of her housing development, she realized she might be too late.

The sky was red and fiery. Frightened double propeller helicopters flew through the sky, shooting at unseen forces below. Buildings were burning and smoke forced itself into her lungs even from a great distance. It looked like Hell itself had descended upon the town of Bluford Springs. (Which, of course, it had, although Lindsay's mother was in no position to be aware of this.)

"Lindsay," she said. She just *knew* her daughter involved in all this. She needed to make sure she was okay.

Lindsay's mother hopped in her car and rocketed out of the driveway. Around her, several frightened neighbors peeked out their windows, wondering what maniac would venture out into this mayhem.

She spun around a few corners and set herself up for a straight down Main Street. She slammed her foot on the gas pedal and took off straight into the depths of the apocalyptic chaos.

As she sailed through red lights at abandonded intersections, Lindsay's mother got a look at the destruction. Some sort of brown mud monsters were tearing through cars and buildings with their squishy limbs as soldiers tried to bomb them into next Tuesday.

As she got even closer, Lindsay's mother got a whiff of the smell and realized that the monsters weren't made of mud. She realized this just before her car plowed through one of them who was standing right in the middle of the street.

Its shitty body splattered all over the car. Lindsay's mother put on the windshield wipers to clear it off the glass as well as possible. She remained steadfast and focused.

I have to get to Lindsay. I have to get to Lindsay.

She continued driving past a stampede of teenagers in tuxes and dresses fleeing the prom. She scanned their faces but Lindsay was not among them.

Of course she wasn't. Lindsay didn't run from horror. She ran straight into it.

Oh, my daughter, she thought. *My deeply disturbed, beautiful daughter.*

Finally, Lindsay's mother made it to the school. The front doors were wide open. Behind the doorway a disturbing blood red light shone blindingly. The noises emenanating from inside were terrible: Bullets, explosions, screams, cries, piercing squeaks, squeals, groans, moans, and booms.

Any sane person would have turned away. But surely, a little crazy ran in Lindsay's family.

Lindsay's mother braced herself and ran inside, straight to the source of all the commotion. She burst into the gym and saw the epic final fight, already in progress.

Her own mother Holly (who was for some reason here instead of sleeping in her bed at St. Carl's), Lindsay, and Teddy stood side by side, double fisting machine guns, marching steadily forward, slaying soldiers as they dropped through an opening in the roof. The soldiers were no match for this front line of determined three.

Elsewhere, Jerry (wait….Jerry was here!) was throwing soldier after soldier onto an ever growing pile across the room. Then, getting bored with his almost too easy defeat of these men, he folded one soldier into a ball and rolled him across the room into his pile of victims, collapsing the pile to pieces like pins on a bowling lane.

At the center of everything was Swampy the swamp monster, that creature of the deep who had wreaked so much havoc over the past year (for we know that havoc just loves to be wreaked) and caught Lindsay up in his web of destruction. He was squashing soldiers like bugs, ripping them into shreds, slurping them up like strands of spaghetti, and spitting their bones out like cherry pits.

Swampy destroyed. Swampy roared. Swampy pounded his chest in victory. Swampy belched.

The soldiers finally realized they were fighting a losing battle. One young and intelligent private, eager to preserve his life, shouted "Let's get the fuck out of here!" The rest of the still living soldiers threw their hands up in relief, glad that *someone* had finally said what they were all thinking.

"WE GIVE UP!" they declared. They ran from the Bluford Springs High School gym as fast as their legs could carry them.

After a minute the gym was silent. Far off sirens and car alarms and screams could be heard in the distance, but the happy winners of the great battle of the 2013 Bluford Springs High School Prom paid those sounds no attention.

"YEAH!" said Teddy. "WE DID IT!"

Holly and Lindsay cheered and hugged each other.

Jerry walked over to Lindsay.

"Ok. Now that that's over, I was in the middle of explaining to you why I disappeared all those years ago."

Lindsay's mother interrupted. "Yes! Why did you disappear all those years ago! I'd love to hear this!"

They all turned. No one had noticed she was there.

"Mom?" said Lindsay.

"Daughter?" said Holly.

"Wife?" said Jerry.

"GRAAA?" said Swampy.

"What is going on here!?" Lindsay's mother asked.

"Well," said Teddy. "Principal Missgivens turned out to be this witch and she had some sort of vendetta against Lindsay and she summoned an army of demons who took the form of giant pieces of poop for some reason, but they all disappeared once we killed her, but the soldiers were still trying to kill James here so we all joined in on the fight."

"Who's James?"

Holly stepped forward. She took Lindsay's mother's hand. "James," she said, "Is your father." She motioned to Swampy.

Lindsay's mother nearly fainted. "Whaaaa?"

Jerry ran over and caught her from falling.

"Are you okay?" he asked.

"What do you care?" she said, angrily.

"*What do I care?* I love you! You're the only thing I care about. You and Lindsay. I left because of how much I love you. I was bitten by a vampire all those years ago and I turned into one myself and I left because I was afraid I would hurt you."

"A vampire?"

"Welcome to the world mom," said Lindsay. "It's a strange fucking place."

"GLUGGG," said Swampy.

"My father??" Lindsay's mother said faintly, looking at Swampy again. She felt severly lightheaded.

The bizarre and confusing family reunion was interrupted just then by the sound of music. Teddy had made his was over to the DJ table and reignited the sound system. Miley Cyrus's power balled "Wrecking Ball" started playing again from the beginning.

"Sorry to interrupt," said Teddy, "but I don't think I can survive another second without dancing with Lindsay."

Lindsay blushed. "Aww, that's so sweet…," she said. Then after a moment, "hey…what was your name again?"

"Teddy."

"Right. Teddy. You're so sweet Teddy."

Teddy put out his hand. "Shall we?"

She took put her arms around him and they swayed romantically to the music.

Holly turned to Swampy. “Remember when we were that young?” she said wistfully.

Swampy bleched.

Holly threw her arms around the monster and they danced to the music, finally enjoying the prom they had been robbed of as teenagers.

Jerry looked at Lindsay’s mother who he was still holding from her near collapse. “Well, everybody else is dancing…” he said.

Lindsay’s mother sighed. “Okay,” she said. “But afterwards we’ve got a lot of talking to do.”

“Understood,” he said.

He pulled her up. As soon as she was in his arms she forgave him for everything. Lindsay’s mother couldn’t help herself. She had always loved Jerry with everything that she was. Plus, he looked just as good as the day he disappeared.

…

Lindsay and Teddy looked around at the other couples and smiled as they danced. Lindsay watched Jerry and her mother. She was deliriously happy to see her parents back together again. Teddy watched Holly and Swampy and winked at his monstrous friend. He was proud that he had done something truly good for someone else.

Then Lindsay and Teddy turned their attention towards each other.

“So you’re friends with my grandfather?” Lindsay said.

“Yeah,” said Teddy. “I sort of was the one who brought him to school here to be your boyfriend because I knew you were in love with him.”

“Really?”

“Yeah. It was part of a long, convoluted series of plans by which I hoped to win your affection.”

"Well you have my affection now," she said.

She leaned in and kissed him.

"Teddy, I should tell you something," Lindsay said. "I'm a really messed up person. I have all sorts of weird mental problems and I know you said you love me and I believe you but I kind of feel like no one would ever really love me if they truly knew who I am inside. So if you stop loving me once you find out who I really am, I'll understand."

"Lindsay, I know exactly who you are," said Teddy. "I've been following you around all year, watching you all the time even though you didn't know I was there. I love everything about you. And I will NEVER stop loving you."

Lindsay teared up at the beauty of his words.

"Oh Teddy," she said. "I think you just might be the one."

They held each other tight. All of the trauma that they had both been through during the past year faded into nothingness. They felt, together, like a long lost key and the lock it was melded for, finally reunited after an eternity of separation. *It was all worth it*, they both thought. All of the death and destruction and calamity in Bluford Springs was worth it so that they could be together at this moment.

"Hey," said Lindsay.

"Yes?" said Teddy.

"Would you like to take my virginity? There's a nice bathroom stall around the corner we could use."

Teddy went red. Goosebumps covered his body. He composed himself.

"I would be honored," he said.

"Oh, you sweet kids," said Chuck, who was still in the room filming. He wiped away a dry vampire tear from his eye. "You're so good together."

Teddy and Lindsay smiled.

"Thanks Chuck," she said.

"Well be right back!" Lindsay shouted out to her grandparents and her parents.

"Ready?" she said to Teddy.

"I've been ready for this since the day I met you," he said.

Lindsay took Teddy's sweaty nervous hand and led him on to the bathroom stall and on to the rest of their lives.

And so they lived, happily ever after.

EPILOGUE

Jacoby sat with his smart phone in lap, watching the live footage of Sam's body burn and char and shrivel into nothing from the fatal garlic stuffed in his mouth.

He smiled from ear to ear.

His plan had paid off. He knew Sam would be too weak to do what would need to be done for the final task and that's why he ensured that Sam would be his final opponent.

He was going to win. He was going to win the NosferatU frat competition. Oh happy day.

"Is everything all right?" asked his prom date Millicent Trundle, who was lying in bed next to him.

"Just fine Millicent, just fine," he said.

Jacoby had asked the ugliest girl in school to prom. He wanted to ensure his victory.

"Let's do this," he said.

Jacoby cast his phone aside and pulled up Millicent's dress.

"Wait, Jacob," she said. "Before we have sex there's something you should know."

"What's that?" he said, uninterested, pulling on her underwear.

"I'm not exactly....human," she said.

"What's that?" he asked.

But just then he saw just what she meant. He removed her underwear. Where her vagina should have been, there was instead a horrifying mouth.

"AHHHHH" he screamed.

But it was too late. Millicent's vagina mouth swallowed him whole and Jacoby was never heard from again.

ACKNOWLEDGMENTS

Special thanks to my mom and sister, Jill and Rachel Dorfman, for their reading and editing work. Thanks to Perry Shall and Jenelle Kleiman for their fine graphic packaging, inside and out.

Thanks to all my family and friends for always being there.

And thanks to all the real life swamp monsters out there, who may never have a chance to have their story told because of society's ceaseless discrimination of their kind.

ABOUT THE AUTHOR

Jeremy Dorfman is a graduate of New York University's Tisch School of the Arts. He can be contacted at jeremyidorfman@gmail.com.

Made in the USA
San Bernardino, CA
28 July 2019